DOCTOR SAX

OTHER WORKS BY JACK KEROUAC
PUBLISHED BY GROVE WEIDENFELD

DOCTOR SAX

Faust Part Three

BY JACK KEROUAC

GROVE WEIDENFELD • NEW YORK

Published by Grove Weidenfeld
A division of Grove Press, Inc.
841 Broadway
New York, NY 10003-4793

Library of Congress Cataloging-in-Publication Data

Kerouac, Jack, 1922–1969.
    Doctor Sax: Faust part three.

    I. Title. II. Title: Dr. Sax
PS3521.E735D63   1987   813'.54   87-25915
ISBN 0-8021-3049-6 (pbk.)

Manufactured in the United States of America

Printed on acid-free paper

First Evergreen Edition 1959
First Black Cat Edition 1975
New Evergreen Edition 1987

10   9   8   7   6   5   4

BOOK ONE

Ghosts of the Pawtucketville Night

1

THE OTHER NIGHT I had a dream that I was sitting on the sidewalk on Moody Street, Pawtucketville, Lowell, Mass., with a pencil and paper in my hand saying to myself "Describe the wrinkly tar of this sidewalk, also the iron pickets of Textile Institute, or the doorway where Lousy and you and G.J.'s always sittin and dont stop to think of words when you do stop, just stop to think of the picture better —and let your mind off yourself in this work."

Just before that I was coming down the hill between Gershom Avenue and that spectral street where Billy Artaud used to live, towards Blezan's corner store, where on Sundays the fellows stand in bestsuits after church smoking, spitting, Leo Martin saying to Sonny Alberge or Joe Plouffe, *"Eh, batège, ya faite un grand sarman s'foi icite"* —("Holy Batchism, he made a long sermon this time") and Joe Plouffe, prognathic, short, glidingly powerful, spits into the large pebblestones of Gershom paved and walks on home for breakfast with no comment (he lived with his sisters and brothers and mother because the old man

3

had thrown em all out—"Let my bones melt in this rain!"
—to live a hermit existence in the darkness of his night—
rheumy red-eyed old sickmonster scrooge of the block)—

Doctor Sax I first saw in his earlier lineaments in the
early Catholic childhood of Centralville—deaths, funerals,
the shroud of that, the dark figure in the corner when you
look at the dead man coffin in the dolorous parlor of the
open house with a horrible purple wreath on the door.
Figures of coffinbearers emerging from a house on a rainy
night bearing a box with dead old Mr. Yipe inside. The
statue of Ste. Thérèse turning her head in an antique Catholic twenties film with Ste. Thérèse dashing across town
in a car with W.C. Fieldsian close shaves by the young
religious hero while the doll (not Ste. Thérèse herself but
the lady hero symbolic thereof) heads for her saintliness
with wide eyes of disbelief. We had a statue of Ste. Thérèse
in my house—on West Street I saw it turn its head at me—in
the dark. Earlier, too, horrors of the Jesus Christ of passion
plays in his shrouds and vestments of saddest doom mankind in the Cross Weep for Thieves and Poverty—he was
at the foot of my bed pushing it one dark Saturday night
(on Hildreth & Lilley secondfloor flat full of Eternity outside)—either He or the Virgin Mary stooped with phosphorescent profile and horror pushing my bed. That same
night an elfin, more cheery ghost of some Santa Claus kind
rushed up and slammed my door; there was no wind; my
sister was taking a bath in the rosy bathroom of Saturday
night home, and my mother scrubbing her back or tuning
Wayne King on the old mahogany radio or glancing at the
top Maggie and Jiggs funnies just come in from wagon boys

outside (same who rushed among the downtown redbricks of my Chinese mystery) so I called out "Who slammed my door (*Qui a farmez ma porte?*)" and they said nobody (*"Parsonne voyons donc"*)—and I knew I was haunted but said nothing; not long after that I dreamed the horrible dream of the rattling red livingroom, newly painted a strange 1929 varnish red and I saw it in the dream all dancing and rattling like skeletons because my brother Gerard haunted them and dreamed I woke up screaming by the phonograph machine in the adjoining room with its Masters Voice curves in the brown wood— Memory and dream are intermixed in this mad universe.

2

IN THE DREAM of the wrinkly tar corner I saw it, hauntingly, Riverside Street as it ran across Moody and into the fabulously rich darknesses of Sarah Avenue and Rosemont the Mysterious ... Rosemont:—community built in the floodable river flats and also on gentle slopes uprising that to the foot of the sandbank, the cemetery meadows and haunted ghostfields of Luxy Smith hermits and Mill Pond so mad—in the dream I only fancied the first steps from that "wrinkly tar," right around the corner, views of Moody Street Lowell—arrowing to the City Hall Clock (with time) and downtown red antennas and Chinese restaurant Kearney Square neons in the Massachusetts Night; then a glance to the right at Riverside Street running off to hide itself in the rich respectaburban wildhouses of Fraternity

5

presidents of Textile (O!–) and oldlady Whitehairs land-
ladies, the street suddenly emerging from this Americana
of lawns and screens and Emily Dickinson hidden school-
teachers behind lace blinds into the raw drama of the
river where the land, the New England rockyland of high-
bluffs dipped to kiss the lip of Merrimac in his rushing roars
over tumult and rock to the sea, fantastic and mysterious
from the snow North, goodbye;—walked to the left, passed
the holy doorway where G.J. and Lousy and I hung sitting
in the mystery which I now see hugens, huger, into something beyond my Grook, beyond my Art & Pale, into the
secret of what God has done with my Time;—tenement
standing on the wrinkly tar corner, four stories high, with a
court, washlines, clothespins, flies drumming in the sun (I
dreamed I lived in that tenement, cheap rent, good view,
rich furniture, my mother glad, my father "off playing
cards" or maybe just dumbly sitting in a chair agreeing with
us, the dream)– And the last time I was in Massachusetts
I stood in the cold winter night watching the Social Club
and actually seeing Leo Martin breathing winter fogs cut
in for aftersupper game of pool like when I was small, and
also noticing the corner tenement because the poor Ca-
nucks my people of my God-gave-me-life were burning
dull electric lights in a brown doom gloom of kitchen with
Catholic calendar in the toilet door (Ah Me), a sight full
of sorrow and labor—the scenes of my childhood– In the
doorway G.J., Gus J. Rigopoulos, and I, Jackie Duluoz,
local sandlot sensation and big punk; and Lousy, Albert
Lauzon, the Human Cave-In (he had a Cave-In chest),
the Kid Lousy, World's Champion Silent Spitter and also

sometimes Paul Boldieu our pitcher and grim driver of later jaloppy limousines of adolescent whim—

"Take note, take note, well of them take note," I'm saying to myself in the dream, "when you pass the doorway look very close at Gus Rigopoulos, Jackie Duluoz and Lousy."

I see them now on Riverside Street in the waving high dark.

3

THERE ARE HUNDREDS of people strolling in the street, in the dream ... it's Sanurday Sun Night, they're all roshing to the Clo-Sol— Downtown, in real restaurants of reality, my mother and father, like shadows on a menu card sitting by a shadow-grill window with 1920's drapes hanging heavy behind them, all an ad, saying "Thank you, call again to dine and dance at Ron Foo's 467 Market Street Rochester,"—they're eating at Chin Lee's, he's an old friend of the family's, he knew me, gave us lichee nut for Christmas, one time a great Ming pot (placed on dark piano of parlor glooms and angels in dust veils with doves, the Catholicity of the swarming dust, and my thoughts); it's Lowell, outside the decorated chink windows is Kearney Square teeming with life. "By Gosh," says my father patting his belly, "that was a good meal."

Step softly, ghost.

4

FOLLOW THE GREAT RIVERS on the maps of South America (origin of Doctor Sax), trace your Putumayos to a Napo-

7

further Amazonian junction, map the incredible uncrossable jungles, the southern Parañas of amaze, stare at the huge grook of a continent bulging with an Arctic-Antarctic —to me the Merrimac River was a mighty Napo of continental importance . . . the continent of New England. She fed from some snakelike source with maws approach and wide, welled from the hidden dank, came, named Merrimac, into the winding Weirs and Franklin Falls, the Winnepesaukies (of Nordic pine) (and Albatrossian grandeur), the Manchesters, Concords, Plum Islands of Time.

The thunderous husher of our sleep at night—

I could hear it rise from the rocks in a groaning wush ululating with the water, sprawlsh, sprawlsh, oom, oom, zoooo, all night long the river says zooo, zooo, the stars are fixed in rooftops like ink. Merrimac, dark name, sported dark valleys: my Lowell had the great trees of antiquity in the rocky north waving over lost arrowheads and Indian scalps, the pebbles on the slatecliff beach are full of hidden beads and were stepped on barefoot by Indians. Merrimac comes swooping from a north of eternities, falls pissing over locks, cracks and froths on rocks, bloth, and rolls frawing to the kale, calmed in dewpile stone holes slaty sharp (we dove off, cut our feet, summer afternoon stinky hookies), rocks full of ugly old suckers not fit to eat, and crap from sewage, and dyes, and you swallowed mouthfuls of the chokeful water— By moonlight night I see the Mighty Merrimac foaming in a thousand white horses upon the tragic plains below. Dream:—wooden sidewalk planks of Moody Street Bridge fall out, I hover on beams over rages of white horses in the roaring low,—moaning

8

onward, armies and cavalries of charging Euplantus Eudronicus King Grays loop'd & curly like artists' work, and with clay souls' snow curlicue rooster togas in the fore front.

I had a terror of those waves, those rocks—

5

DOCTOR SAX lived in the woods, he was no city shroud. I see him stalking with the incredible Jean Fourchette, woodsman of the dump, idiot, giggler, toothless-broken-brown, scarched, sniggerer at fires, loyal beloved companion of long childhood walks— The tragedy of Lowell and the Sax Snake is in the woods, the world around—

In the fall there were great sere brown sidefields sloping down to the Merrimac all rich with broken pines and browns, fall, the whistle was just shrilled to end the third quarter in the wintry November field where crowds and me and father stood watching scuffling uproars of semipro afternoons like in the days of old Indian Jim Thorpe, boom, touchdown. There were deer in the Billerica woods, maybe one or two in Dracut, three or four in Tyngsboro, and a hunter's corner in the *Lowell Sun* sports page. Great serried cold pines of October morning when school's re-started and the apples are in, stood naked in the northern gloom waiting for denudement. In the winter the Merrimac River flooded in its ice; except for a narrow strip in the middle where ice was fragile with crystals of current the whole swingaround basin of Rosemont and the Aiken Street

9

Bridge was laid flat for winter skating parties that could be observed from the bridge with a snow telescope in the gales and along the Lakeview side dump minor figures of Netherlander snowscapes are marooning in the whorly world of pale white snow. A blue saw cracks down across the ice. Hockey games devour the fire where the girls are huddled, Billy Artaud with clenched teeth is smashing the opponent's hockey stick with a kick of spiked shoes in the fiendish glare of winter fighting days, I'm going backwards in a circle at forty miles an hour trailing the puck till I lose it on a bounce and the other Artaud brothers are rushing up pellmell in a clatter of Dit Clappers to roar into the fray—

This the same raw river, poor river, March melts, brings Doctor Sax and the rainy nights of the Castle.

6

THERE WERE BLUE HOLIDAY EVES, Christmas time, be-sparkled all over town almost the length and breadth of which I could see from the back Textile field after a Sunday afternoon show, dinnertime, the roast beef waiting, or *ragout d'boullette*, the whole sky unforgettable, heightened by the dry ice of weather's winter glare, air rarefied pure blue, sad, just as it appears at such hours over the redbrick alleys and Lowell Auditorium marble forums, with snowbanks in the red streets for sadness, and flights of lost Lowell Sunday suppertime birds flying to a Polish fence for bread-crumbs—no notion there of the Lowell that came later, the

Lowell of mad midnights under gaunt pines by the lickety ticky moon, blowing with a shroud, a lantern, a burying of dirt, a digging up of dirt, gnomes, axles full of grease lying in the river water and the moon glinting in a rat's eye —the Lowell, the World, you find.

Doctor Sax hides around the corner of my mind.

SCENE: A masked by night shadow flitting over the edge of the sandbank.

SOUND: A dog barking half a mile away; and river.

SMELL: Sweet sand dew.

TEMPERATURE: Summer mid night frost.

MONTH: Late August, ballgame's over, no more home-runs over the center of the arcanum of sand our Circus, our diamond in the sand, where ballgames took place in the reddy dusk,—now it's going to be the flight of the caw-caw bird of autumn, honking to his skinny grave in the Alabama pines.

SUPPOSITION: Doctor Sax has just disappeared over the sandbank and's gone home to bed.

7

FROM THE WRINKLY TAR corner Moody begins her suburban rise through the salt white tenements of Pawtucketville to reach a Greek peak at the Dracut border wild woods surrounding Lowell, where Greek veterans of American occupation from Crete rush in the early morn with a pail for the goat in the meadow—Dracut Tigers is the name of the Meadow, it is where in the late summer we conduct vast

baseball series in a gray clawmouth rainy dark of Final
Games, September, Leo Martin pitching, Gene Plouffe
shortstop, Joe Plouffe (in the soft piss of mists) temporarily playing rightfield (later Paul Boldieu, p, Jack Duluoz,
c, a great battery all in time when summer gets hot and
dusty again)—Moody Street achieves the top of the hill
and surveys these Greek farms and intervening 2-story
wooden bungalow flats in dreary field-edges of Marchy
old November dropping his birch on a silhouette hill in
silver dusk-fall, craw. Dracut Tigers sitting there with a
stonewall behind, and roads to Pine Brook, wild dark
Lowell so swallowed me doom its croign of holobaws,—
Moody Street that begins a den of thieves near the City
Hall concludes 'mongst ballplayers of the windy hill (all
roar like Denver, Minneapolis, St. Paul with the activities
of ten thousand heroes of poolhall, field and porch) (hear
the hunters crash their guns in skinny black brakes, making
deer covers for their motors)—up goes old Moody Street,
past Gershom, Mt. Vernon and furthers, to lose itself at the
end of the car line, top of the switchpole in trolley days,
now place where busdriver checks yellow wristwatch—lost
in birch woods of crow time. There you can turn and survey
all of Lowell, on a dry bitterly cold night after a blizzard,
in the keen edgeblue night etching her old rosy face City
Hall clock to the prunes of heaven those flashing stars;
from Billerica the wind came blowing dry sun-winds
against moisty blizzard-clouds and ended up the storm
and made news; you see all Lowell ...

Survivor of the storm, all white and still in a keen.

8

SOME OF MY tragic dreams of Moody Street Pawtucketville
on a Spectral Saturday Night—so unreachable and impossible—little children jumping among the iron posts of the
wrinkly tar yard, screaming in French—In the windows
the mothers are watching with wry comments *"Cosse tué
pas l'cou, ey?"* (Dont break your neck, ey?) In a few years
we moved over the Textile Lunch scene of greasy midnight
hamburgs with onion & katchup; the one horrible tenement
of collapsing porches in my dreams and yet in reality every
evening my mother sat out on a chair, one foot inside the
house in case the peaked little porch on top of things and
wires with its frail aerial birdlike supports should fall.
Somehow enjoyed herself. We have one smiling photo-
graph of her on this incredible height of nightmares with
a little white Spitz my sister had then—

Between this tenement and the wrinkly tar corner were
several establishments of minor interest to me because not
on the side of my habitual childhood candy store later becoming my tobacco store—a great famed drugstore run by
a white-haired respectable patriarch Canadian with silver
rims and brothers in the windowshade business and an
intelligent, esthetic, frail-looking son who later disappeared
into a golden haze; this drugstore, Bourgeois', chief in
interest in an uninteresting configuration, was next door to
a vegetable store of sorts completely forgotten, a tenement
doorway, a scream, an alley (thin, looking into grasses
behind); and the Textile Lunch, with pane, bent fisty

13

eaters, then candy store on corner always suspect because
changed ownerships and colors and was always haunted
by the faint aura of gentle elderly neat ladies of Ste. Jeanne
d'Arc church on Mt. Vernon and Crawford up the gray neat
hill of the *Presbitère*, we therefore never patronized that
store for fear of such ladies and that neatness, we liked
gloomy tromping candy stores like Destouches'.

This was the brown establishment of an ailing leper—it
was said he had nameless diseases. My mother, the ladies,
such talk, every afternoon you'd hear great wrankles and
grangles over billowy foams of sewing cloth and flashing
needles in the light. Or maybe it was the gossip of sick
masturbatory children in pimply alleys behind the garage,
horrible orgies and vice by the villainous brats of the
neighborhood who ate fieldstraw for supper (where they
were at my beans hour) and slept in mummies of cornstalk
for the night in spite of all the flashlights of the dream and
of Jean Fourchette the Rosemont hermit stalking over the
corn rows with his vine whip and spit can and come-rags
and idiot giggles in the full of midsleepnight Pawtucketville of wild huge name and softy Baghdad-dense-with-
rooftops-lines-&-wires hill—

"Pauvre vieux Destouches" sometimes they'd call him
because in spite of the horrible reports about his health
they'd pity him for those rheumy eyes and shuffling, dull
gait, he was the sickliest man in the world and had dumb
hanging arms, hands, lips, tongue, not as if idiot but as if
sensual or senseless and bitter with venoms of woe ... an
old dissipate, I can't tell what kick, drug, drunk, illness,
elephantiasis or whatall he had. There were rumors that he

played with the dingdangs of little boys—would go back there in the gloom offering candy, pennies, but with that dull, sick sorrow and weary face, it no longer mattered— obviously all lies but when I went in there to buy my candy I was mystified and horrified as if in an opium den. He sat on a chair, breathing with a bestial dullmouth honk; you had to get your own caramels, bring the penny to his listless hand. The dens I imagined from *The Shadow* magazines that I bought there. They said he played with little Zap Plouffe. . . Zap's father Old Hermit had a cellarful of *Shadows* that one time Gene Plouffe gave me use of (about ten *Shadows* and sixteen *Star Westerns* and two or three *Pete Pistols* I always liked because Pete Pistol looked simple on his covers though hard to read)—buying *Shadows* at Old Leper's candy store had that mixed quality of the Plouffe cellar, there was old dumb brown tragedy in it.

Next to the candy store was a shop, ribbons for sale, ladies of the sewing afternoon with pendant ringlet wigs advertising round blue-eyed mannikin doll-heads in a lace void with pins on a blue cushion . . . things that have turned brown in our father's antiquity.

9

THE PARK RAN CLEAR to Sarah Avenue across backyards of old Riverside Street farms, with a path in the middle of the high grass, the long block wall of the Gershom garage (lovers of evil midnight made blotches and squirting sounds in the weeds). Across the park, at dirtstreet Sarah

Avenue, a fenced-in field, hilly, spruces, birch, lot not for sale, under gigantic New England trees you could look up at night at huge stars through a telescope of leaves. Here the families Rigopoulos, Desjardins and Giroux lived high on the built-up rock, views of the city over back Textile field, high-flats of the dump and the Valley's immortal void. O gray days in G.J.'s! his mother rocking in her chair, her dark vestments like dresses of old Mexican mothers in tortilla dark interiors of stone—and G.J. glaring out the kitchen window, through the great trees, at the storm, and the city faintly etched all redheap white in the glare behind it, swearing, muttering, "What a gad-damn life a man has to live in this hard rock ass cold world" (over the river gray skies and storms of the future) and his mother who can't understand English and doesn't bother with what the boys are saying in afternoon goof hours off school is rocking back and forth with her Greek bible, saying "Thalatta! Thalatta!" (Sea! Sea!)—and in the corner of G.J.'s house I smell the dank gloom of Greeks and shudder to be in the enemy camp—of Thebans, Greeks, Jews, Niggers, Wops, Irishmen, Polocks. . . G.J. turns his almond eyes at me, like when I first saw him in the yard, turning his almond eyes on me for friendship—I thought Greeks were raving maniacs before.

G.J. my boyhood friend and hero—

10

IT WAS IN CENTRALVILLE I was born, in Pawtucketville saw Doctor Sax. Across the wide basin to the hill—on Lupine

Road, March 1922, at five o'clock in the afternoon of a red-all-over suppertime, as drowsily beers were tapped in Moody and Lakeview saloons and the river rushed with her cargoes of ice over reddened slick rocks, and on the shore the reeds swayed among mattresses and cast-off boots of Time, and lazily pieces of snow dropped plunk from bagging branches of black thorny oily pine in their thaw, and beneath the wet snows of the hillside receiving the sun's lost rays the melts of winter mixed with roars of Merrimac —I was born. Bloody rooftop. Strange deed. All eyes I came hearing the river's red; I remember that afternoon, I perceived it through beads hanging in a door and through lace curtains and glass of a universal sad lost redness of mortal damnation . . . the snow was melting. The snake was coiled in the hill not my heart.

Young Doctor Simpson who later became tragic tall and grayhaired and unloved, snapping his—"I think everything she is going to be alright, Angy," he said to my mother who'd given birth to her first two, Gerard and Catherine, in a hospital.

"Tank you Doctor Simpson, he's fat like a tub of butter— *mon ti n'ange* . . ." Golden birds hovered over her and me as she hugged me to her breast; angels and cherubs made a dance, and floated from the ceiling with upsidedown assholes and thick folds of fat, and there was a mist of butterflies, birds, moths and brownnesses hanging dull and stupid over pouting births.

17

11

ONE GRAY AFTERNOON in Centralville when I was probably
1, 2 or 3 years old, I saw in my child self dream-seeing voids
a cluttered dark French Canadian shoe repair shop all lost
in gray bleak wings infolded on the shelf and clatter of
the thing. Later on the porch of Rose Paquette's tenement
(big fat woman friend of my mother's, with children) I
realized the brokendown rainy dream shoeshop was just
downstairs ... a thing I knew about the block. It was the
day I learned to say door in English ... door, door, *porte,
porte*—this shoe repair shop is lost in the rain of my first
memories and's connected to the Great Bathrobe Vision.

I'm sitting in my mother's arms in a brown aura of gloom
sent up by her bathrobe—it has cords hanging, like the
cords in movies, bellrope for Catherine Empress, but
brown, hanging around the bathrobe belt—the bathrobe
of the family, I saw it for 15 or 20 years—that people were
sick in—old Christmas morning bathrobe with conventional
diamonds or squares design, but the brown of the color of
life, the color of the brain, the gray brown brain, and the
first color I noticed after the rainy grays of my first views
of the world in the spectrum from the crib so dumb. I'm
in my mother's arms but somehow the chair is not on the
floor, it's up in the air suspended in the voids of sawdust
smelling mist blowing from Lajoie's wood yard, suspended
over yard of grass at corner of West Sixth and Boisvert—
that daguerreotype gray is all over, but my mother's robe
sends auras of warm brown (the brown of my family)—so
now when I bundle my chin in a warm scarf in a wet gale

—I think on that comfort in the brown bathrobe—or as when a kitchen door is opened to winter allowing fresh ices of air to interfere with the warm billowy curtain of fragrant heat of cooking stove ... say a vanilla pudding ... I am the pudding, winter is the gray mist. A shudder of joy ran through me—when I read of Proust's teacup—all those saucers in a crumb—all of History by thumb—all of a city in a tasty crumb—I got all my boyhood in vanilla winter waves around the kitchen stove. It's exactly like cold milk on hot bread pudding, the meeting of hot and cold is a hollow hole between memories of childhood.

The brown that I saw in the bathrobe dream, and the gray in the shoeshop day, are connected with the browns and grays of Pawtucketville—the black of Doctor Sax came later.

12

THE KIDS YELLING in the tenement yards at night—I remember now and realize the special sound of it—mothers and families hear it in aftersupper windows. They're slaloming the iron posts, I'm walking through them in that spectral dream of revisiting Pawtucketville, quite often I get in from the hill, sometimes from Riverside. I've come wearying out of my pillow, I hear pots rattling in kitchens, complaints of an elder sister in the yard becoming a chant, which the littler ones accept, some with cat meows and sometimes actual cats do join in from their posts along the house and garbage cans—wrangles, African chatters at murky circles—moans of repliers, little coughs, mother-

19

moans, pretty soon too late, go in and play no more, and with my what-woe trailing behind me like the Dragon Net of Bad Dreams I come sploopsing to a no-good end and wake up.

The children in the court pay no attention to me, either that or because I am a ghost they dont see me.

Pawtucketville rattles in my haunted head . . .

13

IT IS A RAINY NIGHT, on the Moody Street Bridge there's poor old millhand Joe Plouffe. The night he was headed for Mill Pond mills with a lunch that he suddenly heaved far up into the night sky— G.J. and Lousy and I were sitting in the Friday evening park grass, behind the fence, and like a million times there goes Joe with lunchpail beneath brown auras of corner lamp with its illumination of every pebble and puddlehole in the street—only to-night we hear a strange yell, and see him throw lunch with a floosh-up of his arms and walk off, as lunch lands, he's going to the bars of wild whiskey instead of the mills of drudgery—the only time we saw Joe Plouffe excited, the other time was in a suppertime basketball game, Joe on my side, Gene Plouffe on G.J.'s, the two brothers start hipping each other, whack, unobtrusive grinning use of hips packing great power that can knock you down and when littler Gene (5:01) gave him a good one bigger Joe (5:02) got red-in-face and slammed him a surreptitious

20

hip that had Gene momentarily stunned and red, what a duel, G.J. and I were trapped pale among the titans, it was a great game—Joe's lunch in fact landed about 20 feet from that very basketball bucket in the tree—

But now it's a rainy night and Joe Plouffe, resigned, huddled, hurries home at midnight (no more buses running) bent against cold March rainwinds—and he looks across the wide dark towards Snake Hill behind the wet shrouds—nothing, a wall of darkness, not even a dull brown lamp.—Joe goes home, stops for a hamburger in Textile Lunch, maybe he ducked in our wrinkly tar doorway to light his butt— Then turned down Gershom in the corner rain and went home (as tragic roses bloom in rainy backyards of midnight with lost marbles in the mud). As Joe Plouffe lifts his heel from the last wood plank of the bridge, suddenly you see a faint brown light come on far in the night of the river—just about on Snake Hill—and beneath the bridge, slouching, dark, emitting a high laugh, "Mwee hee ha ha ha," fading, choking, mad, maniac, caped, green-faced (a disease of the night, Visagus Nightsoil) glides Doctor Sax—along by the rocks, the roars—along the steep dump bank, hurrying—flapping, flying, floating, sweeping to the reedy flats of Rosemont, in one movement removing the rubber boat from his slouched hat and blowing it up into a little rowboat—goes rowing with rubber paddles, red-eyed, anxious, serious, in the gloom of rains and bat-spans and roar hush mist-masts—real river—keeping an eye on the Castle—as over the basin of that Merrimac with eager petite birdy wings bat-boned little Count Condu the Vampire hastens to his baggy dusty crumbled old girl in the unspeakable brown of the Castle door, O ghosts.

14

COUNT CONDU CAME FROM Budapest—he wanted good Hungarian earth to lie still in during the long dull afternoons of the Europe void—so he flew to America by rainy night, by day slept in his six-foot sand box aboard an N.M.U. ship—came to Lowell to feast on the citizens of Merrimac ... a vampire, flying in the rainy night river from the old dump along back Textile field to the shores of Centralville ... flying to the door of the Castle which was located on top of the dreaming meadow near Bridge and 18th. Upon the top of this hill, located symmetrically with the old stone castle-house on Lakeview Avenue near Lupine Road (and the long lost French Canadian hoogah names of my infancy) there stands a Castle, high in the air, the king surveyor of the Lowell monarchial roofs and stanchion-chimneys (O tall red chimneys of the Cotton Mills of Lowell, tall redbrick goof of Boott, swaying in the terminus clouds of the wild hoorah day and dreambell afternoon—)

Count Condu wanted his chickens plucked just right— He came to Lowell as part of a great general movement of evil—to the secret Castle— The Count was tall, thin, hawk-nosed, caped, whitegloved, glint eyed, sardonic, the hero of Doctor Sax whose shaggy eyebrows made him so blind he could hardly see what he was doing hopping over the dump at night— Condu was sibilant, sharp-tongued, aristocratic, snappy, mawk-mouthed like a bloodless simp, mowurpy with his mush-lips swelled inbent and dommerfall as if with a little hanging Mandarin mustache which he didn't have— Doctor Sax was old, his strength of hawkshaw jowls was used on age, sagged a bit (looked a little like Carl Sandburg but shaped with a shroud, tall and thin in a shadow on the wall, not Minnesota road walking open air curly Gawd-damn glad in saintliness days and Peace—) (Carl Sandburg disguised with a dark hat I saw one night in the Jamaica Long Island Negro neighborhood, the Down Stud district, back of Sutphin, walking a long tragic lit up boulevard of islands and mortuaries not far from Long Island railroad tracks, just come in off a Montana freight train)—

The bat dissolved from the air and materialized at the door of the Castle a Vampire Count in evening cape. La Contessa de Franziano, a descendant of Welsh bwerps who fell off a trireme off the coast of Leghorn when it still had its Medieval wall guards, but claiming to be a pure Franconi of the old Medici heirs, came to the door gilt in rapid declining old lace with cobwebs joining threads and dust caking when she bent her back, with a pendant pearl and spider sleeping on it, her eyes all how-low, her voice all verbalisms in a reverberatory vat—"*Dearest* Count, you've come!"—she aims for the door with sobbing arms, opens it to the rainy night and few dull lights of Lowell 'cross the basin—but Condu stands firm, severe, prim, unemotional, Nazi-like, removing a glove—draws breath with a slight poof of the lips and a sniff-up—rattles—

"My dear, unemotional as I allegedly may be I'm sure the antics of the gnome girls don't rival yours when old Sugar Pudding comes home."

"Why Count," tinkles Odessa the slave girl (Contessa in a camp) "how you *do* manage to be vivacious before evening blood—Raoul's only now mixing the Divers—" (Divers of Odds & Ends).

"Is he with his old Toff in the belfry, meaning of course Mrs. Wizard Nittlingen damn blast her thorny old frap."

"I *guess* so—"

"Has my box arrived from Budapest?" queries the Count (a mile away Joe Plouffe makes the Riverside corner before a gust of rain).

"... bureaucratic difficulties, Count, have prevented any likelihood of your box arriving before the Twelvemonth."

"Pash!"—slapping his gloves—"I can see this is going to be another abortive mission to find a fart for old fart face—scrawny-necked individual—who else is here?"

"Blook. Splaf his assistant goon loon. Mrawf the gone duck with his crab head—"

"And?"

"The Cardinal of Acre ... has come to offer his saraband brooch to the skin of the Snake—if he can have a piece of it cut ... for his brooch ..."

"Tell you," smirks the Vamp Count, "they'll be roody well surprised when the peasantry gets a ... sauce of that snake."

"You think it will live?"

"Who's going to kill it to revive it?"

"Who'll want to kill it to survive?"

"The Parisacs and Priests—find them something they have to contend with face to face with the possibility of horror and bloodshed and they'll be satisfied with wooden crosses and go home."

"But old Wizard wants to live."

"In that last form he took I wouldn't bother—"

"Who is Doctor Sax?"

"They told me in Budapest he's just a crazy old fool. No harm will come from him."

"Is he here?"

"Is—presumably."

"Well—and did you have a good journey?" (moderate) "Of course for now I have a box of good American earth for you to sleep in—Espiritu dug it up for you—at a fee— it'll be charged upstairs—and the B equivalent (because he'll never see the money so the only thing he wants is blood) you can leave with me when you get some, and I'll pay him—he's been bitching and bitching—"

"I have some B right now."

"Where'd you get it?"

"A young girl in Boston when I got off the ship at dusk, around 7, snow swirls on Milk Street, but then the rain started, all Boston was slushy, I pushed her in an alley and got her just below the ear lobe and sucked up a good pint half of which I saved in my gold jar for nightcap at dawn."

"Lucky boy—I found myself a sweet sixteen-year-old boy in his mother's window, counting birds at aftersupper blue dusk (the sun just sank in westerly) and I caught him right by the Adam's apple and ate up half his blood he was so sweet—last week it was a—"

"Enough, Contessa, you've convinced me I did excruciatingly the right thing coming here— The Convention won't last long—the Castle will undoubtedly rattle—but (yawn) I want to move on—unless of course the Snake *does* pop up in which case I'll certainly stay to see the horrible spectacle with my own eyes—from a good distance in the air—"

"It'll have to happen at night then, dear Count."

"If you see Mater tell her I'll come in to see her in the morning."

"She's busy at cards with Old Hatchet Craw in the Blue Belfry—entertaining Flamboy the Ambassador so large ... he just·got in from Cravistaw where he stole a polo pony and had it flown to the Maharajah of Larkspur, who sent congratulations— They found a new Dove in the Bengali mountains you know. Supposed to be the Spirit of Gandhi."

"This 'dove' business has gone out of hand," frowned the Count. "*Dovists* ... serious? ... are they? I like my religion practical—blood is good, blood is life, they can act up with their ashes and urns and oily incense ... bloodless theosophists of the moonlight—excalibur dull bottards in a frantic hinch, cock-waddlers on pones and pothosts, rattle-bead bonehead splentiginous bollyongs, cast-offs, bah, flap-slaves and blackbearded bungy doodle frummers of lug and lard. Fat. Dry. Dull. Dead. Spew!—" he spat— "But I'll do anything the High Command wants, of course.

—Have we anything striking for my box design?"

"Oh," gushed the night eyed Contessa dripping an eave from her shoulder's dust, "a fabulous green jade monstrosity of a buckle or belch or insignia of some kind held firmly, well welded, but the main box a gorgeous 12th-century masterpiece, I believe one of Della Quercia's last—"

"Della Quercia!—Ah!"—the Count danced, kiss-a-finger, "let it not be said"—he danced with himself around the decaying foyer all dripping with dust and here and there a bat watching, with hanging African vines of cobwebs in the great center of the hall—"that the Count Condu goes to his well-deserved rest in the fresh and dewy morn (after night times of not ill-considered debauch), goes to his—"

"—quiet spew—"

"—without ostentation, without charm and dignity."

"It's all a matter of taste."

"And money, my dear, money in the blood bank."

15

THE DOOR OF THE GREAT CASTLE is closed on the night. Only supernatural eyes now can see the figure in the rainy capes paddling across the river (reconnoitering those blown shrouds of fogs,—so sincere). The leaves of the shrubs and trees in the yard of the Castle glint in the rain. The leaves of Pawtucketville glint in the rain at night—the iron picket fences of Textile, the posts of Moody, all glint—the thickets of Merrimac, pebbly shores, trees and bushes in my wet and fragrant sandbanks glint in the rainy night—a maniacal laugh rises from the marshes, Doctor Sax comes striding with his stick, blowing snot out of his nose, casting gleeful crazy glances at frogs in mud puddles ... old Doctor Sax here he comes. Rain glints on his nose as well as on the black slouch hat.

He's made his investigations for tonight—somewhere in the woods of Dracut he lifts his door out of the earth and goes in to sleep ... for a moment we see red fires of forges glowing to the pine tops—a rank, rich, mud-raw wind blows across the moon— Clouds follow rain and race the fevered Dame in her moony rush, she comes meditating hysterical thoughts in the thin air—then the trapdoor is closed on the secrets of Doctor Sax, he rumbles below.

He remotes below in his own huge fantasies about the end of the world. "The end of the world," he says, "is Coming ..." He writes it on the walls of his underground house. "Ah me Marva," he sighs... They put Marva in a madhouse, Doctor Sax is a widower ... a bachelor ... a crazy Lord of all the mud he surveys. He tramped the reeds of March midnight in the fields of Dracut, leering at the Moon as she raced the angry marl clouds (that blow from the mouth of the Merrimac River, Marblehead, Nor'West) —he was a big fool forever looking for the golden perfect solution, he went around having himself a ball searching mysterious humps of earth around the world for a reason so fantastic—for the boiling point of evil (which, in his—, was a volcanic thing ... like a boil)—in South America, in North America, Doctor Sax had labored to find the enigma of the New World—the snake of evil whose home is in the deeps of Ecuador and the Amazonian jungle—

28

where he lived a considerable time searching for the perfect dove ... a white jungle variety as delicate as a little white bat, an Albino bat really, but a dove with a snaky beak, and habitating close to Snake Head... Doctor Sax deduced from this perfect Dove, which flew to Tibet for him at will (returning with a brace of herbs strapped to its leg by the Hero Monks of the World North) (H.M.W.N., a Post-Fellaheen organization later acknowledged by the Pope as barbaric) (and by his scholars as primitive) ... deduced that the Snake had part of its body in the jungle ... Came grooking from the Snow North mountains Doctor Sax, educated in a panel of ice and a panel of snow, taught by Fires, in the strangest Monastery in the World, where Sax Saw the Snake

and the Snake saw Sax—

He came hobbling down from the mountain with a broken leg, a cane, a pack, wounds, a beard, red eyes, yellow teeth, but just like an old Montana hobo in the long blue sky streets of Waco—passing thru. And in fact when Doctor Sax did get back to Butte, where he's really from, he settled back to longnight poker games with Old Bull Balloon the wildest gambler in town ... (some say, W.C. Fields' ghost returned he's so much like him, twin to him, unbelievably except for the—) Sax & Bull got into (of course Sax had a Butte name)—into a tremendous game of pool watched by one hundred Butteans in the dark beyond the table lamps and its bright, central green.

SAX (won the break, breaks) (Crash) (the balls spin all over)

SMILEY BULL BALLOON (out of the mouth like a cigar and a

yellow tooth): Say Raymond-O, don't you think this romance has gone far enough?

SAX: Why do you say that Pops? (Neatly rubbing chalk to cue as 8-ball plunks into corner pocket in the mill.) Anything you say Pops.

BULL: Why (bending over the table to take a shot as Sax protests and everybody roars) m'boy it sometimes occurs to me, not that I haven't been to see the doctor late-ly (grunting to take a shot with cue)—the perfect disposition for your well-known little ten dollar ass is over by the table benches there with the Pepsi-Cola box and farmitures, whilst I becalm myself in a dull weed (puffing cee-gar) and aim this rutabaga stick at the proper ball—white—for old yellow number one—

SAX: But I sank the 8-ball!—you can't shoot now!

OLD BULL: Son (patting the flask of Old Granddad in his backpocket with no deprecatory gesture) the law of averages, or the law of supply and demand, says the 8-ball was a goddamn Albino 8-bawl (removing it from pocket and spotting it and lining up white cueball with a flick of his forefinger to a speck on the green beside it, simultaneously letting out a loud fart heard by everybody in the poolhall and some at the bar, precipitating various reactions of disgust and wild cheer, as the Proprietor, Joe Boss, throws a wadded paper at Old Bull Balloon's ass, and Old Bull, position established, whips out a bottle to the light (said flask) and addresses it a short speech before taking a shot—to the effect that alcohol has too much gasoline in it but by God the old Hamp-shire car can go! promptly thereafter re-pocketing

it and bending, neatly and briskly, with amazing sudden
agility, neat and dextrous, fingertip control of his cuestick, good balance, stance, the forefingers all arranged
on the table to hold the cue just so high, just right, pow,
the old man pots the yellow one-ball into the slot, plock,
and everybody settles down from the humor to see a
good game of rotation between two good players—and
though the laffs and yaks continue into the night, Old
Bull Balloon and Doctor Sax never rest, you can't die
without heroes to look after).

This was the Butte background of Doctor Sax—in Butte
Raymond the miner—a miner indeed!—he searched the
mine and ore-source of the Great World Snake.

He looked all over for herbs that he knew someday he
would perfect into an alchemic-almost poison art that
could cast out a certain hypnotic and telepathic light that
would make the Snake drop dead ... a terrible weapon
for some old hateful bitch, people would be dropping dead
all over the streets... Sax figures to blow his powder poof!
for the Snake—the Snake'll see the light—Sax will wish it
dead, the Snake will die from just seeing the telepathic
light ... the only way to transmit messages to a Snake,
where it will understand what you "really" mean ... beware, Doctor Sax. But no,—he himself screams "Palalakonuh beware!" in his noonday fits in the woods with his
afterdinner peps darting his black slouchcape like ink in
the sun, diving under his trapdoor like a fiend ... "Palalakonuh beware!" is written on his wall. In the afternoon
he naps ... Palalakonuh is merely the Aztec or Toltec
name (or possibly Chihuahuan in origin) for the World

Sun Snake of the ancient Indians of North America (who probably trekked from Tibet before they knew they had Tibetan backgrounds or North American foregrounds spreading huge in the World Around) (Doctor Sax had cried "Oh Northern Heroes Trekking from Mongolian Glooms & Bare Korean Thumbs to the Mango Paradises of the New World South, what bleak mornings did you see over the stone humps of Sierra Nueva Tierra as you bowled in a heavy wind with posts, strapped and gear to the night camp to the clanking Prokofiev music of Indian Antiquity in the Howling Void!")

Sax worked on his herbs and powders for a lifetime. He couldn't rush around like The Shadow with a .45 automatic battling the forces of evil, the evil that Doctor Sax had to battle required herbs and nerves . . . moral nerves, he had to recognize good and evil and intelligence.

When I was a little boy the only occasion I happened to make a connection between Doctor Sax and a river (therefore establishing his identity) was when The Shadow in one of his Lamont Cranston masterpieces published by Street & Smith visited the shores of the Mississippi and blew up a personal rubber boat of his own which however was not perfected like the new one concealed in his hat, he'd bought it in St. Louis during the day with one of his agents and it made a bulky package under his arm as they cabbed for the evening scene along the water glancing anxiously at their watches for when to turn into Shadows— I was amazed that The Shadow should travel so much, he had such an easy time potting racketeers in New York Chinatown Waterfront with his blue .45 (glint)

—(roar of The Shadow's Speech in Lead)—(toppling forms of tight coat Chinese gangsters) (falling Tong Wars from the Gong) (The Shadow disappears through Fu Manchu's house and comes out in back of Boston Blackie, whaling with his .45 at the gawkers on the pier, mowing em down, as Popeye comes in a motor launch to carry them away to Humphrey Bogart) (Doctor Sax bangs his knotty cane on the door of an Isadora Duncan-type party in the Castle in the Twenties when the batty lady owned it, when they see who's at the door all greenfaced and leering and blazing-maniac-eyed they scream and faint, his hollow laugh rises to the maddened moon as she screams across those shredded croos in the hue up-night fiending—to the rattle of a million croaks like lizards in a—the toadies—) whoo! Doctor Sax was like The Shadow when I was young, I saw him leap over the last bush on the sandbank one night, cape a-flying, I just missed really seeing his feet or body, he was gone—he was agile then ... it was the night we tried to trap the Moon Man (Gene Plouffe disguised and trying to terrify neighborhood) in a sand pit, with twigs, paper, sand, at one point Gene was treed and almost stoned, he escaped, he flew like a bat in every direction, he was 16, we were 11, he could really fly and was really mysterious and scary, but when he vanished one way and we ran under the lamp a bit so I got a little light blinded I saw and knew Gene the Moon Man over in those trees but on the other and upper bank, by shrubs, stood a tall shadowy figure in a cape, stately, then it turned and leaped out of sight,—*that was no Gene Plouffe*—that was Doctor Sax. I didn't know his name then. He didn't fright-en me, either. I sensed he was my friend ... my old, old friend ... my ghost, personal angel, private shadow, secret lover.

16

AT THE AGE OF SEVEN I went to St. Louis Parochial School, a particularly Doctor Saxish school. It was in the auditorium of this kingdom that I saw the Ste. Thérèse movie that made stone turn its head—there were bazaars, my mother officiated at a booth, there were kisses free, candy kisses and real kisses (with all the local mustachioed Parisian Canadian blades rushing up to get theirs before they run off to join the Army in Panama, like Henry Fortier did, or go into the priesthood on orders from their fathers)— St. Louis had secret darknesses in niches... Rainy funerals for little boys, I saw several including the funeral of my own poor brother when (at age 4) my family lived exactly on the St. Louis parish on Beaulieu St. behind its walls... There were dignified marvelous old ladies with white hair and silver pince-nez living in the houses across the school—in one house on Beaulieu, too ... a woman with parrot on varnished porch, selling middleclass candies to the children (discs of caramel, delicious, cheap)—

The dark nuns of St. Louis who had come to my brother's hoary black funeral in a gloomy file (in rain), had reported they were sitting knitting in a thunderstorm when a ball of bright white fire came and hovered in their room just inside the window, dancing in the flash of their scissors

34

and sewing needles as they prepared immense drapes for the bazaar. Incredible to disbelieve them . . . for years I went around pondering this fact: I looked for the white ball in thunderstorms—I understood mysticism at once— I saw where the thunder rolled his immense bowling ball into a clap of clouds all monstrous with jaws and explosion, I knew the thunder was a ball—

On Beaulieu St. our house was built over an ancient cemetery—(Good God the Yankees and Indians beneath, the World Series of old dry dusts). My brother Gerard was of the conviction, ark, that the ghosts of the dead beneath the house were responsible for its sometimes rattling— and crashing plaster, knocking pickaninny Irish dolls from the shelf. In darkness in mid-sleep night I saw him standing over my crib with wild hair, my heart stoned, I turned horrified, my mother and sister were sleeping in big bed, I was in crib, implacable stood Gerard-O my brother . . . it might have been the arrangement of the shadows. —Ah Shadow! Sax!—While I was living on Beaulieu Street I had memories of that hill, and Castle; and when we moved from there we transferred to a house not far from an across-the-street haunted Pine ground with deserted Castle-manse (near a French bread-bakery back of woods and skating ponds, Hildreth St.). Presentiments of shadow and snake came to me early.

17

ON BEAULIEU STREET I have a dream that I'm in the back-yard on a spectral Fourth of July, it's gray and somehow heavy, but there's a crowd in the yard, a crowd of people like paper figures, the fireworks are being exploded in the grassy sand, pow!—but somehow too the whole yard is rattling, and the dead underneath it, and the fence full of sitters, everything rattling like mad like those varnished skeletal furnitures and the unfeeling cruel uncaring rattle of dry bones and especially the rattle of the window when Gerard said the ghosts had come (and later Cousin Noël, in Lynn, said he was the *Phantome d'l'Opéra* mwee hee hee ha ha, gliding off around the goldfish bowl and glazed fish picture over mahogany mountains in that dreary Lynn churchstreet home of his mother's)—

18

AND YET DESPITE ALL THIS RACKETY GRAY when I grew to the grave maturity of 11 or 12 I saw, one crisp October morning, in the back Textile field, a great pitching performance by a husky strangely old looking 14-year-older, or 13,—a very heroic looking boy in the morning, I liked him and hero-worshipped him immediately but never hoped to rise high enough to meet him in those athletic scuffles of the windy fields (when hundreds of less important little kids make a crazy army benighted by individual twitchings in smaller but not less tremendous dramas, for instance that morning I rolled over in the grass and cut my right small finger, on a rock, with a scar that stays vivid and grows with me even now)—there was Scotty Boldieu on the high mound, king of the day, taking his signal from the catcher with a heavy sullen and insulting look of skepticism and native French Canadian Indian-like dumb calm—; the catcher was sending him nervous messages, one finger (fast ball), two fingers (curve), three fingers (drop), four fingers (walk him) (and Paul Boldieu had enough great control to walk em, as if unintentionally, never changing expression) (off the mound he may grin on the bench)— Paul turned aside the catcher's signals (shake of head) with his French Canadian patient scorn, he just waited till the fingers three (signal for drop), settled back, looked to first base, spit, spit again in his glove and rub it in, pluck at the dust for his fingertips, bending thoughtfully but not slowly, chewing on his inside lip in far meditation (maybe thinking about his mother who made him oatmeal and beans in the gloomy gray midwinter dawns of Lowell as he stood in the dank hall closet puttin on his overshoes), looks briefly to 2nd base with a frown from the memory of someone having reached there in the 2nd inning drat it (he sometimes said "Drat it!" in imitation of B movie Counts of England), now it's the 8th inning and Scotty's given up two hits, nobody beyond second base, he's leading 8-0, he wants to strike out the batter and get into the ninth inning, he takes his time—I'm watching him with a bleeding hand, amazed—a great Grover C. Alexander of the sandlots blowing one of his greatest games—(later he was bought by the Boston Braves but went home to sit with his wife and mother-in-law in a bleak brown kitchen with a castiron stove covered with brass scrolls and a poem in a tile panel, and Catholic French Canadian calendars on the wall). —Now he winds up, leisurely, looking off towards third base and beyond even as he's rearing back to throw with an easy, short, effortless motion, no fancy dan imitations and complications and phoniness, blam, he calmly surveys the huge golden sky all sparkle-blue rearing over the hedges and iron pickets of Textile Main Field and the great Merrimac Valley high airs of heaven shining in the commercial Saturday October morning of markets and delivery men, with one look of the eye Scotty has seen that, is in fact looking towards his house on Mammoth Road, at Cow Field—blam, he's come around and thrown his drop home, perfect strike, kid swinging, thap in the catcher's mitt, "You're out," end of the top of the 8th inning.

Scotty's already walking to the bench when the umpire's called it—"Ha, ha," they laugh on the bench knowing him so well, Scotty never fails. In the bottom of the 8th Scot comes to bat for his licks, wearing his pitching jacket, and swinging the bat around loosely in his powerful hands, without much effort, and again in short, unostentatious movements, pitcher throws in a perfect strike after 2 and 0 and Scotty promptly belts it clean-drop into left over the shortstop's glove—he trots to first like Babe Ruth, he was always hitting neat singles, he didn't want to run when he was pitching.

I saw him thus in the morning, his name was Boldieu, it immediately stuck in my mind with Beaulieu—street where I learned to cry and be scared of the dark and of my brother for many years (till almost 10)—this proved to me *all my life wasn't black.*

Scotty, named that for his thrift among 5¢ candy bars

and 11¢ movies, sat in that wrinkly tar doorway with G.J., Lousy and me—and Vinny.

19

VINNY WAS AN ORPHAN for many years ere his father came back, got his mother out of some tub-washing strait, re-united the children from various orphanages, and re-formed his home and family in the tenements of Moody—Lucky Bergerac was his name, a heavy drinker, cause of his early downfalls as well as Old Jack O Diamonds, got a job repairing rollercoasters at Lakeview Park— What a wild house, the tenement screeched— Vinny's mother was called Charlotte, but we pronounced it Charlie, "Hey Charlie," Vinny thus addressed his own mother in a wild scream. Vinny was thin and skinny boyish, very clean featured and handsome, high voiced, excited, affectionate, always laughing or smiling, always swearing like a son of a bitch, "Jesus Crise goddam it Charlie what the fuck you want me to do sit in this fucking goddam bath tub all goddam day—" His father Lucky outdid him unbelievably, the only eloquence he had was curses, "Jey-sas Crise gawd damn ballbreaking sonofabitch if I ain't an old piece of shit but you look like a goddam fat ass old cow tonight Charlie ..." and at this compliment Charlie would screech with joy—you never heard such a wild screech, her eyes used to blaze out with the intensity of white fire, she was crazy as all get out, the first time I saw her she was standing on a chair fixing a bulb

39

and Vinny rushed up and looked under her dress (he was 13) and yelled "O Jey-sas Crise what a nice ass you got Ma!" and she screeched and whacks him one on the head, a house of joy. Me and G.J. and Lousy and Scotty used to sit in that house all day.

"Jey-sas Crise what a maniac!"

"Is he *crazy*—you know what he did? He stuck his finger up his ass and said Woo Woo—"

"He came fifteen comes, no kiddin, he jumped around jacking himself off all that whole day—the 920 club was on the radio, Charlie was at work—Zaza the madman."

This tenement was located across the street from the Pawtucketville Social Club, an organization intended to be some kind of meeting place for speeches about Franco-American matters but was just a huge roaring saloon and bowling alley and pool table with a meetingroom always locked. My father that year was running the bowling alley, great cardgames of the night we imitated all day in Vinny's house with whist for Wing cigarettes. (I was the only one who didn't smoke, Vinny used to smoke two cigarettes at a time and inhale deep as he could.) We didn't give a shit about no Doctor Sax.

Great big bullshitters, friends of Lucky's, grown men, would come in and regale us with fantastic lies and stories —we screamed at them "What a bullshitter, geez, I never— *is he a bullshitter!*" Everything we said was put this way, "Oh is my old man gonna kick the shit out of me if he ever finds out about those helmets we stole, G.J."

"Ah fuckit, Zagg—helmets is helmets, my old man's in the grave and no one's the worse for it." At 11 or 12 G.J. was so Greekly tragic he could talk like that—words of woe and wisdom poured from his childly dewy glooms. He was the opposite of crackbrained angel joy Vinny. Scotty just watched or bit his inner lip in far away silence (thinking about that game he pitched, or Sunday he's got to go to Nashua with his mother to see Uncle Julien and Aunt Yvonne (*Mon Mononcle Julien, Ma Matante Yvonne*)—Lousy is spitting, silently, whitely, neatly, just a little dew froth of symbolic spit, clean enough to wash your eyeballs in—which I had to do when he got sore and his aim was champion in the gang.—Spitting out the window, and turns to giggle with a laugh in the joke general, slapping his knees softly, rushing over to me or G.J. half kneeling on the floor to whisper a confidential observation of glee, sometimes G.J. would respond by grabbing him by the hair and dragging him around the room, "Ooh this fuckin Lousy has just told me the dirtiest—*is he*—Ooh is he got *dirty thoughts*—Ooh, would I love to kick his ass—allow me, gentlemen, stand back, to kick the ass of Lauzon Cave-In in his means, lookout Slave don't desist! or try to run! frup, gluck, aye, haye!" he's screaming as Lousy suddenly squeezes his balls to break the hair hold. Lousy is the sneakiest most impossible to wrastle snake—(Snake!)—in the world—

When we turned the subject to gloom and evil (dark and dirty and dying), we talked of the death of Zap Plouffe, Gene's and Joe's kid brother our age (with those backstore stories maybe told by malicious mothers who hated the Plouffes and especially the dying melancholy old man in his dark house). Zap's foot was dragged under a milk wag-

on, he caught infection and died, I first met Zap on a crazy
screaming night about the third after we'd moved from
Centralville to Pawtucketville (1932) on my porch (Phebe),
he came rollerskating up on the porch with his long teeth
and prognathic jaw of the Plouffes, he was the first Pawtucketville boy to talk to me... And the screams in the
nightfall street of play!—

"*Mon nom c'est Zap Plouffe mué—je rests au coin dans
maison la*"—(my name it is Zap Plouffe me—I live on the
corner in the house there).

Not long after, G.J. moved in across the street, with
dolorous furnitures from the Greek slums of Market Street
where you hear the wails of Oriental Greek records on
Sunday afternoon and smell the honey and the almond.
"Zap's ghost is in that goddam park," G.J. said, and never
walked home across the field, instead went Riverside-Sarah
or Gershom-Sarah, Phebe (where he lived all those years)
was the center of those two prongs.

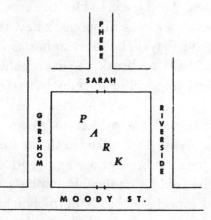

The park is in the middle, Moody's across the bottom.

So I began to see the ghost of Zap Plouffe mixed with other shrouds when I walked home from Destouches' brown store with my *Shadow* in my arm. I wanted to face my duty—I had learned to stop crying in Centralville and I was determined not to start crying in Pawtucketville (in Centralville it was Ste. Thérèse and her turning plaster head, the crouching Jesus, visions of French or Catholic or Family Ghosts that swarmed in corners and open closet doors in mid sleep night, and the funerals all around, the wreaths on old wood white door with paint cracking, you know some old gray ash-faced dead ghost is waxing his profile to candlelight and suffocating flowers in the broongloom of dead relatives kneeling in a chant and the son of the house is wearing a black suit Ah Me! and the tears of mothers and sisters and frightened humans of the grave, the tears flowing in the kitchen and by the sewing machine upstairs, and when one dies—three will die) , , (two more will die, who will it be, what phantom is pursuing *you*?). Doctor Sax had knowledge of death ... but he was a mad fool of power, a Faustian man, no true Faustian's afraid of the dark—only Fellaheen--and Gothic Stone Cathedral Catholic of Bats and Bach Organs in the Blue Mid Night Mists of Skull, Blood, Dust, Iron, Rain burrowing into earth to snake antique.

As the rain hit the windowpane, and apples swelled on the limb, I lay in my white sheets reading with cat and candy bar ... that's where all these things were born.

20

THE UNDERGROUND RUMBLING HORROR OF THE LOWELL NIGHT
—a black coat on a hook on a white door—in the dark—
-o-o-h!—my heart used to sink at sight of huge headshroud
rearing on his rein in the goop of my door— Open closet
doors, everything under the sun's inside and under the
moon—brown handles fall out majestically—supernumer-
ary ghosts on different hooks in a bad void, peeking at my
sleep bed—the cross in my mother's room, a salesman had
sold it to her in Centralville, it was a phosphorescent Christ
on a black-lacquered Cross—it glowed the Jesus in the
Dark, I gulped for fear every time I passed it the moment
the sun went down, it took that own luminosity like a bier,
it was like *Murder by the Clock* the horrible fear-shrieking
movie about the old lady clacking out of her mausoleum at
midnight with a—you never saw her, just the woeful shadow coming up the davenport tap-tap-tap as her daughters
and sisters screech all over the house— Never liked to see
my bedroom door even ajar, in the dark it yawned a black
dangerhole.—Square, tall, thin, severe, Count Condu has
stood in my doorway many's the time— I had an old Victrola in my bedroom which was also ghostly, it was haunted
by the old songs and old records of sad American antiquity
in its old mahogany craw (that I used to reach in and punch
for nails and cracks, in among the needle dusts, the old la-
ments, Rudies, magnolias and Jeannines of twenties time)—
Fear of gigantic spiders big as your hand and hands as big

44

as barrels—why . . . underground rumbling horrors of the Lowell night—many.

Nothing worse than a hanging coat in the dark, extended arms dripping folds of cloth, leer of dark face, to be tall, statuesque, motionless, slouch headed or hatted, silent— My early Doctor Sax was completely silent like that, the one I saw standing—on the sandbank at night—an earlier time we were playing war in the sandbank at night (after seeing *The Big Parade* with Slim Summerville in muddy)— we played crawling in the sand like World War I infantry-men on the front, putteed, darkmouthed, sad, dirty, spitting on clots of mud— We had our stick rifles, I had a broken leg and crawled most miserably behind a rock in the sand . . . an Arabian rock, Foreign Legion now . . . there was a little sand road running through the sand field valley—by starlight bits of silver sand would sparkle—the sandbanks then rose and surveyed and dipped for a block each way, the Phebe way ending at houses of the street (where lived the family of the white house with flowers and marble gardens of whitewash all around, daughters, ransoms, their yard ended at the first sandbank which was the one I was pelting with pitching rocks the day I met Dicky Hampshire —and the other way ending on Riverside in a steep cliff) (my intelligent Richard Hampshire)— I saw Doctor Sax the night of the Big Parade in the sand, somebody was con-voying a squad to the right flank and being forced to take cover, I was reconnoitering with views at the scenery for possible suspects and trees, and there's Doctor Sax grook-ing in the desert plateau of timbers in brush, the all-stars of Whole World strung up behind him à la bowl, meadows and apple trees as a background horizon, clear pure night, Doctor Sax is watching our pathetic sand game with an inscrutable silence— I look once, I look, he vanisheth on falling horizons in a bat ... what great difference was there between Count Condu and Doctor Sax in my childhood?

Dicky Hampshire introduced me to a possible difference ... we started drawing cartoons together, in my house at my desk, in his house in his bedroom with kid brother watching (just like Paddy Sorenson's kid brother watching me and Paddy drawing 4-year-old cartoons—abstract as hell—as the Irish washingmachine wrangles and the old Irish grandfather puffs on his clay upsidedown pipe, on Beaulieu Street, my first "English" chum)— Dicky Hampshire was my greatest English chum, and he *was* English. Strangely, his father had an old Chandler car in the yard, year '29 or '21, probably '21, wood spokes, like some wrecks you find in the Dracut woods smelling of shit and all sagged down and full of rotten apples and dead and all ready to sprout out of the earth a new car plant, some kind of Terminus pine plant with sagging oil gums and rubber teeth and an iron source in the center, a Steel tree, an old car like that is often seen but rarely intact, although it wasn't running. Dicky's father worked in a printing plant on a canal, just like my father ... the old *Citizen* newspaper that went out —blue with mill rags in the alleys, cotton dust balls and smoke pots, litter, I walk along the long sunny concrete rale of the millyards in the booming roar of the windows where my mother's working, I am horrified by the cotton dresses of the women rushing out of the mills at five—the women work too much! they're not home any more! They work more than they ever worked!— Dicky and I covered these millyards and agreed millwork was horrible. "What I'm going to do instead is sit around the green jungles of Guatemala."

"Watermelon?"

"No, no, Guatemala—my brother's going there—"

We drew cartoons of jungle adventures in Guatemala. Dicky's cartoons were very good—he drew slower than I did— We invented games. My mother made caramel pudding for both of us. He lived up Phebe across the sandbank. I was the Black Thief, I put notes in his door.

"Beware, Tonight the Black Thief will Strike Again. Signed, the Black Thief!!!"—and off I'd flit (in broad daylight planting notes). At night I came in my cape and slouch hat, cape made of rubber (my sister's beach cape of the thirties, red and black like Mephistopheles), hat is old slouch hat I have ... (later I wore great big felt hats all level to imitate Alan Ladd *This Gun for Hire*, at 19, so what's silly)— I glided to Dicky's house, stole his bathing trunks from the porch, left a note on the rail under a rock, "The Black Thief Has Struck."— Then I'd run—then I'd in the daytime stand with Dicky and the others.

"I wonder who that Black Thief is?"

"I think he lives on Gershom, that's what I think."

"It might be,—it might be,—then again—I dunno."

I'm standing there speculating. For some odd reason having to do with his personal psychological position (psyche) Dicky became terrified of the Black Thief—he began to believe in the sinister and heinous aspects of the deal

47

—of the—secretive—perfectly silent—action. So sometimes I'd see him and break his will with stories— "On Gershom he's stealing radios, crystal sets, stuff in barns—"

"What'll he steal from me next? I lost my hoop, my pole vault, my trunks, and now my brother's wagon ... my wagon."

All these articles were hidden in my cellar, I was going to return them quite as mysteriously as they disappeared —at least so I told myself. My cellar was particularly evil. One afternoon Joe Fortier had cut off the head of a fish in it, with an ax, just because we caught the fish and couldn't eat it as it was an old dirty sucker from the river (Merrimac of Mills)—boom—crash—I saw stars—I hid the loot there, and had a secret dusty airforce made of cross-beam sticks with crude nail landing gears and a tail all hid in the old coal bin, ready for pubertical war (in case I got tired of the Black Thief) and so—I had a light dimly shining down (a flashlight through a cloth of black and blue, thunder) and this shone dumb and ominous on me in my cape and hat as outside the concrete cellar windows redness of dusk turned purple in New England and the kids screamed, dogs screamed, streets screamed, as elders dreamed, and in the back fences and violet lots I skipped in a flowing cape guile through a thousand shadows each more potent than the other till I got (skirting Dicky's house to give him a rest) to the Ladeaus' under the sandbank streetlamp where I threw surreptitious pebbles among their skippity hops in the dirt road (on cold November sunnydays the sand dust blew on Phebe like a storm, a drowsy storm of Arabic winter in the North)—the Ladeaus searched the hills of sand for

this Shadow—this thief—this Sax incarnate pebblethrower
—didn't find him—I let go my "Mwee hee hee ha ha" in the
dark of purple violet bushes, I screamed out of earshot in
a dirt mole, went to my Wizard of Oz shack (in Phebe
backyard, it had been an old ham-curing or tool-storing
shack) and drop't in through the square hole in the roof,
and stood, relaxed, thin, huge, amazing, meditating the
mysteries of my night and the triumphs of my night, the
glee and huge fury of my night, mwee hee hee ha ha—
(looking in a little mirror, flashing eyes, darkness sends its
own light in a shroud)— Doctor Sax blessed me from the
roof, where he hid—a fellow worker in the void! the black
mysteries of the World! Etc! the World Winds of the Universe!—I hid in this dark shack—listening outside—a madness in the bottom of my darkness smile—and gulped with
fear. They finally caught me.

Mrs. Hampshire, Dick's mother, said to me gravely in
the eye, "Jack, are you the Black Thief?"

"Yes, Mrs. Hampshire," I replied immediately, hypno-
tized by the same mystery that once made her say, when
I asked her if Dicky was at home or at the show, in a dull,
flat, tranced voice as if she was speaking to a Spiritualist,
"Dicky ... is ... gone ... far ... away ..."

"Then bring back Dicky's things and tell him you're
sorry." Which I did, and Dicky was wiping his red wet
eyes with a handkerchief.

"What foolish power had I discovered and been pos-
sessed by?" I asts meself ... and not much later my mother
and sister came impatiently marching down the street to
fetch me from the Ladeau bushes because they were look-

ing for the beach cape, a beach party was up. My mother said exasperated:

"I'm going to stop you from reading them damned Thrilling Magazines if it's the last thing I do (*Tu va arretez d'lire ca ste mautadite affaire de fou la, tu m'attend tu?*)"—

The Black Thief note I printed, by hand, in ink, thickly, on beautiful scraps of glazed paper I got from my father's printing shop— The paper was sinister, rich, might have scared Dicky—

21

"I AM TOO FEEBLE TO GO ON," says the Wizard in the Castle bending over his papers at night.

"Faustus!" cries his wife from the bath, "what are you doing up so late! Stop fiddling with your desk papers and pen quills in the middle of the night, come to bed, the mist is on the air of night lamps, a dew'll come to rest your fevered brow at morning,—you'll lie swaddled in sweet sleep like a lambikin—I'll hold you in my old snow-white arms—and all you do's sit there dreaming—"

"Of Snakes! of Snakes!" answers the Master of Earthly Evil—sneering at his own wife: he has a beak nose and movable jaw-bird beak and front teeth missing and something indefinably young in bone structure but imponderably old in the eyes—horrible old bitch face of a martinet with books, cardinals and gnomes at his spidery behest.

"Would I'd never seen your old fink face and married

you—to sit around in bleak castles all my life, for varmints in the dirt!"

"Flap up you old sot and drink your stinking brandignac and conyoles, fit me an idea for chat, drive me not mad with your fawter toddle in a gloom ... you with your pendant flesh combs and bawd spots—picking your powderies in a nair—flam off, frish frowse, I want peace to Scholarize my Snakes—let me Baroque be."

By this time the old lady's asleep... Wizard Faustus hurries in his wrinkly feet to a meet with Count Condu and the Cardinals in the Cave Room ... his footsteps clang along an iron underhall— There stands a gnome with a pass key, a little glucky monster with web feet or some such —heavy rags wrapped around each foot and around the head almost blinding the eyes, a weird crew, their leader sported a Moro saber and had a thin little neck you'd expect from a shrunk head... The Wizard comes to the Parapet to contemplate.

He looks down into the Pit of Night.

He hears the Snake Sigh and Inch.

He moves his hand three times and backs, he waves a bow with his wrists, and walks down the long sand hill of a grisly part of the Castle with shit in the sand and old boards and moisture down the mossy ratty granite walls of an old dongeon—where gnome children masturbated and wrote obscenities with whitewash brushes like advertisements of Presidents in Mexico.

The Wizard, with a loll of his sensual tongue, dislodges a piece of meat from his front teeth, deep in folded-arm meditation at the head of the gutted bird.

He still bears the horrible marks of his strangulation and occupation by the Devil in the 13th century:—a high collar in the old Inquisition style he wears to partially conceal signs of ravages by Satan in the long ago—an ugly twist—

22

IN THAT ORIGINAL DREAM of the wrinkly tar corner and the doorway of G.J., Lousy, Vinny, Scotty and me (Dicky was never in this gang) (moved to Highlands) there stands across Riverside Street the great iron picket fence of Textile running around the entire grounds connected by brick posts with the year of a Class on it, fast losing posts to space and time, and great shrub trees rising clear around the football and track field part of it—huge footballs transpired in bronze autumns in the field, crowds gathered at the fence to peek through the shrubs, others in the grandstand planks of pipe shrill keen afternoons of ruddy football in fog-bloom pinks of fantastic dusk—

But at night the waving trees made a swish of black ghosts flaming on all sides in a fire of black arms and sinuosities in the gloom—million moving deeps of leaf night— It's a fear to walk along it (on Riverside, no sidewalk, just leaves on ground at roadside) (pumpkins in the dew of Halloween hint, voting time in the empty classroom of November afternoon)— In that field ... Textile let us play in it, one time a friend of mine masturbated in a bottle in the back field and strung it out with jerks of the jar into the air, I scaled a rock at the Textile windows, Joe Fortier slingshot twenty out of existence, tremendous ingratitude to the authorities of the school, at supper summer dusk we rushed out for games of scrub and sometimes double play right on the diamond . . . high grass waved in the redness, Lousy piped from third base, flung me the double play ball, I pivoted on a hinch and flung around back to first with a hitch and dip of my shoulders and a whomp into first high hard straight,—Scotty at short on the next tap scoops up his grasscutter with a motion as still as an Indian about to shit, holds the ball gravely in his meat hand before I know it and is flipping me a softie over the keystone which I have to come in charging synchronized with the Scotty ball a foot off ground, which I do with meat hand and still running (and with passing foot-tap at sack) flick under my left side with all my might to join the firstbaseman's mitt with my straightline loop of reasoning hurl—which he (G.J., eyes semiclosed, cussin, "That fuckin Jack sinks me on purpose with his dusters") scoops mid of earth with a flop of his long leftleg and his other bent in for stretch, a pretty play highlighted by Scotty's calm and his understanding that I would appreciate a *place* on second soft and loopy—

Then we—I invented—I took apart the old Victrola we had, just lifted motor out, intact, and pasted paper around turntable, measured "seconds" and theoretical time-laws of my own related to "seconds" and took it outside to the park, crank and all, to time the athletes of my track meet: G.J., Lousy, Scotty, Vinny, Dicky, even old Iddiboy Bissonnette who'd sometimes join our play with grave seriousness and iddyboy joy ("Hey Iddiboy!")—others—semiseriously grunting out 30-yard dashes to see their "time" (which I had as close to 4 seconds and 3.9 seconds as possible) and to amuse, or cater, to me—to mollify me, I was always giving orders and called the 'big punk' by both Billy Artaud (who is now a loudmouth union leader) and Dicky Hampshire (dead on Bataan)— Dicky wrote "Jack is a big punk" in chalk on the boardfence of a French Canadian Salem street alley as we walked home for noon recess from Bartlett Junior High—

A school which has since burned down—rich trees—on Wannalancitt Street, name of a King—an Indian chief—Pawtucket Boulevard, name of a brave nation— The tragic ice house that burned down also and me and Jean Fourchette offered to help the firemen, we moved hoses, we had walked all the way from Dracut in pyro-maniacal excitement, drooling, "Gee I bet it a good fire, hoh?" (*"Boy mon boy, m'a vaw dire, c'est un bon feu, ce feu la, tu va woir, oui, mautadit, moo hoo hoo ha ha ha"*)—he had a maniac laugh, he was an idiot, underdeveloped mentality, sweet and kind, tremendously dirty, saintly, goofly, hardworking, willing, did chores I guess, a monster idiot Frenchman from the woods— He used to watch those Textile games on Saturday October afternoons through the trees —"moo hoo hoo ha ha, boy mon boy, he sure smear that guy, moo hee hee hee—hoh?"—

I had so (finally) perfected my timing-clock we grew more—we held great gloomy track meets in Textile field at sunset with the last event after dark—a regular cinder racetrack circled the field— I see G.J.—I'm on the sidelines timing him—he's running the Five Lap "Mile"—I see his tragic white shirttails bobbing in the flapshroud of 9 o'clock at summernight far across Textile field somewhere in the shadows of the orange brick castle of its halls and laboratories (with broken windows from Textile homeruns)—G.J. is lost in Eternity, when he rounds (when he flaps on straining in his heartbreaking void trying to catch time with feeble tired boy legs he'll—) I—Ah G.J., he's rounding the last turn, we hear him huffing horribly in the dark, he'll die at the tape, the winds of evening ripple hugely through the shrub trees of the Textile fence and on out over the dump, the river and the summer houses of Lowell—the streets of flashing shadows, the streetlamps—the halls of Textile half-cut in a huge stab of Moody Street light through traceries and mockeries of star and shadow and twining limb, comes clover from Pawtucketville scenting, the Cow Field dusts of ballgames have settled down for the Pawtucketville summernight love of huddled standers—and fallers—G.J. comes twapping down the cinders, his time is miserably slow, he's done all that running for nothing—

He gets sore and sick of my machine— He and Lousy start wrestling— (Meanwhile little George Bouen has started off on his 5 Flap Mile and I started machine and directed takeoff but now I turn from my duties as track official and inventor and leader of commands and puffings) —in this sorrowful huge summer dark with its millionfold stars milking up the pit of night so steep and inky deep with dew— Somewhere in Lowell at this moment my father, big fat Pop, is driving his old Plymouth home from work or an afternoon at Suffolk Downs or in the Jockey Club at Daumier's—my sister, with a tennis racket, is 1935

in the swisheries of tree-haunted courts when tennis is over
and the tennis ghosts pad whitefoot to the home, by water
fountains and waterfalls of foliage— The Huge Trees of
Lowell lament the July evening in a song begins in meadow
apple lands up above Bridge Street, the Bunker Hill farms
and cottages of Centralville—to the sweet night that flows
along the Concord in South Lowell where railroads cry the
roundroll—to the massive lake like archeries and calms of
the Boulevard lover lanes of cars, nightslap, and fried clams
and Pete's and Glennie's ice cream—to the pines of Farmer
Ubrecht Dracut way, to the last craw call crow in the Pine
Brook heights, the flooded wilds and Swamps and swims
of Mill Pond, the little bridge of Rosemont fording a
Waterloo mouth of her backwood Brook in eve remnant
mists—highway lights are flashing, I hear a song from a
passing radio, the crunch of gravel in the road, hot tar stars,
apples to pop signs with crabapples for posts— In the
gloom of all Lowell I rush up to wrestle with G.J. and
Lousy—finally I have Lousy on my shoulder like a sack,
whirling him—he gets tremendously mad, never get Lousy
mad, remember the balls, hanging helplessly in my grip
upsidedown he bites my ass and I drop him like a hot
worm— "Fucking Lousy bit Jack's ass, did he bite his ass!"
(sadly)—"he bit his ass—did he *bite*!"—as we laugh and
wrangle, here comes Georgie Bouen finishing his mile, unknown, ungreeted at the tape, comes puffing to the finish
line in solitary glooms of destiny and death (we never saw
him again) as ghosts wrestle—goof—laugh—all mystery
Huge dripping on our heads in the Antiquity of the Universe which has a giant radar machine haunting its flying

cloud brown night spaces of dull silence in the Hum and
Dynamo of the Tropic—though then my dream of the
Universe was not so "accurate," so modern—it was all black
and Saxish—

Tragedies of darkness hid in the shadows all around Textile—the waving hedges hid a ghost, a past, a future, a
shuddering spirit specter full of anxious blackish sinuous
twiny night torture—the giant orangebrick smokestack rose
to the stars, a little black smoke came out—below, a million
tittering twit leaves and jumping shadows—I have such a
hopeless dream of walking or being there at night, nothing
happens, I just pass, *everything is unbearably over with*
(I stole a football helmet from Textile field once, with G.J.,
the tragedy is in the haunt and guilt of Textile field)
(where also someone hit me in the brow with a rock)—

In the fall my sister would come see me play football
with the gang, sock, crash bang, tackle,—I'd spin touch-
downs for her, for her cheers—this was behind the grandstand as the Textile team scrimmaged with Coach Rusty
Yarvell—great iron reds in the sky, falling leaves flying,
whistles—raw scuffed cold horn chapped sidehands—

But at night, and in summer, or in an April windy rain
wetly waving, this field, these trees, that terror of pickets
and brickposts,—the brooding silence—the density of the
Pawtucketville night, the madness of the dream,—the race
being concluded in a vat gloom, there is evil in the flashing
green round of brown night— Doctor Sax was everywhere
in this—his glee supported us and made us run and jump
and grab leaves and roll in the grass when we went home—
Doctor Sax gets into the blood of children by his cape ...

his laughter is hidden in the black hoods of the darkness where you can suck him up with air, the glee of night in kids is a message from the dark, there is a telepathic shadow in this void bowl slant.

23

I SLEPT AT JOE FORTIER's—many's the time I could feel the goose pimples of his cold legs or the leather of his tar black heel, as we lay in dank barns and attics of his various homes in the Doctor Sax midnights of ghost stories and strange sounds—

I first met Joe when he lived on Bunker Hill Street a stone's throw practically from West Sixth and Boisvert where the brown bathrobe warmed me in the sky at my mother's neck— His mother and my mother worked side by side at the great St. Louis Paroisse bazaar—together they once visited the stone mansion castle on the Lakeview hill near Lupine Road that is symmetrical to Snake Hill Castle (and among the serried black pines of whose slope-grounds Gerard had slid in snows of my infancy, I remember I was afraid he'd hit a pine tree)— His mother and mine went in the "Castle" to see about some church affair, they came out saying the place was too spooky for the bazaar—my mother said there were niches of stone in the halls (the old sun must have shone red through hallway dusts on these stone hollows in the Hook, as I was being born across the pines outside)—

Joe and I explored all the possible haunted houses in

town. Chief of our great houses was when he lived on Bridge Street near 18th, in an old gray rickety manse in a V of leafy streets in autumn—across Bridge Street, over the stone lawn wall, rose the slope side of pines and drearies, exactly like the lawn of the Lakeview Castle—to the Haunted House which was but a shell, a wreck of plasters, beams, broken glass, shit, wet leaves, forlorn legs of old centerpieces, rusted piano wires in a ping (like in an old abandoned freighter used as a buoy you still find Captain's Mess has scrollwork in the beams, and the sun shines in all joy morn of sea like it did off Malaya or Seattle so long ago)— There were ghosts in that old House Shell—roofs decaying—pissing was a thrill among these decadent beams and bulge crack walls— Something namelessly, shroudily obscene and wild—like drawings of great cocks of the length of snakes, with dumb venom spittles—we tugged at boards, shifted bricks, broke fresh plaster islands, kicked out glass chips and—

At night, summer's nights, with the family downstairs in the big kitchen (maybe my own mother or father there, others, a young priest just down from Canada who loves to woo de ladies—we are four levels up to the attic, we only hear faint roars of laughter below)—in the Lowell night we lay relaxed in pissy mattresses, with treeswish at the window, telling stories ("Shee-cago! shee-cago!"), playing with our ding dongs, squirming, throwing legs up in air, rushing to the window to look out at commotions—to look out at our Haunted House in the multiform black and white flashing Lowell night... What owls? hoos and voodoos in the midnight? What old maniac in white hair is come to pluck the rusty piano springs in a maze of midnight? what Doctor Sax crawling along the black, shaded, cowled, peloted, zinging speedily at low-height to his mysteries and fear—

Together, by huge afternoon of world clouds, we explored reservoirs in the hill of Lowell so high, or made camps outside sewage pipes in brown tragic matted fields —in the backfields of St. Louis school—in a tree we sit, call it Fresh Air Texicab,— I fly kites in the field—

Joe comes to my house one Sunday morning after church but I'm eating breakfast so in his white knickers while waiting he goes down the cellar and shovels up a pail of coal for my Ma—we pose outside with Henry Troisieux and my cat, in dull Sunday afternoon,—behind us wave the Doctor Sax trees . . . the record of old nights in the sleeping barns, in the cold attic, in the mystery, in the dream, Joe and me— Old buddies of the lifetime of boyhood— Yet Joe avoided shrouds, knew no mystery, wasn't scared, didn't care, strode along, lumberjack boots, in rainy mornings in church, Sunday, he's spent last week exploring a little river, wants this afternoon to find his cave in the pine woods—go build a tent, fix the car in rainy dim-mists all day with cans and smudge rags and no refreshments—

Joe had turrets and attics in his house but he wasn't afraid of sailing ghosts . . . his phantoms were reality, work and earn money, fix your knife, straighten the screw, figure for tomorrow. I played dismal private games in his backyard, some mythic hassel with myself involving how many times around the house and water—while he's busy fixing something for his use. Come night, shadows creep, Sax

60

emerges, Joe just rocks on the porch talking of things to do and every now and then leaning over and scratching his leg and going "Hyoo hyoo hyoo! you shore did get sore that time—hoo hoo!"

24

THE NOISE OF THE BIG FAMILY PARTIES could only be heard faintly up in Joe's fourth story attic but O! when it was at my house, the cottage on West Street earlier or later on, wow, the whoops and screams of the ladies as madcap Duquette would get Blanche to put all the lights out and start playing spooky music on the piano, up riseth a face powdered in white flour, framed in an empty picture frame, with flashlight under chin, oogoogoogoo, the bursts of howling laughter would just practically knock me outa my bed one flight above— But at least I had the satisfaction of knowing that no real shades would come to get me in the midst of such strong adult mockery and racket— Gad, that was a gang: they called themselves *La Maudite Gang* until one of the couples died leaving them twelve couples instead of thirteen so it became *The Dirty Dozen*— Poor priest LaPoule DuPuis was involved with them, he was the last unmarried son of a huge Quebec family that according to tradition felt it would be *damnée* if someone in the house didnt belong to the priesthood so madcap sexfiend LaPoule was retired piously behind the cloistral wall, to some extent, a woman wasnt safe in the same room

with him— One Saturday night he got dead drunk after
pirouetting with all the ladies at a big roaring party and
passed out before midnight (woulda stopped drinking at
midnight anyway, as he was saying Mass in the morning)—
Come morning Joe's father hauls LaPoule into the shower,
shoves black coffee down his throat, then calls the whole
gang to come see the fun at eleven o'clock Mass—

They're all there, the Duluozes, the Fortiers, the Du-
quettes, the DuBois, the Lavoisiers, the lot, all in the front
pews, and out comes LaPoule in chasuble with the solemn
altar boys and weaves and totters to his work— Every time
he turns his bloodshot suffering eyes to the front pews,
there's my father or Joe's, or Ma and the other crazy women
giving him surreptitious little mocking waves of the hand
(like in some hilarious blasphemous French movie not yet
made) and he in turn waves back as if to say "For krissakes
keep it low" but they think he's spoofing back at them and
all through the Mass Joe's father you can hear his spluttrous
inheld explosions of dont-laugh— My father makes everything worse by waving his strawhat between his legs, or
Blanche crosses her eyes at LaPoule just as he's raising a
host at the communion rail—mad gang—the poor fellow
laboring to kneel, altar boys clutching at his arm as he
almost falls over, as good a man of gold and God I'd say
as the most postrous Bishop ever levied frowns on his flock
—LaPoule at our wild parties loved to tell the joke (which
was actually a true story) about the parish priest in Canada
who wouldnt pardon some guy for a sin and in revenge the
guy smeared shite on the rail of the pulpit so here it is Sun-

day morning the priest is about to begin: "Today, ladies and gentlemen, I want to speak about religion, la *nature* de la religion—Religion," says he, beginning, putting his hand on the rail, "religion . . ." he brings his hand up to his nose, puts it down again . . . "religion is—" once again he brings his hand to his nose, frowning in preplexity, "*la religion—mais c'est d'la marde!*" Which joke was one of those that used to send off Joe's big happy mother Adelaïde into such a scream you could hear it clear down the river rocks and inevitably blasted my cat off my pillow and sent me wondering out of dreams— The mad gang, the time they had a party at the beach and after the near-tragedy of Pa and Mr. Fortier swimming out too far and almost drowning (Salisbury Beach) even then enough gayety in the gang, that, as Mrs. Fortier is frying the porkchops on the camp cottage stove and everybody's feeling kinda gloomy, Duquette comes up in his bathing suit, plucks pubic hairs from under his trunks and sprinkles them into the sizzling pan saying "They need a little spice"—so that the gang laughter rang by the sea, and talk about your modern day neighbors complaining to the police about noisy parties, these parties were revolutions and cannonades, it'll never happen again in America (besides all the swishing trees have been cut down, so dreaming boys cant lean their chins on midnight window-sills any more)—O Moon Lowell— And my mother making coffee in our old 15-cup drip grind aluminum pot, and the poker games in the kitchen lasting till doomsday—Joe and I'd sometimes come down and peek from the staircase at all this Riot Loveliness—

25

WHEN JOE LIVED on Bunker Hill Street and we were 8, 9, we explored first thing the banks of the Merrimac in that part along Lakeview Avenue then-Polish slums where the river swam dirtily, meekly without rock-roar along the huge red walls of Boott Mills—we'd on rainy Sunday afternoons in February run down there to kick at ice floes and rusty empty kerosene cans and tires and crap— One time we fell in to our hips, got wet—Big brother Henry shat against a tree, he actually did, squatted and aimed an explosion on a lateral line, horrible. We found fat lovers disentangling huge dimpled lady legs and hairy manlegs out of an intercourse in a litter of movie magazines, empty cans, rat rags, dirt, grass and straw halfway up the slope in the bushes ... a gray afternoon in summer, they were delightfully engaged in a field dump by the river ... and at night came back, darker, wilder, sexualler, with flashlights, dirty magazines, jiggling hands, sucks, furtive listens to the Sound of Time in the river, the mills, the bridges and streets of Lowell ... wildeyed in heaven they screwed, and went home.

Joe and I ransacked the river down there ... the darker and rainier the better the time... We fished out crap from the stream. An unknown and forgotten morning took place in the yard of a rickety two story house corner of Lakeview and Bunker Hill where we threw firewood and balls all up and down the air and mothers yelled at us, new friends,—like the forgetting of the memory of next Monday morning

in school—ugh it's impossible to forget the horror of school
. . . coming . . . Monday—

One afternoon—in the ghost yards of St. Louis, the
crunchly gravels of recess, banana smells in the lockers, a
nun combing my hair with the water of the pissoir drip-
pipe, dank dark gloom and sins of corridors and corners
where also (on the girl side) my sister Nin dashed in eternities echoing of her own horror—one afternoon as the
whole school stood silent in the noon gravel, listening and
fidgeting, Joe, who'd done some *pécher* (sin) during the
recess, was being whanged with a big ruler with iron rims
on the ass in the Sister Superior's office—shrieking and
howling he was, when I asked him about it later he said
"It hurt" and didn't make any excuses for the howling he
did. Joe was always a big cowboy. We played in some old
Farmer's (Farmer Kelly's) field—he had a solemn farm-
house on West Sixth with attendant hugetree and barns,
100-years-old farm, in the middle of middleclass cottages
of Centralville, behind his great fields spread, apples, hollows, meadows, some corn close in, fences,—with the St.
Louis parish on his flank (rectory and church and school
and auditorium and battered sadfield of recess) (St. Louis,
where my brother's funeral darkened in a fitful glimmer
before my eyes . . . in a dim far loneliness far from here and
now . . . forgotten rains have shrouded and re-shrouded
the burial grounds) . . . Farmer Kelly—his old lamplit oil
house flimmered in a glub of night trees when we passed
going from my house to Joe's, we always wondered what
kind of an old mysterious hermit he must be, I knew far-

65

mers and farm life from Uncle John Giradoux in the Nashua
woods where I went in summers ... to a cobwebbed Sax
of forest trees—

A kid across the street from Joe's died, we heard wailing;
another kid in a street between Joe's and mine, died—rain,
flowers—the smell of flowers—an old Legionnaire died, in
blue gold horrors of cloth and velvet and insignias and
paper-wreaths and the cadaverous death of satin pillows—
Oh yoi yoi I hate that—my whole death and Sax is wound
in satin coffins— Count Condu slept in one all day below
the Castle—purple lip't—they buried little boys in them—I
saw my brother in a satin coffin, he was nine, he lay with
the stillness and the face of my former wife in her sleep,
accomplished, regretted—the coffin streaks, spiders join his
hand below—he'd lay in the sun of worms looking for the
lambs of the sky—he'd gook a ghost no more in those
shroudy halls of sand incarnate dirt behung in drapes of
grain by level deep doop dung—what a thing to gape at—
AND THROUGH ROTTING SATIN.

I gave up the church to ease my horrors—too much candlelight, too much wax—

I prefer rivers in my death, or seas, and other continents,
but no satin death in Satin Massachusetts Lowell—with the
bishop of St. Jean de Baptiste Stone, who baptized Gerard,
with a wreath in the rain, beads on his iron nose, "Mama
did he baptize me?"

"No he baptized Gerard," I wished— I was just a little
too young to have been baptized by a Saint of the Hero
Church, Gerard had, and so baptized, saint did thus die
—rain across the Rouault Gray Baroque Strasbourg Cathe-

dral façade Big Minster Face of St. Jean Baptiste church on Merrimac St. at Aiken's sad end—rising stone heap from the tenements of Moody Street—grooking rivers piled beneath.

Doctor Sax traversed the darknesses between pillars in the church at vespertime.

26

FINALLY VINNY BERGERAC moved to Rosemont—from that tenement on Moody to the swampy interiors and lowlands of Rosemont, a rosecovered cottage flat on the dreaming lurps and purls of the Merrimac... Fact is, they had a swimbeach on that shore, Joe and I went swimming, three times a day in the white sand dumped there—where regularly you saw lumps of human shit floating—I have nightmares of swallowing a cud of crap when I get up on my half rock and point hands to dive, by God I learned to dive by myself by half submerging to my waist—but here's these turds floating in the river of time and I'm ready to sprowf myself one up, flubadegud— The beach was located in reeds down by the easternmost lost fender of the dump where the rats scurried in a dull gloom of vague smokes smoldering since Xmas week—in the summer mornings of freshness and boyhood we sallied forth into the vast dewy day in a clew pale of happy easters, two kids in a wild swale, having times we'd never forget—I be Buck Jones, you be Buck Jones—all boys want to grow up into hardy weathered characters thin and strong who when they do grow old throw dark seamy faces to the shroud, blot your satin up and roll it away—

Doctor Sax is hiding in the dark room waiting for it to turn from gray afternoon, late, with quiet child singings in the block (on Gershom, Sarah) (as I peek from dark dumb dull drapes of afternoon)— Sax hides in that darkness coming from behind the door, soon it will be night and the shadows will deepen darker and hoo doo you— Gods of the Fellaheen Flagebus level of fly-away dung bottles blue with bags and scrawny cross black striped old Bohemian carpet of the clock-sprale-pot—

We heard the Henry Armstrong fights through roots of broken leaves, we lay on the sofa upside down in dark summer evenings with the window open and only the radio dial for a light, deep browngloom red glow, Vinny, G.J., Lousy, Scotty, me, Rita (Vinny's kidsister) and Lou (his kidbrother) and Normie (next oldest brother, blond, nervous)—Mother Charlie and Father Lucky out, she at graveyard shift of mill, he as bouncer in a French Canadian nightclub (full of cowbells)— We in the summer evening indulged ourselves in various listens to the radio (Gangbusters, The Shadow—which is on Sunday afternoon and always dismally short of the mark)—(Orson Welles greatprograms of Saturday night, 11 P.M. Witches' Tales on faint stations—) We all talked of screwing Rita and Charlie, the women in the world were only made to bang— There was an orchard in back, with trees, apples, we kicked among them—

One night we had a juvenile homosexual ball without realizing what it was and Vinny leaped around with a sheet over his head and yelled "Oook!" (the effeminate shrieking ghost as compared to the regular "Aouooo!" of the regular virile dumbghosts) (eek, Dizzy); also I remember vaguely G.J.'s and my disgust with the whole thing. It was that madcap Vinny, that's who it was. A horrible moron by name of Zaza hung around Vinny, he was almost 20, Zaza indeed—that was his real name, it was a regular Arabian country epic—along the dump he'd drooled since childhood, spermatazoing in all directions, jacking off dogs and worst of all sucking off dogs—they'd seen him try it under a porch. Doctor Sax the White-haired Hawk knew these things—The Shadow always knows—um hee hee he ha— (echo hollow chamber hello ripple anybody there-y-ere-y-ere-ere- Like? hike? hike?)—(as the tank recedes)—that's The Shadow's laugh—Doctor Sax lurked under porches watching these operations, from the cellar, made notes, sketched, mixed herbs, come up with a solution to kill the Snake of Evil—which he used on the last climactic day—the Day the Snake was Real—and stove up—and hurled a honk of angers at the wailing world but later—

Ali Zaza indeed—a moronic French Canadian sexfiend, he is now in a madhouse—I saw him masturbate in the livingroom one rainy afternoon, he did it in public to amuse Vinny who watched at his leisure like a Pasha and sometimes gave instructions, and munched on candy—no pariah the schoolboy be—but a Persian super Luminary of the Glittering Courts— "Come on Zaza madman, faster—"

"I go fast I can."

"Go, Zaza, go—"

The whole gang: "Come on Zaza, come!"

"Here he comes!"

We all laugh and watch the horrible sight of an idiot youth pumping up his white juices with his jerking fist in a dazzle of frenzies and exhaustion of the spirit . . . nothing else to resort to. We applaud! "Hooray for Zaza!"

"Thirteen times last Monday—he came each time exactly, no lie—Zaza has an endless supply of come."

"That's Zaza the crazy one."

"He'd rather jerk off than die."

"Zaza the sex fiend—look! he's startin again—Gol dang son of a bootch—Zaza's at it again—"

"Oh his record's longer than this—"

(To myself: "*Quel*—what a damn fool.")

I believe eight-year-old Lou must have seen—no, as Vinny always made sure his kidbrothers weren't involved in any dirty play . . . he protected them with sanctimony and gravity.—His sister much less—as primitive people do—

It was later when Vinny moved to Moody Street again, farther downtown, in the humbuzzing around St. Jean de Baptiste that we began to have less childlike pursuits haunted by darkness and goofs— Later we simply forgot dark Saxes and hung ourselves on the kick of sex and adolescent lacerated love . . . where everafter the fellows disappear. . . There was a great big whore called Sue, 200 pounds, friend of Charlie's, came calling at Vinny's, to sit in rockingchair and yak but would sometimes throw her dress up to show us herself when we made cracks from a safe distance. The existence of this huge woman of the world reminded me that I had a father (who visited her purple doorways) and a real world to face in the future

—whoo! It snowed on shroudy New Year's one two three as we laughed about that!

27

SATURDAY NIGHT WAS the time of the balloon in the sky when I'd listen to Wayne King, or some of those great André Baruch orchestras of the thirties (our first radio had a great shit-colored false-paper-disc speaker round and strange)—sit back, imagine—stoned beyond eternity as I listened to the for-the-first-time-to-me individual pieces of music and instruments,—all of it by the literal flower-vase of the Golden Davenport Thirties when portly Rudy Vallee was a dalliance dawn cuteboy of rosy moon saws by a lake, coo owl—lost in Saturday night reveries, earlier of course it's always the Hit Parade, fanfare number one song hit, boom, crash, the title? *Film Your Eyebrows in my Song, Tear*—with an upswing of the band and crash of events as I turn over my page of Saturday night funnies fresh from the wagons of the boys in the exciting Sat night streets in which also I cut along considerably, one night with Bruno Gringas arm in arm wrestling all the way up the bright market of Moody from City Hall to Parent's meat store (where Ma bought everything)—the butcher himself looked good enough to eat, the store was so rich— Pursy times, when I'd a 20¢ cake splurge, and they were the biggest cakes then—black night shadows of Sat night wound with fiery lights of stores and traffic make a huge arrangement of lacelike blackery to splarse and intersplash the views and heels of spiny real people in clothes interwiling with the wild blue dark, disappear—the mystery of the night, which is a dew of grain—

Great White Sheets of the house being ironed by my mother on the big round table in the middle of the kitchen— She drinks tea while working,— I'm in the solemn furniture of the livingroom, my mother's brown chairs, with leather, and wood, big and thick, inconceivably solid, the table is a massive plank on a log, round—reading *Tim Tyler's Flying Luck*— My mother's past furnitures have almost been forgotten, certainly lost, O lost—

On Saturday night I was settling down alone in the house with magazines, reading *Doc Savage* or the *Phantom Detective* with *his* masky rainy night— *The Shadow Magazine* I saved for Friday nights, Saturday morning was always the world of gold and rich sunlight.

28

NOT LONG AFTER WE MOVED TO PHEBE from Centralville, and I had met Zap Plouffe, I was playing at latedusk in the yard with aftersupper buzzes and slamming screendoors everywhere—with Cy Ladeau and Bert Desjardins in their part of their own childhood which is so antique to me that they seem unbelievably monstrous and assumed more normal shapes in the age molds of later years— Bert Desjardins it was impossible to see young, twelve, his long tall weeping brother Al... I saw him cry boohoo in front of a whole gallery of porch sitters composed of Gene and Joe Plouffe and others in the midst of an eclipse of the sun that partly I'm looking at through my darkburnt glass from the dump and partly ignoring to gape at this spectacle of Al Desjardins sobbing in front of the gang (from some Al Roberts kick in the ass, Al's sittin there giggling, he was a great catcher and longball hitter)—as the darkness fills all the brown windows of the neighborhood for an instant in the fiery summer afternoon— Bert Desjardins no less eccentric —playing—he walked across the Moody Street Bridge with me the first morning I went to St. Joseph brothers school —the rail was on our left, iron, separating us from the 100-foot drop to the roaring foams of the rocks in their grisly eternity (that became white be-maned hysterical horses in the night)—he said "I remember my first day at school, I wasn't tall enough to look over the thick bar of that rail, you're going to grow just like I did right over it—in no time!" I couldn't believe it.

Bert was in the same school. I don't know what I did —irked a kid, at recess—I was in love with Ernie Malo, it was a real love affair at eleven—I tiptoed on his fence heartbreakingly across the street from school—I hurt him once with my foot on the fence, it was like hurting an angel, at Gerard's picture I said my prayers and prayed for Ernie's love. Gerard made no move in the photo. Ernie was very beautiful to my eyes—it was before I began to distinguish between sexes—as noble and beautiful as a young nun—yet he was just a little boy, tremendously grown up (he became a sour Yankee with dreams of small editorships in Vermont)—· A kid known as Fish darkly approached me as I was lifting my foot off the last Moody

Bridge plank approaching Textile and the walk in fields and dumps to home—came up to me, "Well, there you are," and punched me in the face, and walked away as I blubbered. I staggered home aghast in weeps—by walls and under orangebrick chimneys of the painful eternity—to my mother—I wanted to ask her why? why should he hit me? I vowed to hit Fish back for a lifetime and never did—finally I met him delivering fish or gathering garbage for the city, in my yard, and didn't think anything of it—could have hit him in the gray—the gray's forgotten now—and so the reason's gone too—but the tragic air is gone—a new clime dew occupies these empty spaces of Nineteen O Two Two we're always in— All this to explain Bert Desjardins —and playing with Cy Ladeau in the yard.

I threw a piece of slate skimming in the air and accidentally caught Cy at the throat (Count Condu! he came in the night flapping over the sandbank and cut Cy in the neck with his eager blue teeth by sand moons of snore) (the time I slept at Cy's with Cy and Big Brother Emil when folks drove to Canada in '29 Ford—moon was full the night they left)— Cy cried and bled into my mother's kitchen with that wound, fresh varnish just moved in he spills blood on, my mother coaxes him to stop crying, bandages him, slate so neat and deadly everybody's mad at me—they say the Castle Hill's called Snake Hill because it's got so many little garter snakes hangin around—snaky slate— Bert Desjardins said "You should not do that."— Nobody could understand it was an accident, it was so sinister—like the paper I used to Black Thief Dicky, sinister —that gray's forgotten too, as I say Cy and Bert were dreadfully young in a long-ago of moving Time that is so remote it for the first time assumes that rigid post or posture death-like denoting the cessation of its operation in my memory and therefore the world's—a time about to become extinct —except that now it can never be, because it happened, it— which led to further levels—as time unveiled her ugly old cold mouth of death to the worst hopes—fears—Bert Desjardins and Cy Ladeau like any prescience of a dream are unerasable.

29

AND THERE'S ME—playing my baseball game in the mud of the yard, draw a circle with a rock in the middle, for 3rd, for ss, 2nd base, first, for outfield positions, and pitch ball in with little selfward flick, a heavy ballbearing, bat is a big nail, whap, there's a grounder between the rock of 3rd and ss, basehit into left because also missed rolling through infield circles—there's a flyball to left, plops down into left field circle, he's out, I played this and hit such a long home-run that it was inconceivable, heretofore the diamond I'd drawn in the ground and the game I was playing were synonymous with regular distances and power-values in baseball, but suddenly I hit this incredible homerun with the small of the nail and drove the ball which was my great race champion $1,000,000 Repulsion in its bedroom-in-the-winter-life, now it's spring, blossoms in center field, DiMaggio's watching my apples grow—it goes sailing across an intervening stadium, or yard, into the veritable

suburbs of the mythical city locating the mythical ballfield
—into the yard of the Phebe Street house where we used
to live—lost in the bushes there—lost my ball, lost Repulsion, the whole league ended (and the Turf was bereft of
its King), a sinister end-of-the-world homerun had been
hit.

I always thought there was something mysterious and
shrouded and foreboding about this event which put an
end to childish play—it made my eyes tired— "Wake up
now Jack—face the awful world of black without your
aeroplane balloons in your hand."—Behind the thudding
apples of my ground, and his fence that shivers so, and
winter on the pale horizon of autumn all hoary with his
own news in a bigmitt cartoon editorial about storing up
coal for the winter (Depression Themes, now it's atombomb bins in the cellar communist dope ring)—a huge goof
to grow sick in your papers—behind winter my star sings,
zings, I'm alright in my father's house. But doom came like
a shot, when it did, like the foreboding said, and like is
implied in the laugh of Doctor Sax as he glides among the
muds where my ballbearing was lost, by March midnight
that overlaps with a glare mad of her bloodened sun-scapes
in the set with the iron groo brush at dusk call fogs, across
marshy surveys— Sax strides there soundless on the apple
leaf in his mysterious dream-diving night—

When at sweet night I round all my kittens up, my cat,
round my blanket up, he slips in, does exactly three turns,
flops, motor runs, s' ready to sleep all night till Ma calls
for school in the morning—for wild oatmeal and toast by
steaming autumn mornings—for the fogs shimmering up

from G.J.'s mouth as he meets me in the corner, "Crise it's *cold!*—the goddam winter's got his big ass farting from the North before the ladies of the summer pick their parasols and leave."

—Doctor Sax, whirl me no Shrouds—open up your heart and talk to me—in those days he was silent, sardonic, laughed in tall darkness.

Now I hear him scream from the bed of the brim—

"The Snake is Rising Inch an Hour to destroy us—yet you sit, you sit, you sit. Aïeee, the horrors of the East—make no fancy up-carves to the Ti-bet wall than a Kangaroo's mule eared cousin— Frezels! Grawms! Wake to the test in your frails— Snake's a Dirty Killer—Snake's a Knife in the Safe— Snake's a Horror—only birds are good—murderous birds are good—murderous snakes, no good."

Little booble-face laughs, plays in the street, knows no different— Yet my father warned me for years, it's a dirty snaky deal with a fancy name—called L-I-F-E—more likely H-Y-P-E... How rotten the walls of life do get—how collapsed the tendon beam...

BOOK TWO

A Gloomy Bookmovie

SCENE 1 TWO O'CLOCK—strange—thunder and the yellow walls of my mother's kitchen with the green electric clock, the round table in the middle, the stove, the great twenties castiron stove now only used to put things on next to the modern thirties green gas stove upon which so many succulent meals and flaky huge gentle apple pies have been hot, whee—(Sarah Avenue house).

SCENE 2 I'm at the window in the parlor facing Sarah Avenue and its white sands dripping in the shower, from thick hot itchy stuffed furniture huge and bearlike for a reason they liked then but now call 'overstuffed'—looking at Sarah Avenue through the lace curtains and beaded windows, in the dank gloom by the vast blackness of the squareback piano and dark easy chairs and maw sofa and the brown painting on wall depicting angels playing around a brown Virgin Mary and Child in a Brown Eternity of the Brown Saints—

SCENE 3 With the cherubs (look closeup) all gloomy in their little sad disports among clouds and vague butterflies of themselves and somehow quite inhuman and cherub-like ("I have a cherub tells me," says Hamlet to the Rosencranz and Guildenstern track team hotfooting back to Engla-terre)—(I'm rushing around with a wild pail in the winters in that now-raining street, I have a scheme to build bridges in the snow and let the gutter hollow canyons under ... in the backyard of springtime baseball mud, I in the winter dig great steep Wall Streets in the snow and cut along giving them Alaskan names and avenues which is a game I'd still like to play—and when Ma's wash is icy stiff on the line I march it down piecemeal on a side dredge into the drifts of the porch and shovel Mexican gloriettas around the washline merrygoround pole).

SCENE 4 The brown picture on the wall was done by some old Italian who has long since faded from my parochial school textbooks with his brown un-Goudt inks and inkydinky lambs about to be slaughtered by stern Jewish businesslike Mose with his lateral nose, won't listen to his own little son's wails, would rather—the picture is still around, many like it— But see close, my face now in the window of the Sarah Avenue house, six little houses in the entire dirt street, one big tree, my face looking out through dew-drops of the rain from within, the gloomy special brown Technicolor interior of my house where also lurks a pisspot gloom of family closets in the Graw North—I'm wearing corduroy pants, brown ones, smooth and easy, and some sneakers, and a black sweater over a brown shirt open at collar (I wore no Dick Tracy badges ever, I was a proud professional of the Shades with my Shadow & Sax)— I'm a little kid with blue eyes, 13, I'm munching on a fresh cold mackintosh apple my father bought last Sunday on the Sundaydriving road in Groton or in Chelmsford, the juice just pops and flies out of my teeth when I cool these apples. And I munch, and chaw, and look out the window at the rain.

SCENE 5 Look up, the huge tree of Sarah Avenue, belonged to Mrs. Flooflap whose name I forget but sprung God-like Emer Hammerthong from the blue earth of her gigantic grassy yard (it ran clear to long white concrete garage) and mushroomed into the sky with limb-spreads that o'ertopped many roofs in the neighborhood and did so without particularly touching any of em, now huge and grooking vegetable peotl

Nature in the gray slash rain of New England mid-April—
the tree drips down huge drops, it rears up and away in an
eternity of trees, in its own flambastic sky—

SCENE 6 This tree fell down in the Hurricane finally, in 1938,
but now it only bends and sinews with a mighty woodlimb
groan, we see where the boughs tear at their green, the junc-
ture point of tree-trunk with arm-trunk, tossing of wild forms
upside down flailing in the wind,—the sharp tragic crack of
a smaller limb stricken from the tree by stormhound—

SCENE 7 Along the splashing puddles of grassyard, at worm
level, that fallen branch looks enormous and demented on its
arms in the hail—

SCENE 8 My little boy blue eyes shine in the window. I'm
drawing crude swastikas in the steamy window, it was one of
my favorite signs long before I heard of Hitler or the Nazis—
behind me suddenly you see my mother smiling,—"*Tiens*,"
she's saying, "*je tlai dit qu'eta bonne les pommes* (There, I
told you they were good the apples!)"—leaning over me to
look out the window too. "*Tiens, regard, l'eau est deu pieds
creu dans la rue* (There, look, the water's two feet deep in the
street)—*Une grosse tempête* (a big storm)— *Je tlai dit pas
allez école aujourdhui* (I told you not to go to school today)—
Wé tu? comme qui mouille? (See? how it rains?) *Je suis tu
dumb?* (Am I dumb?)"

SCENE 9 Both our faces peer fondly out the window at the
rain, it made it possible for us to spend a pleasant afternoon
together, you can tell how the rain pelts the side of the house
and the window—we don't budge an inch, just fondly look
on—like a Madonna and son in the Pittsburgh milltown window—only this is New England, half like rainy Welsh mining
towns, half the Irish kid sunny Saturday Skippy morning, with
rose vines—(Bold Venture, when May came and it stopped
raining, I played marbles in the mudholes with Fatso, they

piled up with blossoms overnight, we had to dig em out for every day's game, blossoms from trees raining, Bold Venture won the Derby that Saturday)— My mother behind me in the window is oval faced, dark haired, large blue eyes, smiling, nice, wearing a cotton dress of the thirties that she'd wear in the house with an apron—upon which there was always flour and water from the work with the condiments and pastries she was doing in the kitchen—

SCENE 10 There in the kitchen she stands, wiping her hands as I taste one of her cup cakes with fresh icing (pink, chocolate, vanilla, in little cups) she says, "All them movies with the old grandmaw in the West slappin her leetle frontiers boy and smackin him 'Stay away from dem cookies,' Ah? la old Mama Angelique don't do that to you, ah?" "No Ma, boy," I say, *"si tu sera comme ça jara toujours faim* (No Ma, boy if you was like that I'd always be hungry)" *"Tiens—assay un beau blanc d'vanilla, c'est bon pour tué* (There, try a nice white one of vanilla, it's good for you.)" "Oh boy, *blanc sucre!* ("*. . . . .*") (Oh boy, white sugar!)" *"Bon,"* she says firmly, turning away, *"asteur faut serrez mon lavage, je lai rentrez jusquavant' quil mouille* (Good, now I've got to put away my wash, I got it in just before it rained)"—(as on the radio thirties broadcasts of old gray soap operas and news from Boston about finnan haddie and the prices, East Port to Sandy Hook, gloomy serials, static, thunder of the old America that thundered on the plain)— As she walks away from the stove I say, from under my little black warm sweater, *"Moi's shfué's fini mes race dans ma chambre* (Me I's got to finish my races in my room)"—*"Amuse toi* (amuse yourself)"—she calls back —you can see the walls of the kitchen, the green clock, the table, now also the sewing machine on the right, near the porch door, the rubbers and overshoes always piled in the door, a rocking chair facing the oil heat stove—coats and raincoats hanging on hooks in corners of the kitchen, brownwood

waxed panelling on the cupboards and wainscots all around—
a wooden porch outside, glistening from rain—gloom—things
boiling on the stove—(when I was a very little kid I used to
read the funnies on my belly, listen on the floor to boiling
waters of stove, with a feeling of indescribable peace and
burble, suppertime, funnies time, potato time, warm home
time) (the second hand of the green electric clock turning
relentlessly, delicately through wars of dust)—(I watched that
too)—(Wash Tubbs in the ancient funnypage)—

SCENE 11 Thunder again, now you see my room, my bedroom
with the green desk, bed and chair—and the other strange
pieces of furniture, the Victrola already to go with *Dardanella*
and crank hangs ready, stack of sad thirties thick records,
among them Fred Astaire's *Cheek to Cheek, Parade of the
Wooden Soldiers* by John Philip Sousa— You hear my footsteps unmistakably pounding up the stairs on the run, pleup
plop ploop pleep plip and I'm rushing in the room and closing
the door behind me and pick up my mop and with foot heavy
pressed on it mop a thin strip from wall near door to wall
near window—I'm mopping the race track ready—the wall-
paper shows great goober lines of rosebushes in a dull vague
plaster, and a picture on the wall shows a horse, cut from a
newspaper page (*Morning Telegraph*) and tacked, also a
picture of Jesus on the Cross in a horrible oldprint darkness
shining through the celluloid—(if you got close up you could
see the lines of bloody black tears coursing down his tragic
cheek, O the horrors of the darkness and clouds, no people,
around the stormy tempest of his rock is void—you look for
waves—He walked in the waves with silver raiment feet, Peter
was a Fisherman but he never fished that deep—the Lord
spoke to dark assemblies about gloomy fish—the bread was
broken ... a miracle swept around the encampment like a
flowing cape and everybody ate fish ... dig your mystics in
another Arabia. . .). The mop I am mopping the thin line

with is just an old broomhandle with a frowsy drymop head, like old ladies' hair at the hair stylists—now I am getting down briskly on my knees to sweep away with my fingertips, feeling for spots of sand or glass, looking at the fingertips with a careful blow,—10 seconds pass as I prepare my floor, which is the first thing I do after slapping the door behind me— You saw first my one side of the room, when I come in, then left to my window and the gloomy rain splattering across it— rising from my knees, wiping fingers on pants, I turn slowly and raising fist to mouth I go "Ta-ta-ta-tra-tra-tra-etc."—the racetrack call to the post by the bugler, in a clear, well modulated voice actually singing in an intelligent voice-imitation of a trumpet (or bugle). And in the damp room the notes resound sadly— I look goopy with self-administered amazement as I listen to the last sad note and the silence of the house and the rain click and now the clearly sounding whistle of Boott Mills or Goop Mills coming loud and mournful from across the river and the rain outside where Doctor Sax even now is preparing for the night with his dark damp cape, in mists— My thin trail for the races began at a cardboard inclined on books—a Parchesi board,—folded, to the Domino side to keep the Parchesi side from fading (precursor to the now Monopoly board with checkers on other side)—no wait, the Parchesi board had a black blank side, down the huck of this all solid and round raced my marbles when I let them slip down from under the ruler— Lined on the bed are the eight gladiators of the race, it's the fifth race, the handicap of the day.

SCENE 12 "And now," I'm sayin, as I bend low at the bed, "and now the Fifth Race, handicap, four year olds and up etc."—"and now the Fifth Race of the gong, come on *Ti Jean arrete de jouer* and get on with the—they're headed for the post, the horses are headed for the post"—and I hear it echoing as I say it, hands upraised before the lined up horses on the blanket, I look around me like a racing fan asking himself, "Say, it shore is gonna rain soon, they're headed for the post?"—which I do— "Well son, better bet five on Flying Ebony the old gal'll make it, she didn't do too bad against Kransleet last week." "Okay Pa!"—striking new pose—"but I see Mate winning this race." "Old Mate? Nah!"

SCENE 13 I rush to the phonograph, turn on *Dardanella* with the push hook.

SCENE 14 Briskly I'm kneeled at the race-start barrier, horses in left hand, ruler barrier clamped down at starting line in right hand, *Dardanella*'s going da-daradera-da, I have my mouth open breathing in and out raspily to make racetrack crowd noises—the marbles pop into place with great fanfare, I straighten em around, "Woops," I say, "look—out—l-o-o-k-o-u-t no—NOPE! Mate broke from the starter's helper—back he goes—Jockey Jack Lewis exasperated on his back—set em up straight now—'the horses are at the post!'—Oh that old fool we know that"— "'They're off!'" *"What?" "They're off!—hoff!"* crowd sigh—boom! they're off— "You made me miss my start with that talk of yours—*and it's Mate taking an early lead!*" And off I rush following the marbles with my eyes.

SCENE 15 Next scene, I'm crawling along all stridey and careful following my marbles, and I'm calling em fast "Mate by two lengths"—

SCENE 16 POW flash shot of Mate the marble two inches ahead of big limping Don Pablo with his chipholes (regularly I held titanic marble-smashing ceremonies and "trainings" and some of the racers came out chipped and hobbled, great Don Pablo had been a great champion of the Turf, in spite of an original crooked slant in his round—but now chipped beyond repair—an uncommon tender fore hock, crock, wooden fenders of gloomy mainsmiths smashing up the horn in the horse's hoof on gray afternoons on Salem Street when

87

still a little horseshit perfumed the Ah Afternoons of Lowell—
tragic migs frantic in a raw bloom of the floor, of the flowery
linoleum carpet just drymopped and curried by the racetrack
trucks— "Don Pablo second!" I'm calling in the same low
Doctor Sax crouch—"and Flying Ebony coming up fast from
a slow start in the rear—Time Supply" (red stripes on white),
(no one else will ever name them), blam, no more time, I'm
already leaning over with my arm extended to lean falling
on the wall over the finish line and hang my face tragically
over the pit of the wood homestretch in entryway with wide
amazement and speechless—just manage, wide-eyed, to say—
"—s-a-a-a-,"—

SCENE 17 The marbles crashing into wall.

SCENE 18 "—Don Pablo rolled over and crashed in—gee,
chipped, he's so heavy! *Don Pablo-o!*" with hands to my head
in the great catastrophe of the "fans" in the grandstand. (One
morning in that room there had been such glooms, no school,
the first official day of racing, way back in the beginning,
the dismal rainy 1934's when I used to keep history of myself—started that long before Scotty and I kept baseball history of our souls, in red ink, averages, P. Boldieu, p., .382 bat,
.986 field—the day Mate became the first great winner of the
Turf, capturing a coveted misty prize of lost afternoons (the
Graw Futurity) beyond the hills of Mohican Springs racetrack "in Western Massachusetts" in the "Mohawk Trail
country"—(it was only years later I turned from this to the
stupidities and quiddities of H.G. Wells and Mososaurs—in
these parentheses sections, so (-), the air is free, do what you
will, I can—why? whoo?—) the gray dismal rains I remember,
the tragic damp on my windowpane, the flood of heat pouring up through the transom near the closet, my closet itself,
the gloom of it, the doom of it, the hanging balloons of it,
the papers, boxes, smatterdurgalia like William Allen White's

88

closet in Wichita when he was 14—my yearning for peanut
butter and Ritz crackers in the late afternoon, the gloom
around my room at that hour, I'm eating my Ritz and gulping
my milk by the wreckage of the day— The losses, the torn
tickets, the chagrined footsteps disappearing out the ramp,
the last faint glimmer of the toteboards in the rain, a torn
paper rolling dismally in the wet ramps, my face long and
anxious surveying this scene of gloomy jonquils in the floor-
frat—that first bookkeeping graymorning when Mate won the
Stakes and from the maw-mouth of the Victrola the electric
yoigle yurgle little thirties crooners wound too fast with a
slam-bash Chinese restaurant orchestra we fly into the latest
1931 hit, ukeleles, ro-bo-bos, hey now, smash-ah! *hah!* atch
a *tcha!* but usually it was just, "Dow-dow-dow, tadoodle-
lump!"—"Gee I like hot jyazz"—

　　Snazzz!)

　—but in that room all converted into something dark, cold,
incredible gloomy, my room on rainy days and all in it was
a saturation of the gray Yoik of Bleak Heaven when the sides
of the rainbow mouth of God hang disfurdled in a bloomy
rue—no color . . . the smell of thought and silence, "Don't
hang around in that stuffy old room all the time," my mother
had said to me when Mike came for our Dracut Fields Buck
Jones appointment and instead I was busy running off the
Mohican Futurity and digging back into earlier records of
my antiquity for background material for the little newspaper story announcing the race . . . printed by hand on
gloomy gray-green sheets of Time.

EIGHTH RACE: Claiming $1500, for 4 year olds and up. Six
　　　　　　furlongs
Post: 5:43 TIME 1:12 4-5
　　　CAW CAW (Lewis)........ $18.60　7.40　3.80
　　　FLYING HOME (Stout) ....　　　　2.40　2.30
　　　SUNDOWN LAD (Renick)..　　　　　　11.10

89

ALSO RAN: Flying Doodad, Saint Nazaire, a-Rink,
Mynah, a-Remonade Girl, Gray Law, Rownomore,
Going Home. Scratched: Happy Jack, Truckee.
a-Jack Lewis entry.

—or my newpapers would have headlines:

REPULSION ARRIVES FOR BIG 'CAP

Lewis Predicts Third Straight
VICTORY FOR THE KING

TIPS BY LEWIS

APRIL 4, 1936—Mighty Repulsion arrived today by van from his resting-place at Lewis Farms; accompanying him were Jack Lewis, owner and jockey,

TODAY

S Springs, 3rd

CARMAK

trainer Ben Smith and his trusty Derby-cups and assistants.

Bright skies and a fast track preceded the arrival of these tremendous luminaries upon the scene of a great week's end of racing with a thousand dollars pouring from individual pockets of wild jockey club bets, while less swanky Turf fans (like me and Paw from Arkansas) hang on the rail, railbirds, steely-eyed, far-seeing, thin, from Kentucky, brothers in the blood on the score of hosses and father and son in a tragic Southern family left destitute only with two horses that sometimes I'd actually rig races by putting solid champion types in 'workouts' among less luminous luminary marbles, and call the winner on my 'Tips' corner for that honor and also for hardboot father-and-son who need the money and have followed my, Lewis', advice— I was Jack Lewis and I owned the greatest horse, Repulsion, solid ballbearing a half inch thick, it rolled off the Parchesi board and into the linoleum as smooth, and soundless but as heavy as a rumbling ball of steel all tooled smooth, sometimes kicked poor aluminum-marbles out of sight and off the track at the hump bump of the rampbottom—sometimes kicked a winner in, too—but usually rolled smoothly off the plank and mashed any little glass or dust on the floor (while smallest marbles jiggled in the infinitesimal lilliputian microcosmos of the linoleum and World)— and zoomed swiftly all shiny silver across the race-course to its appointed homestretch in the rockly wood where it just assumed a new rumbling power and deep hum of floorboards and hooked up with the finish line with a forward slam of momentum—a tremendous bull-like rush in the stretch, like Whirlaway or Man O War or Citation—other marbles couldn't compete with this massive power, they all came tagging after, Repulsion was absolute king of the Turf till I lost him slapping him out of my yard into the Phebe Avenue yard a block away —a fabulous homerun as I say, turned my world upside down like the Atombomb—Jack Lewis, I, owned that great Repulsion, also personally rode the beast, and trained him, and found him, and revered him, but I also ran the Turf, was Commissioner, Track Handicapper, President of the Racing Association, Secretary of the Treasury—Jack Lewis had nothing lacking, while he lived—his newspapers flourished—he wrote editorials against the Shade, he was not afraid of Black Thieves— The Turf was so complicated it went on forever. And in a gloom of ecstasy. —There I am, clutching my head, the fans in the grandstand go wild. Don Pablo at 18-1 upset the applecart, nobody expected he'd even make it to the wall with his half gait and great huge chips, he'd a been 28-1 if it wasn't for his old reputation as a battered veteran before he was chipped— *"He went and done it!"* I'm saying to myself in astonishment—boom!

SCENE 19 I'm at the Victrola putting in a new record, swiftly, it's *The Parade of the Wooden Soldiers*, everybody's leaving the racetrack—

SCENE 20 You see me marching up and down where I stand, moving slowly around the room, the races are over, I'm marching out of the grandstand but also shaking my head quizzically from side to side like a disgruntled bettor, tearing up my tickets, a poor child pantomime of what sometimes I'd seen my father do after the races at Narragansett or Suffolk Downs or Rockingham— On my little green desk the papers are all spread, my pencil, my editorial desk running the Turf. On the back of that desk still were chalkmarks Gerard had made when he was alive in the green desk—this desk rattled in my dreams because of Gerard's ghost in it—(I dream of it now on rainy nights turned almost vegetable by the open window, luridly green, as a tomato, as the rain falls in the block-hollow void outside all dank, adrip and dark . . . hateful walls of the Cave of Eternity suddenly appearing in a brown dream and when you slow the drape, fish the shroud, shape your mouth of mow and maw in this huge glissen tank called Rainy,—you can see the void now). —Pushed against the corner by the Victrola, my little pool table—it was a folding pool table, with velvet green, little holes and leather pockets and little cues with leather tips you could cue-chalk with blue chalk from my father's pool table at the bowling alley— It was a very important table because I played The Shadow at it— The Shadow was the name I gave to a tall, thin, hawknosed fellow called St. Louis who came into the Pawtucketville Social Club and shot pool sometimes with the proprietor my father . . . the greatest poolshark you ever saw, huge, enormous hands with fingers seemingly ten inches long laid out spread-claw on the green to make his cue-rest, his little finger alone sprouted and shot from his handmountain to a distance of six inches you'd say, clean, neat, he slipped the cue right through a tiny orifice between his thumb and forefinger, and slid on all woodsy shiny to connect with that cue-ball at cue-kiss—he'd smack shots in with no two cents about it, fwap, the ball would cluck in the leather hole basket like a dead thing— So tall, shroudy, he bent long and distant and lean for his shots, momentarily rewarding his audience with a view of his enormous gravity head and great noble and mysterious hawk nose and inscrutable never-saying eyes— The Shadow— We'd see him coming in the club from the street—

SCENE 21 And in fact this is what we see now, The Shadow St. Louis is coming into the Social Club to shoot pool, wear-ing hat and long coat, somehow shadowy as he comes along the long plywood wall painted gray, light, but's coming into an ordinary bowling alley four of which you see to the left of The Shadow, with only two alleys going and two pinboys at work (Gene Plouffe and Scotty Boldieu, Scotty wasn't a regular like Gene but because he was the pitcher on our team my father let him make a few extra pennies spotting at the alleys)— A low ceiling cellar is what the joint is, you see plumbing pipes,— We are watching The Shadow come in and up the plywood walls from our seats at the head of the alleys, Coca Colas, scoresheet boards that you stand at, by the rack, and the duckpin balls in the rack and the duckpins set up down the alley squat and shiny with a red band in their goldwood—rainy Friday 6:30 P.M. in the P.S.C. alleys, we see smoke shroudens even the shroudy Shadow as he moves up, we hear murmurs and hubbubs and echo-roars of the hall, click of pool games, laughter, talk ...

SCENE 22 My father's in the little cage office at the rear near the Gershom street-door, smoking a cigar behind the glass counter, it rises from him in a cloud, he is frowning angrily at a piece of paper in his hand. "Jesus Christ now where did *this* thing come from?—" (looking at another)—"is that a?—" and he falls into scowling meditation with himself over these two little pieces of paper, the other fellows in the office are talking ... there's Joe Plouffe, Vauriselle, and Sonny Alberge —everything's jumping— We are only looking in at the door, can't see the entire office, in fact we are looking in at the office from about six feet up in the door a foot from it on a stone step level with the office floor, we are just about as

93

high as The Shadow's nose as we look in with The Shadow whose hawk visage slants from us in a Huge. My father never looks up, except briefly, coldly, to see who it is, then a mere look of the eye signifying greeting—in fact no greeting at all, he just looks up and down again with that bemused perused expression my father always had, as though something was reading him and eating him inside and he all wrap't and silent in it. So St. Louis, his face doesn't budge anyway, just addresses the three—"*Ca vas?* (it goes?)"—"*Tiens, St. Louis! Ta pas faite ton 350 l'autre soir—ta mal au cul* (you didn't make your 350 t'other night, you got a sore ass)." This being said by Vauriselle, a tall, unpleasant fellow that my father didn't like—no answer from St. Louis who has just a fixed hawklike grin. Now Sonny Alberge, tall and athletic and handsome, became Boston Braves shortstop in a few years, with a big clean-teeth smile, a real bumpkin boy in his prime at home, his father was a little sad shrivelly man who adored him, Sonny responded to his father like an Ozark hero grave and Billy-the-Kid tender, but with French Canadian stern gravity that knows what's coming to everybody in Heaven later on inside Time—it's ever been so in the bottom of my soul, the stars are crying down the sides of Heaven—Sonny says to   Louis—"*Une game?*" St. Louis' grin though moveless gains significance, and he opens his blue hawklike lips to say with sudden surprising young man voice "*Oui*"—and they look at one another the challenge and cut out to bowl— Vauriselle and Joe Plouffe (always a short solid wry listener and chieftain among the heroes of Pawtucketville) follow— my father's left alone in the office with his papers, looks up, checks the time, slaps cigar in mouth and cuts out following the boys in a thing-to-do of his own, fiddling for keys, bemused, as someone yells out at him in the next view

SCENE 23 (as he steps down from office with fat busy proprietor key look at chain from pocket), from the auras of smoke

and pooltable glow a dark shaded man with a cuestick in
the pissy background of cans and wood is calling "Hey, Emil,
il mouille dans ton pissoir (it's raining in your toilet)—*a tu
que chose comme un plat pour mettre entours?* (got anything
like a pan to put under?)" There's another poolshark in the
dark green background of blue rain evening in the golden
club with its dank stone floor and shiny black bowling balls—
In smoke—shouts (as Emil my father is muttering and nodding yes) (and St. Louis, Joe, Sonny, Vauriselle cross the
scene in file, like Indians, Shadow's removing his coat)—
*"Pauvre Emil commence a avoir des trou dans son pissoir,
cosse wui va arrivez asteur, whew!—foura quon use le livre
pour bouchez les trous* (Poor Emil's starting to have holes in
his pissery, what's gonna happen now, whew! we'll have to
use the book to block the holes!!!)" *"Hey la tu deja vu slivre
la*—(Hey didja ever see that book?)" a poolshark in the light,
young Leo Martin saying to LeNoire who lived directly across
the street from the club, on Gershom, adjoining Blezan's
store, in a house that always seemed to me haunted by sad
flowerpots of linoleum eternity in a sunny void also darkened
by an inner almost idiot gloom French Canadian homes seem
to have (as if a kid with water on the head was hiding in
the closet somewhere)—LeNoire a cool little cat, I knew his
kidbrother and exchanged marbles with him, they were related to some dim past relation I'd been told about—ladies
with great white hair periwigs sewing in the Lowell rooms,
wow— LeNoire: (we're watching from the end of the plywood wall, but almost on alley Number One at this spread-
out smoky scene and talk) *"Quoi?—Non. Jaime ra ca, squi est?*
(what, no, I'd like that, where's it?" LeNoire says this from
a crouch over his cueball— He was a very good bowler too,
St. Louis had trouble beating him bowling—faintly we see
brown folding chairs along the Gershom wall, with secret
dark sitters but very close up to the table and listening to

95

every word—a Fellaheen poolhall if there ever was one— The door opens quickly and out of the rain and in comes I, silent, swift, gliding in like The Shadow—sidling to the corner of the scene to watch, removing not coat nor budging, I'm already hung up on the scene's awe.

SCENE 24 *"Tiens, Ti Jean, donne ce plat la a Shammy,"* my father is saying to me, turning from the open storage room door with a white tin pan. "Here, Ti Jean, give this pan to Shammy." My father is standing with a peculiar French Canadian bowleggedness half up from a crouch with the pan outheld, waiting for me to take it, anxious till I do so, almost saying with his big frowning amazed face "Well my little son what are we doing in the penigillar, this strange abode, this house of life without roof be-hung on a Friday evening with a tin pan in my hand in the gloom and you in your raincoats—" *"Il commence a tombez de la neige,"* someone is shouting in the background, coming in from the door ("Snow's startin to fall")—my father and I stand in that immobile instant communicating telepathic thought-paralysis, suspended in the void together, understanding something that's always already happened, wondering where we were now, joint reveries in a dumb stun in the cellar of men and smoke ... as profound as Hell ... as red as Hell.—I take the pan; behind him, the clutter and tragedy of old cellars and storage with its dank message of despair—mops, dolorous mops, clattering tearstricken pails, fancy sprawfs to suck soap suds from a glass, garden drip cans—rakes leaning on meaty rock—and piles of paper and official Club equipments— It now occurs to me my father spent most of his time when I was 13 the winter of 1936, thinking about a hundred details to be done in the Club alone not to mention home and business shop—the energy of our fathers, they raised us to sit on nails— While I sat around all the time with my little diary, my Turf, my hockey games, Sunday afternoon tragic football games on the toy pooltable white chalkmarked . . . father and son on separate toys, the toys get less friendly when you grow up—my football games occupied me with the same seriousness of the angels—we had little time to talk to each other. In the fall of 1934 we took a grim voyage south in the rain to Rhode Island to see Time Supply win the Narragansett Special—with Old Daslin we was . . . a grim voyage, through exciting cities of great neons, Providence, the mist at the dim walls of great hotels, no Turkeys in the raw fog, no Roger Williams, just a trolley track gleaming in the gray rain— We drove, auguring solemnly over past performance charts, past deserted shell-like Ice Cream Dutchland Farms stands in the dank of rainy Nov.—bloop, it was the time on the road, black tar glisten-road of thirties, over foggy trees and distances, suddenly a crossroads, or just a side-in road, a house, or barn, a vista gray tearful mists over some half-in cornfield with distances of Rhode Island in the marshy ways across and the secret scent of oysters from the sea—but something dark and rog-like.— *I had seen it before* . . . Ah weary flesh, burdened with a light . . . that gray dark Inn on the Narragansett Road . . . this is the vision in my brain as I take the pan from my father and take it to Shammy, moving out of the way for LeNoire and Leo Martin to pass on the way to the office to see the book my father had (a health book with syphilitic backs)—

SCENE 25 Someone ripped the pooltable cloth that night, tore it with a cue, I ran back and got my mother and she lay on it half-on-floor like a great poolshark about to take a shot under a hundred eyes only she's got a thread in her mouth and's sewing with the same sweet grave face you first saw in the window over my shoulder in that rain of a late Lowell afternoon.

God bless the children of this picture, this bookmovie.

I'm going on into the Shade.

97

BOOK THREE

More Ghosts

1

HE CAME TO ME out of Eternity—it is Sunday afternoon in Lowell, absolutely unphotographable it is that I am sitting in my room in good Sunday clothes just home from a drive to Nashua, not doing anything, semi beginning to preside dully and absently over perhaps my slamdash hockeybang game which is a whole lot of marbles fighting over a little puck marble to kick it in the goal thereby killing two birds w.o.s. by making it also the official betweenseason Ceremony of racehorse-chipping, racehorse-*destinying*, things have to change in an organic picture of the world, my Turf was just like that, horses had to go through processes of prime and decay like real horses—but instead of really bothering (whether also it's basketball or football game, football was a crude Pro iron smash thru the line, I ceased because too many of my racehorses were dying split in half in this carnage)—tired of games, just sitting there, over my pooltable, late red Sunday afternoon in Lowell, on the Boott Mills the great silent light shrouded the redbrick in a maze of haze sorrow, something mute but about

101

to speak lurked in the sight of these silent glowing mills seen on dumb-Sundays of choked cleanness and odors of flower ... with just a trace of the red earth grain by grain crawling out of the green and coming back into real life to smash the Sunday choke life, return earth to the issue, with it *night* later on ... something secretively wild and baleful in the glares of the child soul, the masturbatory surging triumph of the knowledge of reality ... tonight Doctor Sax will stalk—but it is still the hour when Sunday yet lives, 5 P.M. October, but the hour when red silence in the entire city (above the white river roar) will make a blue laugh tonight ... a long blue sepulchral laff— There stands a great red wall of mystery—I get hungup looking at a speck of dust on a marble in a corner, my mind is blank, suddenly I remember when I was a little kid of five on Hildreth I used to make the Great Bird pursue the Little Man, the Little Man is running on two fingers, the Great Bird who has come out of eternity swoops down from heaven with his finger-beak and lowers to pluck him up ... my eyes rounden in the silence of this old thought—unphotographable moment—"*Mende moi donc cosse qui arrive* (I wonder what's happening)" I'm saying to myself— My father, having labored up the stairs, is standing in the door puffing, redfaced, strawhat, blue eyed, "*Ta tu aimez ta ride mon Ti Loup?* (Did you enjoy your ride my Little Wolf?)"

"*Oui* Pa—"

He's going into his tragic bedroom for something—I've dreamt of that gray room—"*dans chambre a Papa*"—('n' Papa's room).

"*Change ton butain,*" he says, "*on va allez manger sur*

102

Chin Lee. (Change your clothes, we're going to eat at Chin Lee's.)"

"Chin Lee?!! O Boy!"

It was the ideal place on sad red Sundays... We drove, with Ma and Nin, in the old '34 Plymouth, over the Moody Street Bridge, over the rocks of eternity, and down Merrimac Street, in parlous solitudes of the Sabbath, past the church St. Jean Baptiste, which on Sunday afternoons seems to swell in size, past City Hall, to Kearney Square, Sunday standers, remnants of the littlegirl gangs who went to shows in new ribbons and pink coats and are now enjoying the last red hours of the show-day in the center of the city redbrick Solitudes, by the Paige Clock showing Bleak Time,—to the snaky scrolls and *beansprouts* of the Chinese dark interior rich heartbreaking family booth in the restaurant, where I always felt so humble and contrite ... the nice smiling Chinese men would really serve us that food of the smell so savory hung in the linoleum carpet hall downstairs.

2

THE VERY SKELETAL of the tale's beginning— The Paquins lived across on Sarah in a Golden Brown House, a 2-story tenement but with fat owf-porches (piazzas, galleries) and purty gingerbread eaves and *Screens* on the porches making a dark Within ... for long fly-less afternoons with Orange Crush... Paquin brothers were Beef and Robert, Big Beef of the ass-waddling down the street, Robert was a freckled earnest giant good intentioned with all, nothing wrong with Beef, freckled too, goodnatured, my mother says she was sitting on the porch one evening and Beef came out with the moon to talk to her, told her his deepest secrets about how he wanted to just go out and enjoy nature as far as he was concerned—or some such—she my mother sat there reigning over wild conversations, Jean Fourchette the idiot came stompin by with his firecrackers and google giggled in the late sun afternoon streets of Fourth July Lowell 1936 and made monkey ginsy dances for the ladies whose children most likely by this time were all downtown disbanding among crowds of the Fourth July South Common Fireworks and Carnival, great nights —tell you about it—Jean Fourchette saw my mother sitting on the porch in a scrape of eve and asked her if she was lonely would she like to be entertained by some fireworks, she said okay, and old mad Jean set everything-he-had-in-his-pocket-off—plop plow, scatter, zing; cross—he entertained the ladies of Sarah Avenue not twenty minutes before the opening bomb gong down at the Common across the soft July rooftops of Lowell clear from white tene-mental creameries of Mt. Vernon porch to crazy rick-ass Bloozong Street across the river over by the dye works, over by the tanners, over by your Loo-la, Lowell—over by your long hoo-raws, roar old old rohor—rohor motor clodor closed door—on the pajama leg hanging, ding, with the white hoozahs flangeing right, they made left on a wide swing, beat the time with every wing, the ring, saw nothing in the heaven eyes but silver-star-bells, of all descriptions, saved but never knew it, he tried every means to explain to the odd festival of types gathered around his shoe-horn, "Looka here ladies and genelmen,"—as me and G.J. and Vinny and Scotty are scuffling around at the Carnival—(my mother is smiling at Jean Fourchette)(Boom!) the fireworks are beginning, the whore-caster by the stream is showing you how the horses race in the wild hullah, they had— There were races run with wooden flap-horses leaping ahead on the turn of dice—they spun the dice so fast (in cages) you could see horses leap ahead in their win—a crazy inanimate wild living race like you'd imagine angels run ... when they feel—X was the mark where the bing-lights played, in the night mist a top hatted clown presided over the toteboard— Farther on we smelt shit in grass, saw cameras, ate popcorn, blew the string balloons to heaven— Night came shrouding bluely with flap off arms in the hiar-zan— Hanging moss (like the moss in the Castle hanging as you hear a kid whistle for his balloon)(in the grass the littler kids are wrestling in a Tiny Tim Dim you can hardly see—big souls from little acorns— Wrangling toots on all sides of pipe steams, furt-fut peanuts for sale, furtive hipsters of the time, underfoot shammysoft dusts)— Beef Paquin, now, years later, I see huddled in a football hood coat heading home from the mills in mid December, bending to the wind round Blezan's corner, advancing homeward to hamburger supper of the upper clime, the golden rich consistency of his mother's kitchen— Beef is going into Eternity at his end without me—my end is as far from his as eternity— Eternity hears hollow voices in a rock? Eternity hears ordinary voices in the parlor. On a bone the ant descends.

105

3

THE SCENE IS IN THE CASTLE, in one of the more sumptuous rooms facing the forests of Billerica, as March Hare clouds race to the black,—speaking just then ("Of course that doesn't indicate that anything is going to come of these attempts") was (it is evening) Count Condu, impeccably dressed, just-risen from the coff of eve, the Satin Doombox with its Spenglerian metamorphosed scravenings on the lid. The recipient of his speech is the witty, gay ambassador for the Black Cardinal, our good friend Amadeus Baroque —sitting with his legs underneath, on an elegant *longue*, with a sip drink, titterlipped in listen.

"Yes my dear Count, but you do know don't you how pre-POSTEROUS it will be for *any* of these things"— (his slavering glee)—"to have any effect on anyone, Ghod!—it will have to—"

"Second, I show you—"

"—*pos*itively—"

"—heretics in the church is what they are—houndmasters of The Francis horn, phantom-grieved, golupally in their shrouds, think they can make everybody dangle—it's this is up, these Dovists betray the decadence—any organization gets decadent—"

"But my dear, so baroque—I *don't* mean to use my name —so gay—"

"Which after all you measure everything by. I wanted strength in the party, blood—no Zounds and arses in their follifications, making pear pillows in the shade—well, poop along they can— I don't see any reason why, if the Wizard of Nittlingen is willing to—*allow* it shall we say, I go along, have no preference in the matter—" He turned away, pursed over his key-chain . . . key to his coffin, gold.

"Dovists are after all mere lovers of—no different than the Brownings of other Romes, groaners of other gabbles —I *mean*—"

Count Condu stood at the stone window staring severely into the night; in Baroque's elegant chambers it was possible to relax, so he wore his malagant—hood-like his head loomed over his shoulders as if winged— A knock on the door, Sabatini ushered in young Boaz the son of the Castle Caretaker who was an old mysterious goof always hiding in the cellar— Young Boaz, with his long dark feet and leer, strangely satanically handsome like a clay head stretched, sophisticated son of a hermit, "Oh—!—Baroque is here."

"I should say, dearie, it's my room."

"*Your* room! I thought it was Count Condu's. Well may I close the door—?"

"No, flit to an eve," muttered the Count in his cup.

"The wildest news," said Boaz.

"And now—?" perked Baroque expectantly (he wore his brocaded white silk tunic pajamas à la Cossack with a great bloodclot in red thread over the heart, he smoked from elegant holder, "perfumed of course," a brilliant wit in the Ark Galleries of the Rack where he'd been for a while before descending (not to take courses in a taxi school) to forfend the later migamies for his mother's estate and save the day, and find himself a Sugar Daddy at the same time so here he was) (the Wizard's brother, meek ill-tempered oldqueen Flapsnaw, we never saw him around).

107

"And now," provided Boaz, "they have officially denounced the Dovists as underground heretics of the Free Movement—"

"*Free* movement," snorted Condu— "some kind of dysentery? Would be rather a joke if the Snake should spew out like a great wet fart watering and be-splattering the earth with a piece of its own good riddance—"

In the window, suddenly, unbeknownst to all of them, Doctor Sax appears, dark, merged with the balcony, shrouded, silent, as they talk.

"*Such* a notion," laughed B. "That doves, are kin, to snakes, my *dear!*"

"They infer it from doves' and snakes' proximities."

"Infer without proof is less than infer without proof for no reason—these people show ignorance without charm."

"Well foo you too," said Boaz bowing and slapping his white gloves together. "Maybe they'll rain *you* out sometime in a blap, then where will your verdigris be? out in the garden under an onion."

"Onions show stones"—Baroque threw in.

"It'd be better if fancy iterators re-fancied their anvil on a wit."

"*Touché.*"

The Doctor Sax vanished—out in the yard it could be heard, a faint triumphant distant ha ha ha ha ha of inside secret sureness in the black—around the bird bath his shroud slanted to a fade—the moon croaked—Blook wandered in the back Garden with a garland of peanut butter twigs in his hair, put there by Semibu the suspicious dwarf, 'twas to ward away the Onion. Blook had a orror of onion—

In the belfry of the castle triumphant leered the panic Bat—a Spider hung from the wall facing the river with his silvery moonlight thread all dusty, a stately lion descended the stairs in the cellars where the Zoo was kept, a truckload of Gnomes came flipping through the wire—(in underground tunnels).

Condu, looking out the window, mused.

Baroque read the little booklet of Dovist poem in his bed.

Boaz sat stiffly writing his elegy for the dead, at the table, by the lamp.

"On the Day," read Baroque, "clouds of Seminal Gray Doves shall issue forth from the Snake's Mouth and it shall collapse in a Prophetic Camp, they will rejoice and cry in the Golden Air, 'Twas but a husk of doves!'"

"It'll husk *them*," spoffed Condu splurtering in his laughbeard hands,—"phnuff—what?"

"I expect," said Boaz looking up, "the Snake will devour them that deserve it," but he said it in such a way Condu couldn't tell if this was an ordinary friendly statement or not—

"Simply—*divine!*" concluded Baroque closing the book. "It's *so* refreshing—we need *any* kind of revival, my dear, because you know it's got great yoiky elements of Coney Island Christian in it." He leaned over and turned on his favorite record . . . Edith Piaf dying.

Count Condu was gone—he had transformed himself to his bat-form, while no one looked, and into the moon he Flew—Ah me, Lowell in the night.

Jack Kerouac

4

THERE WAS AN ALLEY DOWNTOWN among the soft redbrick
of Keith's Theater and the Bridge Street Warehouse, with
a red neoned candy store of antique Saturday nights of
funnies still smelling of ink and strawberry ice cream sodas
all pink and frothy with a dew on top, in Dana's—across
the street from the alley— In the alley itself there were
cinders, leading to the stage door— Something there was
so fantastically grad sad about this alley—in it the living
W.C. Fields had walked, headed from a rainy afternoon
stint in the 6-Act Vod Bill (with gaping masks ha-ha)—
twirling that Old Bull Balloon cane, W.C. Fields and the
tragic Marx Brothers of early times swaying precariously
from immense ladders and goofing in an awful holocaust of
Greatstage Sorrow all huge with drapes and jello rippling
flop props in the middle of the day, 1927—in 1927 I saw the
Marx Brothers, Harpo on the ladder—in 1934 I saw Harpo
on the screen, *Animal Crackers*, in a dark and unbelievably
Doctor Sax garden where Neo-Like God-Like the rain and
sunshine just mixed for a Cosmic Joke by Chico "Don't go
out that door, it's raining—try this one"—tweet tweet birds
—"see?" and Harpo drops silverware in the dark, God how
Joe and I in the dark balcony sat transfixed by this picture
of our joint dreams snoring in the dark attics of our boyhood together ... brothers of the frantic snazzle in the
Wood, at 8, when, with Beauty the immense Shepherd dog
of the Fortiers, and little Philip Fortier nicknamed Snorro,
we took off on a 20-mile hike to Pelham New Hampshire to
slide up and down the hayloft of some dairy farmer—there

110

were dead owls skewered on the pine, gravel pits, apples, distances of green Normandy fields into a mist of New England Inscrutable Space mystery—in the imprint of the trees on the sky in the horizon, I judged I was being torn from my mother's womb with each step from Home Lowell into the Unknown . . . a serious lostness that has never repaired itself in my shattered flesh dumb-hanging for the light—

But Joe never had anything to do with that alley of tragedy harpo marx hurrying by greasepaint Variety oldprint brown crackly, with masks on a shiny ballroom in the menu,— Nights of 1922 when I was born, in the glittering unbelievable World of Gold and Rich Darkness of the Lowell of my prime father, he would escort my mother Tilly the Toiler of his weekly theatrical column (with whom he argued in verbose slang about the quality of the shows) ("Boy O boy, next Wednesday we gets to see *The Big Parade*, with Karl Dane, Dead Hero John Gilbert—") —escort my mother to the show among the black cardboard throngs of long ago in 1920's of U.S.A., the grawky sad loop of the City Hall clock illuminating or staring sadly at penyons of real endeavor in another air, another time— different outcries on the street, different feelings, other dusts, other lace—other funnies, other drunk lamp posts— the inconceivable joy that creams up in my soul at the thought of the little kid in the funnies under his blanket quilt at midnight New Year's when thru the blue sweetness of his window in comes the bells and horn cries and honks and stars and slams of Time and Noises, and the blue fences of the quilt night are dewy in the moon, and

111

strange Italian rooftops of parliament tenements in Courts that are in old funnies—the redbrick alley where my father in big strawhat walked, with B.F. Keith's circuit ads sticking out of his pocket, smoking a cigar, not a smalltime businessman in a smalltown, a man in a straw hat hurrying in a redbrick alley of Eternity.

Beyond, the back railroad tracks of the Warehouse, some switch tracks to the cotton mills, the Canal, the Post Office to the right across it—rampy lots, box crate heats of afternoon, the dark dank rich redbrick Georgian alley street like a great street in self-interior Chinatown between wholesale offices and printing plants—my father swung his groaning old Plymouth of the Kraw Time around the little corner, tooting—coming to the inky darkness of the warehouse of his plant, where on a Saturday night in a dream-tragic holdups or moldups are taking place and my father's busy with one of his interminable aides at some huge hassel of the crock, there's no telling what it is I really see in that dream—into the future really. Dreams are where participants in a drama recognize one another's death—there is no illusion of life in this Dream—

Long long ago before tot-linoleums of Lupine Road and even Burnaby Street there was, and will be, inconceivable rich red softnesses in the consistency of the air on going-to-the-show nights. (One of those nameless little bugs, so small you don't know what they are, so tiny, flew by my face.)

Some kind of brown tragedy it was, in the plant,—the spectral canal flows by in its own night, brown gloom of midnight cities presses the windows in, dull lamps as

of poker games illuminate the loneliness of my father—
just as in Centralville he's completely unavailable in the
Lakeview Avenue night of old—O the silence of this—he
had a gymnasium there, with boxers, real life fact— When
W.C. Fields has boarded the destiny train, for sooty miles
to Cincinnati, my father hurries in the B.F. Keith alley
opens the door, goes in on lost endeavors wined from the
Canal of sperms and oil that flows between the mills,
under the bridge— The mystery of the Lowell night ex-
tends to the heart of downtown, it lurks in the shadows of
the redbrick walls— Something in old musty records in
the City Hall—an old, old book in the library files, with
prints of Indians—a nameless laugh by the purities of
the wave mist on the river bank, at dead of March or
April night—and empty winds of winter night under the
Moody Bridge, around the corner of Riverside and
Moody, sand grit blowing, here comes old Gene Plouffe
in the dawn grim cold headed for work in the mills, he's
been sleeping in his shroud and brown night in the old
house of Gershom, the moon's whipped to one side, cold
stars gleam, shine down on empty Vinny Bergerac tenement court where now the washlines creak, The Shadow
creeps,—the ghosts of W.C. Fields and my father emerge
together from the redbrick alley, straw be-hatted, headed
for the lit-up blackwalls of the night of the cross eyed cat,
as Sax grins . . .

BOOK FOUR

The Night the Man with the Watermelon Died

1

AND NOW THAT TRAGIC HALO, half gilt, half hidden—the night the man with the watermelon died—should I tell—(Oh Ya Ya Yoi Yoi)—how he died, and O'Curlicued on the planks of the bridge, pissing death, staring at the dead waves, everybody's already dead, what a horror to know —the sin of life, of death, he pissed in his pants his last act.

It was a baneful black night anyway, full of shrouds. My mother and I walked Blanche home to Aunt Clementine's house. This was a dreadful drear brown house in which Uncle Mike was dying these past five, ten, fifteen years, *worse*—next door to a garage for hearses leased by one of the undertakers around the corner on funereal Pawtucket Street and had a storage room for—coffins—

Gad, I had dreams rickety and strange about that barn garage—hated to go to Mike's for that reason, it was God-awful the scene of marijuana-sheeshkabob cigarettes he smoked for his asthma, Cu Babs— The thing that got Proust so all-hung-out—on his frame of greatness— Right Reference Marcel—old Abyssinian Bushy Beard—Uncle Mike

117

bliazasting legal medical tea in his afternoons of gloom-special meditation—brooding by brown window drapes, sadness— He was an extremely intelligent man, remembered whole spates of history, talked at great length with his melancholy rasping breath about the beauties of the poetry of Victor Hugo (Emil his brother always extolled the *novels* of Victor Hugo), Poet Mike was the saddest Duluoz in the world—that is very sad. I saw him cry countless times—"*O mon pauvre Ti Jean si tu sava tout le trouble et toute les larmes epuis les pauvres envoyages de la tête au sein, pour la douleur, la grosse douleur, impossible de cette vie ou on's trouve daumé a la mort—pourquoi pourquoi pourquoi—seulement pour suffrir, comme ton père Emil, comme ta tante Marie*—for nothing, my boy, for nothing,—*mon enfant pauvre Ti Jean, sais tu mon âme que tu est destinez d'être un homme de grosses douleurs et talent—ca aidra jamais vivre ni mourir, tu va souffrir comme les autres, plus*"—(Saying: "Oh my poor Ti Jean if you know all the trouble and all the tears and all the sendings of the head to the breast, for sadness, big sadness, impossible this life where we find ourselves doomed for death—why why why—just to suffer, like your father Emil, like your aunt Marie—for nothing—my child poor Ti Jean, do you know my dear that you are destined to be a man of big sadness and talent—it'll never help to live or die, you'll suffer like the others, *more*"—

"*Napoleon était un homme grand. Aussie le General Montcalm a Quebec tambien qu'il a perdu. Ton ancestre, l'honorable soldat, Baron Louis Alexandre Lebris de Duluoz, un grandpère—a marriez l'Indienne, retourna a*

*Bretagne, le pere la, le vieux Baron, a dit, criant a pleine
tête, 'Retourne toi a cette femme—soi un homme honnete
et d'honneur.' Le jeune Baron a retournez au Canada, a la
Rivière du Loup, il avais gagnez de la terre alongez sur
cette fleu—il a eux ces autres enfant avec sa femme. Cette
femme la etait une Indienne—on ne sais pas rien d'elle ni
de son monde— Toutes les autres parents, mon petit, sont
cent pourcent Français—ta mère, ta belle tite mère Angy,
voyons donc s'petite bonfemme de coeur,—c'etait une
L'Abbé tout Français au moin qu'un oncle avec un nom
Anglais, Gleason, Pearson, quelque chose comme ca, il y
a longtemp—deux cents ans—"*

Saying: "Napoleon was a great man. Also the General
Montcalm at Quebec even though he lost. Your ancestor,
the honorable soldier, Baron Louis Alexandre Lebris de
Duluoz, a grandfather—married the Indian woman, returned to Brittany, the father there, the old Baron, said, yelling
at the top of his voice, 'Return to that woman—be an honest
man and a man of honor.' The young Baron returned to
Canada, to Rivière du Loup (Wolf River) he had been
granted land along that river—he had his other children
with his wife. That woman was an Indian—we know nothing about her or her people— All the other parents, my
little one, are one hundred percent French—your mother,
you: pretty little mother Angy, poor little goodlady of the
heart—she was a L'Abbé, all French except for one uncle
with an English name, Gleason, Pearson, something like
that, it's a long time ago—two hundred years—"

And then:—he would always finish with his weeping and
woe—terrible agonies of the spirit—*"O les pauvres Duluozes*

119

*meur toutes!—enchainées par le Bon Dieu pour la peine—
peut être l'enfer!"—"Mike! weyons donc!"*

Saying: "O the poor Duluozes are all dying!—chained by
God to pain—maybe to hell!"—"Mike! My goodness!"

So I says to my mother *"J'ai peur moi allez sur mononcle
Mike* (I'm scared me of going to Uncle Mike's ...).*"* I
couldn't tell her my nightmares, how one dream had it that
one night in our old house on Beaulieu when somebody
was dead Uncle Mike was there and all his Brown relatives
(by Brown I mean all gree-darkened in the room as in
dreams)— But he was horrible, porcine, fat, sickfaced,
bald, and green. But she guessed I was a slob with fear
concerning nightmares. *"Le monde il meur, le monde il
meur* (If people die, people *die*)" is what she said—"Uncle
Mike has been dying for ten years—the whole house and
yards smell of death—"

"Especially wit de coffins."

"Yeh, especially wit de coffins and you gotta remember
honey Aunt Clementine has suffered all these many years
trying to keep ends together... With your Uncle sick and
lost his grocery store—remember the big barrels of pickles
in his grocery store in Nashué—the sawdust, the meat—
what with having to bring up Edgar and Blanche and
Roland and Viola *pauvre tite bonfemme—Écoute, Jean, ai
pas peur de tes parents—tun n'ara plus jamais des parents
un bon jour.* (... and Viola poor little woman—Listen,
Jean, don't be afraid of your parents—you won't have any
more parents one fine day.)"

So one night, from the Phebe house, we walked Blanche
(who later in such a walk insisted on bringing my dog

Beauty because she's afraid of the dark and as the little beast escorted her home it rushed out and got run over by Roger Carrufel of Pawtucketville who was somehow driving an Austin tinycar that night and the low bumper killed it, previously on Salem Street at Joe's lawn door it got run over by an ordinary car but rolled with the wheels and never got hurt—I heard the news of its death at precisely that moment in my life when I was lying in bed finding out that my tool had sensations in the tip—they yelled it up to me thru the transom, *"Ton chien est mort!* (Your dog is dead!)"* and they brought it home dying—on the kitchen floor we and Blanche and Carrufel with hat in hand watch Beauty die, Beauty dies the night I discover sex, they wonder why I'm mad—)—So now Blanche (this is before Beauty was born, 2 years earlier) wants me and Ma to walk her home, so we go, a beautiful soft summer night in Lowell. The stars are shining in the deep,—millions. We cross the great darknesses of Sarah Avenue by the park, with hugetree sighs above; and the baleful flickering dark of Riverside Street and the Textile ironpicket shrouds and on to Moody and across the Bridge. In the summerdark, far below, the soft white horses of the thrush-foam over rocks are surging in a Nightly Tryst with Mystery and Mists that Crash off Rocks, in a Gray Anathema Void, all raw-roar-roo . . . a wild Ionian sight and frightening—we turn at Pawtucket and move up past the gray tenement and the Hospital St. Joseph's where my sister had appendicitis and the Funeral homes of the dark Flale there after you pass the curve of gooky rickety Salem curvacueing in—huge mansions appear, solemn, sitting in state on lawns, all behung with signs— "R.K.G.W.S.T.N. Droux, Funeral Director"—with hearses, lacy windows, warm rich interiors, dank chauffeur like hearse garages, shrubs around the lawn, the great slopes of the river and the canal falling away from the black lawn to grand darkness and lights of foam and night—ha river! My mother and Blanche are discussing astrology as they walk under the stars. Sometimes they lapse into philosophy—"Isn't it a perfectly beautiful night Angy? Oh my *fate!*—" sighing—Blanche had tried to commit suicide from the Moody Bridge—she had told us among gloomy pianos—she played piano and told her moods, she was an elegant visitor to our house that sometimes my father found infuriating especially because she was teaching us so well—explaining Rachmaninoff's *Rustle of Spring* and playing it—a beautiful blonde woman, well preserved—old Shammy had his eye on her, he lived in that old white house on Riverside across Textile ironpickets under an immense 1776 tree and we always talked about Shammy as we passed at night the house where he lived with his wife (Sad Harmonies of Love Night Lowell)—

The Grotto—it Hugely Mooked ahead of us, to the right . . . that baleful night. It belonged to the orphanage on the corner of Pawtucket Street and School Street at the head of the White Bridge—a big Grotto is their backyard, mad, vast, religious, the Twelve Stations of the Cross, little individual twelve altars set in, you go in front, kneel, everything but incense in the air (the roar of the river, mysteries of nature, fireflies in the night flickering to the waxy stare of statues, I knew Doctor Sax was there flowing in the back

darks with his wild and hincty cape)—culminating, was
the gigantic pyramid of steps upon which the Cross itself
poked phallically up with its Poor Burden the Son of Man
all skewered across it in his Agony and Fright—undoubtedly this statue moved in the night— . . . after the . . . last
of the worshippers is gone, poor dog. Before seeing Blanche
in home to the horrible brown glooms of her dying father's
house—we go to this Grotto, like we often do, to get some
praying in. "*Wishing*, I'd call it more," Blanche said. "Oh
Angy, if I could only find my ideal man."

"What's the matter with Shammy, he's an ideal man."

"But he's married."

"If you love him that ain't his fault—you gotta take the
bad with the worse." My mother had a great secret love for
Shammy—she told him and everybody so—Shammy re-
ciprocated with great kindness and charm— When he
wasn't at the Club bowling or shooting pool, or home
sleeps, or driving his bus, he was at our house having big
parties with Blanche and my father and mother and sometimes a Textile student Tommy Lockstock and my sister
—Shammy had a real affection for Blanche—

"But he's only a truck driver," she'd say. "There's nothing
really *fine* about him." She probably meant he was just
dumb and silent, Shammy was, nothing much troubled
him, he was a goodlooking peaceful man. Blanche wanted
Rachmaninoff in her teacups.

"Oh the irony of life."

"Yeah," my mother'd echo, "the iyony of life, *oui*"—and
bundle along with Blanche's arm in hers in coats for the
latenight mist, and I, Ti Jean, walking beside them some-

times listening but most of the time watching the dark shadows in the night, from Sarah park to the Funerals and Grottos of Pawtucket, looking for The Shadow, for Doctor Sax, listening for the laugh, "mwee hee hee ha ha," looking for that lawn where G.J. and I and Dicky Hampshire wrestled, the place where Vinny Bergerac and Lousy threw popcorn at each other etc. and also wrapped deep in that dream of childhood which has no bottom and instantly soars to impossible daydreams, I've got the whole city of Manhattan paralyzed, I'm going around with a super-buzz-ing-current in me that knocks everything out of its way and also I'm invisible and taking money out of cash registers and striding along 23rd Street with fire in my head and making the elevated highways ring with my electricity, on steel and stone etc.— Across the street, just before we go in the Grotto, is the store Uncle Mike briefly owned before he got too sick and for a while Edgar ran it and one summer night I heard him say that new word "sex appeal" and all the ladies laughed—

As we're turning from the sidewalk into the darkness of the Grotto (it's about eleven o'clock) Blanche is saying "If he only'd made some money somehow, if he'd been rich like some men do with store,—instead the squalor of those years and that house, really Angy I was born for something much grander, don't you feel it in my music?"

"Blanche I always did say you was a very great painist —there!—a great artist, Blanche, I understand you, when you make a mistakes on the piano I always know, it's always been so—ain't it?"

"You do have a good ear, Ange," conceded the Princess.

"You damn tootin right—ask anybody if I ain't got a good ear, Ti Jean, I tell you," (turning to me) *"a toutes les fois que Blanche fait seulement quainque un ti mistake sur son piano, pis je'll sais tu-suite, . . . Hah?"* (Repeating what she said.)

And I jump up athletically to catch a branch of the overhead tree in answer and to prove my world is more action —so engrossed have we been in our conversation, we're in the Grotto!—deep, too,—halfway to the first Station of the Ghost. The first of the stations faced the side of a funeral home, so you kneeled there, at night, looking at faint representations of the Virgin, hood over head, her sad eyes, the action, the tortured wood and thorns of the Passion, and your reflections on the subject become mirrored from the funeral home where a dull light fixed in the ceiling of an overpass rain garage for hearses shines dully in the gravelly gloom, with bordering dewy grassplots and shrubs to give it the well-tended look, and the drapes in the windows showing, incredibly, where the funeral director himself lives, in his House of Death. *"This is our home."* Everything there was to remind of Death, and nothing in praise of life —except the roar of the humpbacked Merrimac passing over rocks in formations and arms of foam, at 11:15 P.M. Among the shrubs of wild grotto and senary funeral home I know there in the green opulence of dollars and in the grotto sorrows of rocks and plaster . . . gravel croaked and on-led for persetury investigators in the wrong roil road to the flaminary immensities and up-fluge of the poor bedighted, be-knighted Crown and Clown of sorrowmary doom in This anyway-globe . . . the Jesus most admirable in his

125

height—in all this Doctor Sax I knew, I saw him watching from a shroud in the bushes by the river ... I saw him flit across the moonlit rocks of the summerriver to come and see the visitors in the Grotto. I saw him flit from Station with his cape now hanging from the orphan home walls with a keen eye on our doings... I saw him flit from Station to Station, from the backs of em, in terrible blasphemy prayer in the dark with everything reversed—he was only following to see me, it was later when the Snake was ready and Sax brought me to see, which was the final thing that happened and I covered my eyes for fear of what I saw—

We made the stations to the ultimate foot of the Cross, where my mother kneeled, prayed, and worked a step up the cross-mount, to show me how some people did it all the way up—to the foot of the Cross itself, tremendous ascents to blasphemous heights in the river breeze and views of long land vistas— We tramped back arm-in-arm down the gravel path running thru the grotto dark, to the lights of the street again, where we bade Blanche adieu.

I always liked to get out of there ...

And headed towards home— There was a full moon that night.

(The following full moon, August month the next, I had my bus pass stolen from me as I stood with it clasped behind me in the glittering lights of Kearney Square and a sad bully of the Lowell alleys rushed up and stole it and ran through the crowd. "The full moon," I cried, "twice in a row—it's giving me—death, and now I get robbed, O Mama, God, what you,—hey," and I rushed in the terrible clarity of the August full moon to hide myself from it ...

126

as I ran home across the Moody Bridge the moon made the mad white horses foam all beautiful and close and shiny so that it was almost inviting—to jump in—everybody in Pawtucketville had the perfect opportunity to commit suicide coming home every night—that is why we lived deep lives—)

The full moon this night was the moon of death. We, my mother and I rounded the corner of Pawtucket and Moody (cattycorner across the home of the French Canadian St. Joseph's parochial Jesuit brothers, my fifth-grade teachers, gloomy men in their black mid sleep now), and stepped on the planks of the Moody Street Bridge and headed over the canal which after a huge stonewall offered the rest of the waterbed dug in primord-rock to the river that dug it with its lovekiss tongues—

A man carrying a watermelon passed us, he wore a hat, a suit in the warm summer night; he was just on the boards of the bridge, refreshed, maybe from a long walk up slummy swilly Moody and its rantankling saloons with the swinging doors, mopped his brow, or came up through Little Canada or Cheever or Aiken, rewarded by the bridge of eve and sighs of stone—the great massive charge of the ever stationary ever yearning cataracts and ghosts, this is his reward after a long dull hot dumb walk to the river thru houses—he strides on across the bridge— We stroll on behind him talking about the mysteries of life (inspired we were by moon and river), I remember I was so happy— something in the alchemy of summernight, Ah Midsummer Night's Dream, John a Dreams, the clink of clock on rock in river, roar—old gloor-merrimac figalitating down the

127

dark mark all spread—I was happy too in the intensity of something we were talking about, something that was giving me joy.

Suddenly the man fell, we heard the great thump of his watermelon on wood planks and saw him fallen— Another man was there, also mysterious, but without watermelon, who bent to him quickly and solicitously as by assent and nod in the heavens and when I got there I saw the watermelon man staring at the waves below with shining eyes (*"Il's meurt*, he's dying," my mother's saying) and I see him breathing hard, feeble-bodied, the man holding him gravely watching him die, I'm completely terrified and yet I feel the profound pull and turn to see what he is staring at so deadly-earnest with his froth stiffness—I look down with him and there is the moon on shiny froth and rocks, there is the long eternity we have been seeking.

"Is he dead?" I said to my mother. As in a dream we adjourn behind the dead man, who sits near the rail with his stare, holding his belly with his wrist, all slumped, distant, in the throes of that which is carrying him far away from us, something private. Another man vouchsafed an opinion:

"I'll get an ambulance at St. Joseph's here, he may be alright."

But my mother shook her head and made that sneer you see the world wide around, in California or in China, "No, *s't'homme la est fini* (no, that man there is finished)"— *"Regard—l'eau sur les planches, quand qu'un homme s'meurt ils pis dans son butain, toute part* ... (Look, the water on the planks, when a man dies he pees in his clothes, everything goes.)"

Indubitable proof of his death I saw in that tragic stain that in the moonlight was spectralized milk, he was not going to be alright at all, he was already dead, my mother's was no prophecy it was a known thing from the start, her secret snaky knowledge about death as uncanny as the Fellaheen dog that howls in the muddy alleys of Mazatlan when death has laid its shroud on the dead in the dark. I had intended to look at the dead man again—but now I saw he was really dead and taken—his eyes had turned glassy on the milky waters of the night in their hollow roar cold rock—but it was *that* part of the giant rocks below he chose to die his fixed gaze on—that part which yet I see in dreams of Lowell and the Bridge. I shuddered and saw white flowers and grew cold.

The full moon horrified me with her cloudy leer. "*Regard, la face de skalette dans la lune!*" cries my mother— "*Look, the face of a skeleton in the moon!*"

2

THUMPING TREES IN THE WILD WOOD beyond the bridge rail, the forests of the rock bank of Merrimac, where oft I'd seen old Sax-heart urge his oiky-cloiky fly along the black sides, headed for a perfidy of dirt—in mists of raw March— wild glee—

The history of the Castle goes back to the 18th century

129

when it was built by a mad seafarer named Phloggett who
came to Lowell looking for a sea-like expanse of the Merrimac and decided on the Rosemont basin and built his
old haunted rockheap on the top of the Centralville hill
where it backsloped to its Pelhams and Dracuts (many's
the time we'd run around there Joe and me picking green
apples from the ground by stone walls and finding rusty
fenders to piss on in the heart of every forest)—a ruinous
old bones of a house, with turrets, stone, entryways gothic-
ized, a gravel driveway which was put in by its 1920's
occupants for roadsters of the Ripe—Old Epzebiah Phloggett, he was a seafarer, for all we know he was a slavetrader
— He sailed from Lynn in the molasses and rum fleet—
Retired he went to his Lowell castle—not known as Lowell
then, and wild—nothing but the Pawtucket Indians sending up their calm wigwams at eve with a puff of smoke—
Old Smogette Phloggett occasionally made hikes with his
footmen to see the Indians, at the Falls—where the river
left its shale shelf that has served it since before Nashua
and now drops blonk into the wornaway rock—rock as soft
as silk when you touch it in hot dry summers— Phloggett
didn't have much to do with the Indians, he occasionally
bought a young squaw and brought her to the Castle and
back again in a week— There was something evil in the
bottom of his dirty old soul ... some snaky secret Sax
knew about later— He had a long old antiquarian telescope
eye-glass that he unfurled on gray March mornings on the
West balcony and pointed to the wild wide Merrimac as
it ancestral plowed its original forest-trail thru the site of
Now-Lowell—not a house—New England was alone in the

woods of time. Where Dracut Tigers field now is, back
of homeplate, in the shrubs and stub pines, a red man
Indian stalked in the silent morn—the birds that luted in
the dew, and pointed rosy eyes to the new Promised East,
are now the birds that fritter on the branch of dust—ancestral voices in the mute mist of morning, without fanfare
or cry, quiet, it was bound to be there a long time— Phloggett trains his telescope on these woods, on the hump-rise
of the sandbank in its wild golden isle mid green,—the huge
tree across the street from my Sarah Avenue house stood
then with the same majesty and height above the solid
grunchy vastness green of the Pawtucketville forest—no
dream-skyscrapers sprung from Mt. Vernon Street—
George Washington was a boy stalking deer in Virginia flat
forests— In the Gaspé peninsula up north the first of the
American Armorican Duluozes was wrangling with his
squaw on the Wolf River morns—over by Pine Brook, in the
18th century, peaceful, tepees were pitched in the sward
carpet of the spring, over the pine hill the crows cawed, a
hunter came tramping home over the field—a young Indian
boy dove brown and naked with his tuft-hair and red-stone
bracelet into the cool pool of life—it was centuries later
I came by there with Sebastian and Dicky Hampshire and
we sang poems to the rising sun—African alligator adventures took place along Pine Brook (Slow Waters) clear
to the Rosemont (Ohio River at its Cairo) junction with
(Swift Waters) Merrimac in the drowsy afternoons of Indian children— Fellaheen singers with greasy manes and
capes made mournful Hebraic cries along the *merced* walls
of Cadiz, in the 18th century morn— The whole world,

fresh and dewy, rolled to the sun—as it will tomorrow morning so golden—

Old Epzebiah Phloggett the owner of Phlogget Hill Castle—Snake Hill Castle it eventually became, because of the overabundance of small snakes and garter snakes to be found on that hill—little Tom Sawyers of early Lowell pre Civil War went angling up that hill from the old Colonial slums of Prince Street or Worthen where Whistler was born, found the snakes, renamed the hill— Phloggett died in solitude and black loneliness in the primordial castle . . . some ghastly thing was buried with him. It was years later the cool lake of the basin was rippled by the oars of the Thoreau brothers, and Henry himself up-glanced the Castle with a snort so profound with contempt he never wrote it—besides, his eye was in the water lily, his hand was on the Upanishads—

For a very real snaky reason the unnamably evil owner of the Castle died—of snakebite. Buried no one knew where —derelict castle gooked alone.

Phloggett had sold Black Ivory to the Kings.

In the 19th century it was bought from some firm in Lynn by a landed family from Lynn, contemptuous of the manufacturing gentry but forced to face the early mills across the water; it became their summer place. Oil paintings were hung on the walls, in niches, family portraits, the fireplace roared, the genteel sons stared at the Merrimac with after dinner sherries—from the sun-red west balcony in March dusks, and were bored. Post chaises couldn't make it to the Castle, bad road—so finally the family got bored—and then the sicknesses began, they all died of something or other. It began to be realized the Castle was never meant for human occupation, it had a hex. The family (Reeves of Lynn) (they'd renamed it Reeves Castle) packed and got out, depleted—the mother, a daughter and three sons dead, one an infant—all of them had been on a summer at the Lowell Castle—the father and his remnant son went to Lynn, got moldered with Hawthorne's bones nearabouts—

And the Castle was a derelict heap without windows and full of bats and kidcrap flaps for a hundred years.

In 1921 it was bought up by the only kind of person who would want it. Bought up cheap, dusty records in Lynn had been eaten by termites, with seals and ribbons collapsing—only the land was good. (But full of snakes.) Bought up by Emilia St. Claire, a dotty Isadora Duncan woman in a white cult robe with roadsters from Boston on weekends—renamed it Transcendenta she did

> Transcendenta!
> Transcendenta!
> We shall dance
> A mad cadenza!

Mwee hee hee ha ha, Doctor Sax was ready for them all—

One clear Saturday morning the citizens of Lowell saw the mad Miss St. Claire (a terribly rich woman with a house in Cuba and an apartment house in St. Petersburg, Russia, where her mother had stayed on after the 1917 Bolshevik Revolution—) wandering in the marble-statued gardens of the castle grounds, a mad sight to see, pissing off rocks on the heights around the valley little boys could

133

see her, a white dot moving in the distant yard— Bottles of whiskey were found in the yard by little boys who played hookey to explore the Castle Grounds and play blackjack in a shitty bay window. One night long ago, in the thirties, in the height of the Depression a young man who was walking home from the mills at midnight, down by the canal at Aiken near Cheever in Little Canada, headed home to Pawtucketville to a wretched furnished room over the Textile Lunch (name was Amadeus Baroque) saw a curlicueing yellow sheaf of papers sliding in the coldmoon January wind of the French Canuck ruts in frozen mud so like Russia, by creaking saloon signs, grit winds, canal frozen solid— What would anybody do seeing this thing, it was though it talked and begged to be picked up the way it sidled to him like a scorpion—with its dry sheaves crack-a-lak—a rustling clink-dry voice in the winter solitudes of bitter Human North—he picked it up with his fingertips, he stooped to pluck it in his bearish coat, he saw it had writing on it

DOCTOR SAX, AN ACCOUNT OF HIS ADVENTURE WITH THE HUMAN INHABITANTS OF SNAKE CASTLE—Written & Arrang'd by Adolphus Asher Ghoulens, With a Hint Contain'd of Things Which Have Not Yet Seen Their End

—he briefly had time to read that ghoulish title, and undertucked the eerie manuscript which he'd plucked from tenemental coldnorth night of desolation like the Lamb is plucked from black hills by the Grace of the Lord, and went home with it.

Arriving there, he unfurled his snaky mysteries—there

had already come a hunch to this intelligent young mill-worker that satisfied his taste for ambition. He did not know then that he held in his hands the only existing piece of writing from the pen of Doctor Sax, who confined himself to alchemies and outcries as a rule—this bit of foddle wildwawp had been briefly sketched with quill feather in his underground forge-works and red sleep-hole (under a hermit of ark shack on the Dracut Tigers road, he had a stonewall around, a fence, a garden with vegetables and herbs, a good big dog, and a scraggly single pine)—on a night when drunk—after a visit for a poker game from Old Bull Balloon of Butte and Boaz the caretaker of Snake Hill Castle who'd stayed on long after Miss St. Claire had departed from the Castle forever—(in the manuscript Boaz is the butler, Miss St. Claire's butler, it shows how Sax met Boaz for the first time). Old Bull Balloon incidentally came once a year for a game with Sax, Bull traveled a lot—the game was always held in Doc Sax's shack in Dracut Tigers road—that is, in the underground room, where the giant black cat guarded the laboratory secrets of the doctor—

This was the story, on yellowed blotchy papers with rusty staples and stained with winter, garbage, and sand shrouds—Baroque read and laughed (Doctor Sax was no sophisticated writer):—

Emilia St. Claire was a woman of whimsy; in this she was a tyrant, indeed a lovable tyrant. She could afford to be a tyrant for she was rich. Her family had left her millions. She had a chateau in France (at most, she had a dozen chateaux in Europe); she had a mansion in New York City on Riverside Drive; a villa in Italy overlooking Genoa; it was

135

rumored she had a marble retreat on an isle near Crete. (But this is not certain.)

Her whimsy demanded the baroque, the unusual, often the weird, sometimes even the perverted; she had seen too much to be satisfied with the ordinary. Like Isadora Duncan, she wept for the Russian peasant and conducted Oriental salons in her parlours.

Emilia St. Claire did not care for New England, not in any overbearing sense, but there lived in Boston (the Hub of Culture) a clique of her friends who were at all odds some of the most interesting people in the entire world. For this reason, when Emilia St. Claire returned from Athens one March in 1922, she went directly to her place in New England from Pier 42 in New York, driven by her chauffeur Dmitri (an Irishman from Chicago). The "place" was a turreted, all-stone mansion situated on a hill in the northern part of Massachusetts; on clear days, one could gaze from the northern wings and see the Merrimac River winding down from New Hampshire. Emilia St. Claire was not too fond of her newly-acquired New England haven, but she had grown a bit weary of the unusual and had decided to come there for a little of the healthy, robust New England weather that is famous the world over. March, in New England, is like a gust of something raw and moist and feverish; there is the heavy, pungent thaw of dark muds; above, pale clouds, dark clouds flee across the ghostly heavens in terror. March is terror!

Emilia St. Claire, seated in her morning room, drank the tea which had been fetched her by the tall young butler Boaz and smiled at the scene before her eyes, the torn, gaping skies, the steaming marshes, the birch, the bent spruces. She thought rather fondly of the name she had given to her New England retreat: "Transcendenta."

"Transcendenta in the gray morning," mused Emilia St. Claire to herself, sipping the tea.

Transcendental Transcendental
We shall dance a mad cadenza!

The unusual! Ha! Doctor Sax would certainly provide her with that!

Doctor Sax lived in a wooden shack behind the hill upon which reposed the noble bulk of Trancendenta which was originally Reeves Castle. If one were to approach· the shack from the back, from the side, from the front—nothing would be revealed. The shack was as square as a perfect block; it suggested nothing. In the yard were rows of vegetables and strange herbs. A tall, tall pine stood in the front. There was no fence; weeds, millions of weeds stretched along the property of Doctor Sax. (Was it his? No one knows.) March nights, the mist would rise and completely obliterate the shack, leaving only the arched rib of the pine protruding above, nodding sadly in the unholy weather. If one were to approach the shack, Ah! there now a light glowing in one of the two windows, with reddish smoky look that light! Should we approach and gaze within? What vials, what skull heads, what stacks of ancient paper, what red-eyed cats, what haze of what eerie smoke! Horrors, no, we shall leave the discovery to . . . Emilia St. Claire.

After a few days telephoning and writing, friends began to drift into Transcendenta to be hosted by the fabulous Miss St. Claire. Dark-eyed young dramatic students roved the rooms, garlanded amongst their wild black locks of hair with New England flowers. Strange young women in slacks lounged on the divans and indolently provided resumées of latest Art for Emilia St. Claire. One was a poet; the other a pianist. One was an artist; the other a sculptor. There, now, in the livingroom, an interpretative dancer! There now, in the pantry (devouring cold chicken) —a celebrated ballet impresario. Now, coming up the drive in a roadster, a drama critic, a composer, and their mistresses. Oh! there's Polly Ryan! (Have you met Polly? She wears Bohemian dresses, her mascara is applied for deft mystery, she insults everyone, she is a dear.) Tall, swaying Paul (so tall he sways) with his long hands that speak of the stage (the hands! the hands transparent!); the torch singer from Paris with three of her men, one a naive pickpocket they say; the curious young student from Boston College who has been lured by the glitter of the weekend and perhaps leisure and good food and a bit of time for study (Roger dragged him along—Roger thought he was so virile, so self-sufficient!). Soon now, the household will be complete. Where Emilia St. Claire goes, there, by the grace of God, go nonconformists! the intellectuals! the rebels! the gay barbarians! the dadaists! the members of the "set"!

"Let's be gay!" sang Emilia St. Claire. "I want you all to be frightfully mad! I feel so the need for something different!"

They all proceeded to be gay, mad, different. The interpretative dancer rushed upstairs to don her Thousand-and-One Nights dancing regalia. Sergei's beautiful hands, at the keyboard, drew forth the enchantment of a Zaggus suite. An evil Gidean in bored tones described his recent experience with the Monster of the Congo and an angelic Damascan waif in Sadi-bel-Abi: with razors and ropes. Polly insulted the young Boston College student: "Really, do you study engineering? I mean really?"

"Yes!" smiled the B.C. lad (while Roger beamed). "I'm studying for a fellowship at M.I.T. I brought some of my calculus homework up here to do a little work . . . ha! ha!

ha! . . . I hope I can find time to study. Do you go to school?"

"And do you also study Aquinas? I mean, really really?"

"Sure! Ha ha!"

Polly turned away.

"Ha ha!" cried the B.C. student, his voice breaking on the last "ha." Roger turned on Polly and hissed very much like an adder:

"You lascivious bitch!"

"Oh really Roger don't hurl your effeminate fury at me," complained Polly wearily.

Emilia St. Claire laughed gayly.

"You Bostonians," she whispered raptly. "You impossible, wonderful people."

The interpretative dancer entered the room and began to sway her nude hips while little bells tinkled in her hands. She danced, she danced! Soon, sweat was pouring from her flesh like lust. They all watched intently. A foul odor filled the room; smoke, liquors, lust, perfumes, incense from the jade Buddhas. Boaz the butler peered from behind a curtain and watched. There was no sound except the little tinkling bells, the sandaled feet, and the heavy breathing.

The East! the East! they thought. Wherefore? Tinkle, tinkle.

But outside, a mad moon peered from time to time through the ripping clouds. The wind moaned, the spruces creaked, all things were in their dark vestment. A figure approached along the drive. It crossed the lawn and neared the window. It peered inside.

Transcendenta! Transcendenta!
We shall dance a mad cadenza!

Polly roamed towards the window with a Fatima held tenderly between white, frail fingers. She said to Joyce:

"My dear, when are you going to introduce that 'interesting' friend of yours?"

"Oh Polly," sang Joyce, her dark eyes glittering, "you'll be simply fascinated. He has such poise!"

"What does he <u>do</u>?"—behind Polly's words the room gurgled with conversation, lilted with little laughter; glasses tinkled, the piano tinkled, voices tinkled.

"Oh, he does nothing," said Joyce airily, "he just does nothing."

"But does he <u>really</u>?" intoned Polly indolently, and she walked to the window slowly; the eyes of the men, from their chairs, couches, standing near the fireplace, near the punch bowl, followed the slow coil of her lavish body, the full flesh that seemed to press for release from the tight velvet gown, they watched her creamy back with its sensual cleft down towards a round bursting hind (like that of a great cow abloom from summers of heavy fodder); they took note of the shoulders like two gleaming ivories, of the breastbone like the plains of snow before the mount; they watched. Their eyes gleamed. Polly's limbs rolled lazily. She stopped at the window to gaze out at the wild night.

She screamed!

He he he he! He he he he he! She screams! She screams!

Doctor Sax was at the window. His eyes were emerald green, and they flashed at the sight of her. They lit with delight at her scream. When she fainted to the floor, Doctor Sax hurled his cape around his shoulder and glided swiftly to the front entrance. He wore a large slouch hat the very color of the night. In an instant he was ringing furiously at the door, rapping the oak panels with his knotty cane.

They all thought Polly had taken a fit of some sort (she was apoplectic, you know); they carried her to the

140

divan and brought water. Boaz yawned involuntarily and went to the door, his long black shoes creaking along the gloomy carpeted hall. He opened the door with a careful flunkey's flourish.

A foul wind, abreath with the rank mud of the marshes, poured into the musty hallway. The caped figure stood.

Boaz screamed like a woman. Doctor Sax entered snarling.

"I am Doctor Sax!" he howled at the butler. "I shall announce myself!"

Doctor Sax swept into the salon, his cape flowing and looping, his slouch hat half concealing a secret, malevolent leer. His countenance was purplish, he had red hair and red eyebrows, his eyes were fierce green and they flashed with joy. He was very tall. He swept his black cane at all of them and emitted a happy growl. "Greetings!" he howled. "Greetings to one and all! May I join your charming company, eh? May I join you all?"

Transcendenta! Transcendenta!
We shall dance a mad cadenza!

Screams! Screams! Screaming, the women fell, one by one! Ha ha! They fell, they fell! The men paled, some of them buckled to the floor, some stood transfixed with horrors. Emilia St. Claire swooned upon the divan! Hee hee hee! Hee hee hee hee hee!

Doctor Sax swept to the decanter and poured himself a drink of Napoleon brandy. He whirled and faced them all; only a few men stood trembling.

"What ails thee, my spright?" demanded Sax approaching one of the more stalwart survivors. The latter toppled over and swooned with a groan. Doctor Sax looked around, his green eyes flashing beams of venomous light.

He was amused, nay delighted!

"Interesting ye be, pale neighbors, so surely can'st be-

141

grudge me wee hospitality!" No answer. "Eh?" he demanded. "EH?" he howled, turning to the young butler Boaz who had staggered after him down the hall and was clutching to shrouded curtains. But a malignant smile from Doctor Sax sent this young man fleeing up the hallway and out into the insane March night with his long black shoes flapping.

Doctor Sax ran after him to the door, flying and beating his swirling robed shadow:

"He flees! He flees! Heh heh heh! To the vampire mists imbecilic flees! Heh heh heh!"

Doctor Sax paused for an instant at the entrance and surveyed the havoc in the salon with immense delight. Only one young man stood stalwartly swaying, the young student from Boston College. Gleefully, Sax rubbed his cane against a purple jowl; his fire-brows contracted together over a hawkish nose. Tremendously, he began to laugh; there was no end to his joy; his private knowledge of the world pealed forth from purple lips, publishing to all who were aware the secret wisdom, the huge malevolent humour, the undreamed information that crouched concealed in that unholy head beneath that black slouch hat. Then, with a final chortle of glee (and here now, for the first time, one could detect a touch of loneliness in his tone), he spun on his heel and glided forth from Transcendenta merging with the night like night, disappearing in the weird gloom of the thicket, pausing, for just a moment, to laugh once more a great peal of mockery to the world. And he was gone.

Doctor Sax had paid his compliments to Emilia St. Claire and her guests, and, as he had come, so had he left, secretly, with a huge delight that confounded all of the knowledge, reason, and purpose that man had gathered about his life. He knew something that no other man knew; a something reptilian; pray, was he a man?

Through the open door poured a foul moist breeze of fecund, muddy swamps. The moon stared insanely, for an instant, through a cleavage in the 'March skies. All was silent, save for a few groans from the stricken mortals.

Hee hee hee hee hee!

Doctor Sax had paid his compliments.

Hee hee hee hee hee!

Now they begin to regain consciousness, there is a stirring of stunned minds.

Let us all laugh.

Hee hee hee hee hee!

(finis)

Another strange event and tied up with this, after Emilia St. Claire moved out of Reeves Castle, March (1932), about seven, eight years and four, five months later in the sunk hot bed of July summer by which time the Wizard and his forces of Evil gathered from all over the world (expenses paid) (by Satan below) had had plenty of time to ruin the balance of the world with strokes of good luck, a particularly propitious May (having nothing to do with the sweet rose that flows so merry in the blue night from Weirs of the upper Marrocrock Roil in Manchestaire, the Aristook Falls, up-ledges near great granite Stone Face, Laconia, Franconia, Notch,—not the May of the Odyssey of the Rose but the May of Demter Hemter Skloom criss-crossing in the aerial sky over the gnomic ever-to-be-seen-from-all-parts-of-town Castle like a blue smoke shroud castle in the clear real air of Lowell—I remember opening my eyes from Giant Pillow Sleeps and seeing that gnomic shape atop the far gray river hill as if I could see through

143

the walls of my bedroom at the river)—their work, so
well done, they broke the fancy chain of reality and there
was an earth tremor. All Lowell felt it. I was going to
store before school in the dewcool March morning and
there in the ground of the park where it was flattened
from kid scuffle stands and marble piggly was a huge crack
jagging across the earth, an inch thick. Up at Snake Hill
the crack was three inches thick (by Saints of Red Sun)
and almost thicker below— Some of us drove over to see,
at the foot of Snake Hill near the old ironpickets and granite
gate walls of the deserted castle groups of the Social Club
gang huddled around kicking at the crack. Through the
pines, up to the castle (in that selfsame door where Condu
flew down to the Countess that opening night)—there
stands Boaz the old caretaker, he's turned the main hall
of the castle his smoky shack for dogs and soul—huddles
over a potbelly stove with wood in it, by the staircase, an
old cot along the underpinnings, hanging Arabian Gypsy
drapes of old hermit decoration, a Jean Fourchette of the
Castle Solitudes instead of dump and smoke wrecks—a
Saint, the old man was a red-eyed saint, he'd seen too much,
there was a crack down his Tree, a Gulf in his cataracts—
that first view of Sax as so ably reported by Sax himself
made his hair turn gray overnight—muttering, he stood in
the door looking down at Vauriselle, Carrufel, Plouffe and
all of us earthquake investigators. No comment.

It was an incident worth noting—that abyss cracking
open.

3

MY MOTHER AND I, bless her soul, raced from that scene of moony death on the damned bridge and rushed home. *"Bien,"* she said, *"c'est pas'l diable pleasant* (Well, it's not the devil pleasant!)"—"Let's get out of here"— Corner where that kid Fish had socked me in the face, there it was, ironic rejoinder to skeletal moons— At home my hair stood on my head. Something was somehow wreathy purple and gloomy about our house that night. My sister was in the kitchen, kneeling at the table funnies of dull supper weekdays, my pop was in his chair by the Stromberg Carlson radio (by the driveway, by the dog), the sandbank brooded its Doctor Sax secrets in banefuller night than ever— We told pop about the dying man . . . gloomy music played in my soul . . . I remembered the turning Thérèse statue head, the fish heads cut off in the cellar, doors yawning open in the closet of night, black spiders crawling in the dark (huge black ones)(like I saw at the Castle when everything exploded), fantastic grooking clothes-lines whiteshrouded in the night, washlined neighborhoods hung with sheets, ookeries in the elfin celt, *the smell of flowers the day before somebody dies*—the night Gerard died and all the weeping, yelling, arguing in the bedrooms of the Beaulieu Street house in the brown glooms of Uncle Mike's family (Mike, Clementine, Blanche, Roland, Edgar, Viola, all were there) and my mother crying, in the yard the cousins are setting off our firecrackers against our wishes, it's midnight my father's harassed and worried

145

"Alright Ti Jean and Nin can go to the Dudley's," (Aunt Dudley was there too, awful millings of broken relatives and excited-by-death relatives fumigating in the attic row, all the things I had ever missed and never knew to find, the constant fear I had that either or both of my parents would die) (this mere thought was all I needed to know of death)—"Well don't worry about it," my father is saying —sits glooming with pouty lips shining in the kitchen lights of 1934 night in summer, expects me— Suddenly we hear a great thud that shakes the neighborhood, as though the watermelon ballooned world huge had fallen in the street outside to again remind me, and I go *"Oooh coose que ca?"* and for a moment they all listen with heartbeats like me, and again, it goes THUD, shaking the earth, as though old hermit Plouffe in his cellar on the corner was driving home his secret with explosive blasts of the furnace of hell (could he have been an accomplice of Sax's?)—the whole house, ground shakes—I know now it is the voice of doom coming to prophesy my death with proper fanfare—

"It's nothing but old Marquand striking the log with his ax *frappe le bucher avec son axe*—" and it struck, *thud*, we all ealized so it was. But then I swore there was something mighty peculiar about Marquand with his ax this late, I'd never heard him before this late, death had kept him up, he had a contract this night to rhyme his ax with the funerals of my fear, besides of which immediately next to old Plouffe and his house was full of drapes, death, beads, his yard was full of flowers, something I didn't understand about the smells of other houses and the concomitant doom and dull within—

But suddenly we heard a great moan rising from underground, next door— We all started with fear. "M-o-o-o-o-a-n"—

"O-w-w-w-w-" —the goddam Moon Man had materialized himself into husky death in the grain real ground— It was staring me in the face—"Ooooo"—the Man of Death, not content with his bridge, had come spooking after me to moan at my mother's doormat and haunt the A M R E S Y of the night.

Even my mother—"*Mende moi donc, mais cosse qu'est ca! s't'hurlage de bonhomme*—(My goodness what is *that*! that howling of old man!)"—for a moment I think it crossed her head too that the man who died on the bridge was still after us—his spirit didn't want to give up without a fight— craziness crossed her eyes in a flash, in mine it was stuck —I goofed. That whole night I refused to sleep alone, slept with my mother and sister—I think my sister got sick and tired and transferred to my bed in middle of night, I was twelve— In Centralville it had always, I'd every night crawl in between them when the dark made me cry (Ah sweet Christmas midnights when we found our toys richly placed by they now returning from church on the snowy porch as we roll in our pajamas under the carpet tree)— Suddenly in Pawtucketville I no longer feared the dark, nameless religious ghosts of malign funeral intent had given way to the Doctor Sax honorable shroud ghosts of Pawtucketville, Gene Plouffe and the Black Thief— But now death was catching up again, Pawtucketville too was doomed and brown to die—it was only the next day that we learned the horrible moaning had been done by Mr. Mar-

quand who had a fit in his cellar after chopping wood—
he'd got a message of death from the bridge and from
me— He died quite recently after that ... it always is true,
you smell the flowers before someone dies— My mother
stood in my father's room sniffing suspiciously, old Mr.
Marquand was sending his roses all the way from next
door— In the young you can see the flowers in their eyes.

I lay huddled against the great warm back of my mother
with open eyes up-peeking from the pillow at all shadows
and leafshades on the wall and at the screen, nothing could
harm me now ... this whole night could only take me if
it took her with me and she wasn't afraid of any shade.

Luckily after that, and by unconscious arrangement, in
a flu epidemic my mother and I were semiquarantined in
bed for a week where (mostly it rained) I lay reading *The
Shadow Magazine*, or feebly listening to the radio downstairs in my bathrobe, or blissfully sleeping with one leg
thrown over my mother in the night time—so secure did I
become that death vanished into fantasies of life, the last
few days were blissful contemplations of the Heaven in the
ceiling. When we were well again, and got up, and joined
the world again, I had conquered death and stored up new
life. Beautiful music, regale me not in my bier heaps—please
knock my coffin over in a fist fight beer dance bust, God—

4

MELL, RIVER ROSE, MELL . . .

The sandbank dipped low at one point, over which we'd
rode wild cowboys,— I had a dream of the last houses on

Gershom overflowing to as far as that low dip, full of German police dogs—

There were Saturday mornings when a muddy brown pool was joyous to the test of squatting kids . . . as dewy and mornlike as brown mud water can get,—with its reflected brown taffy clouds—

The ring closes round, you can't continue forever—

Dust takes a flyer, and then folds under—

Doctor Sax made a special trip to Teotehuacan, Mexico, to do his special research on the culture of the eagle and the snake—Azteca; he came back laden with information about the snake, none about the bird— In the stately block-walls of the Pyramid de Ciudadela he saw the stone snake heads with Blake sunflower collars leering up from hell with the same coy horror of Blake's figures, the round button eyes over the prognathic gated jaws, the wulp-hole within, the Leer of the Stone bone—other heads were apparently eagle heads, and had the same beady reptilian nameless horror—(on the windy top of the Pyramid of the Sun, just now, as I looked up from my chores near Mrs. Xoxatl's washlines waving in the lower levels of the same wind, I saw the tiny movement and drowsy flutter of the priest up there cutting out some victim's heart to inaugurate another 20-day festival for his rackets, the procession is wind-whipped on the slant waiting for him to finish—blood, a beating heart, is offered to the sun and snake—)

I saw the picture *Trader Horn*, the blackened-by-runners hill in the brown field of Africa—lasi lado, lasi lado, they came running over the round hillside in a fiendish horde all waving their ant spears and screeching in the wild sun

149

of Africa, horrible black Fuzzy Wuzzies of the bush let alone your desert, they wore dirty bones across their breasts, their hair stuck out a foot like Blake Snake halos and they wielded spears and hung people upside down on crosses in fires—the hill resembled *exactly* the dreaming farm hill on the top of Bridge Street where I saw that Castle rising like a gray smoke—over its bare bald top (in the movie there it was) came this mass of screaming demons with their teeth and bamboos—with their drought— I was convinced the end of the world was coming and these demons were going to come swarming over a sunny hill like that in every town and city in the United States, I thought they were as numberless as ants and poured from Africa in frantic caravans up a wall and down the moiling side—uproars and armies of fiends cataracting across the world howling lasi lado, lasi lado, lasi lado— It seemed to me a drought would come, parch the earth, reduce Lowell and the world to nothingness-parturience with everybody starving and thirsting to death and weeping for rain, and suddenly over that burnt-gold hill under the swarms of puff-white bigclouds leaning over in the blue eternity afternoon that I'd be gazing at from a terrace on the earth on my back with a blade of grass in my mouth . . . would come the gigantic first rank of the bluggywuggies waving antennae like so many cockroaches, and then the second rank, the solid wave spilling all crinkly over the hill in screeching savagery and black, then the full thing.

This was enough to drive me panicky fullspeed from my own mind—I was a scared kid.

It was therefore easy to see the Castle on that hill, and to prophesy the Snake.

DOCTOR SAX (striding in the moonlight with his shroud, an eerie constitutional by the moonbranch, meditatively holding his cane to his jowl) (facing the white horses of the horizon moon night) (the caves of darkness and long hair in the East beyond) "Ah—will my cloak ever flare and flutter in the darkness and great wind of Satan rearing from the earth with his—ugh! Therefore *meet* ... that I have dedicated my life to the search and study of the Snake ... for no—these mortals who here com-*bat* the hour of their sleep with traditional wings of angels ... and moo their caps, or flaps—these Lowell, these mortality-rates—the children, the brown shroud of night—*meet* that I protect them from horrors they can not know—if they *do* know, paff, the angular rides I'll have to take to simplify myself, end the Mission of the Ideal. No (standing now severe and quiet on second base at One A.M.)—I'll simply jump into the pit.

"They think a pit exists not?

"Ah!"—(for suddenly he sees me, and ducks).

BOOK FIVE

The Flood

1

DOCTOR SAX STOOD on the dark shore, a ledge above the waters—it was March, the river was flooded, ice floes were thundering against the rock—New Hampshire had poured its torrents to the sea. Heavy snows had melted in a sudden soft weekend—gay people made snowballs—the runners were noisy in the gutters.

Doctor Sax, holding his shroud around his shoulder firmer, utttered a low laugh beneath the roar of waters and stepped closer to the edge—

"Now a flood will bring the rest," he prophesied. Just barely you can now see him, gliding off between the trees, bound for his work, his "mwee hee hee ha ha" floats back sepulchral and glee-mad, the Doctor has rushed to work to find his spider-juices and bat powders. "The day of the Great Spider," is come—his words ring beneath the Moody Street Bridge as he hustles off to his Dracut Tigers shack —one lorn pine stands above his bier-shaped house, into which, with a doorslam, he vanishes like ink in inky night, his last laugh trailing to any suspect ear in the March—

faintly in the air, following his laugh, you hear the distant dumb roar of the swollen river.

"River! river! what are you trying to do!" I'm yelling at the river, standing on the ledge among bushes and rocks, beneath me great ice floes are either slipping in big lumps over a rock-dam in the holocaust or floating serenely in temporary dark drownpools or crashing square and headstone against the bier of rock, the ship side of the shore, a rock armor of the earth Merrimac Valley— The carnage of huge rains in a snow flood. "Oh rose of the north, come down!" my soul I cried to the river—

And from a small bridge at the north fairyplace where the river was 30 feet broad—up somewhere far north of Lake Winnepesaukee, north of gaps in the White Mountains, the Merrimac had an infant childly phase of beginning from an innocent bubbling-up in the Sandy pines, where fairy tale people made moos around Child Marrimack—from the little bedangled bridge a lover boy in a Hans Christian Andersen fairytale dropped a rose into the stream—it was Saturday night and his little Gretchen had stood him up to go out with Rolfo Butcho—Hero Boy was defeated, would never see her ruby lips again or make with the stash in her pantaleens, never would the stars shine on the soft grease of her thighs, he was sunk to digging holes in the ground and ramming it bloody in, so he threw the rose away— The rose was meant for mary—and down it comes in the Merrimac Valley—following that eternal waterbed— down by Pemigawasset, down by Weir, down by weird, down by the poems of the night.

156

THE POEMS OF THE NIGHT

So falls the rain shroud, melted
By harps; so turns the harp gold,
Welded by mell, roll-goldened
By caramel, softened by Huge.
The weary tent of the night
Has rain starring down the wallsides,
A golden hero of the up atmospheres
Has sprung the leak in the ambiguity
That made the heavens fore-fall.

    So the pollywogs grow
    And the bigger frogs croak,
    By the May Pole in the mud
    Crazy Lazy swings her crutches—
    Was the wife of Doctor Sax
    Gave up him for a crud.

Maybelle Dizzitime, a gal of many
Fancies, swings her shadow ape
In the cloaks of midnight whamsy;
The ball of the pollywog may-time,
The dance of the flooded mall
Crack went the Castle underground
Cank cantank old Moritzy
Flames his froosures in the dank,

    Dabbely doo, dabbely dey,
    The ring has got the crey.
    Ringaladout, ringalaree,
    Ringala Malaman,
    Ringala Dee.

The hooded urchins of the pissed river
Are making melted marbles of the mud;
Rain, Rain, Sleeping Shrouded Falls,
The manager of the Pittsburgh Pirates
Is sleeping in his craw.
The boss of the winter stove league
Has given up his chaw.

    So Sax in his Ides Does Bide,
    Comes Melting like Mr. Rain
    With a Shake of the Fritters,
    Drops his Moistures One by One.

The Golden Rose
That in the wave's
Repose—
	The Angel with the
	  Wetted Wings,
	  The Nose

The Lark & Lute
in Every Mist
	The Cark that in
	  the Harried Anxious
	  Flows to East

The Hoods of Windfall
Blown with Rain
	The gammerhooks
	  of cloud-rise
	  in the moon.

The Ice Floes
Bonging at
the Falls,
	The Whistle of
	  an Arcadian
	  Fluke

The Eyes of Eagles on the Main—	Flaws in Heaven Are no Pain.

Demi mundaine dancers at the broken hall ball,
Doctor Sax and Beelzabadoes the whirling polka
Gallipagos—

The crickets in the flower petal mud
Throng at the Water Lilies, Thirst
for fair—

Cring Crang the broken brother boys
See Mike O'Ryan in the river rising,
Tangled.

The Spiders of the evil Hoar
are coming in the flood

Every form shape or manner
the insects of the wizard blood

The Castle stands like a parapet,
Kingdoms enthralled in air

Saturday Heroes of the windy field
Bare fist-glasses to the *mer*—

The Merrimac is roaring,
Eternity and the Rain are Bare

Down by White Hood Falls,
Down by the darkened weirs,
Down by Manchester, down by Brown,
Down by Lowell, Comes the Rose—
Flowing to its seaward, brave as knights,
Riding the humpback Merrimac
Rage excites

159

So doth the rain droop open,
    more like a rose
Less adamantine
    Than ang

Liquid heaven in her drip
    eatin rock
    mixing kip

Eternity comes & swallows
    moisture, blazes sun
    to accept up

Rain sleeps when the rain is over
Rain rages when the sun keels over
Roses drown when the pain is over

The water lute sides of Rainbow
Heaven—
Rang a dang mam-mon
Sing your blacking song.

THE SONG OF THE MYTH OF THE RAINY NIGHT

Rose, Rose
Rainy Night Rose

Castle, Castles
Hassels in the Castle

Rain, Rain,
Shroud's in the Rain

Makes her Luminescence
Of folded Incandescence

Raw red rose in wetted night
"I had all to do
With that dreaded essence."

Pitterdrop, pitterdrop,
Rain in the woods

Sax sits Shrouded
Meek & crazy
Rumored in his trousers
Naked as a baby

"Rainy drops, rainy drops,
    Made of loves,
Snake's not real,
    'Twas a husk of doves

"The rain is really milk
The night is really white
The shroud is really seen
By the white eyes of the light
A young & silly dove
Is yakking in the sky
The dream is cropping under
The muds & marble mix
Petals of the water harp,
Melted lutes,
Angels of Eternity
And pissing in the air

"Ah poor life and paranoid gain,
    hassel, hassel, hassel,
    man in the rain

"Mix with the bone melt!
Lute with the cry!
So doth the rain blow down
From all heaven's fantasy."

—Deep in myself I'm mindful of the action of the river, in words that sneak slowly like the river, and sometimes flood, the wild Merrimac is in her lark of Spring lally-da'ing down the pale of mordant shores with a load of *humidus aquabus aquatum* the size of which was one brown rushing sea. By God as soon as the ice floes were past, the brown foam fury waters came, thundering in midstream in one lump bump like the back of a carnival Caterpillar pitching green muslin-hunks and people screaming inside—only this was chickens, drowned chickens garnished the middle of the rill-ridge roar in centerriver—brown foam, mud foam, dead rats, the roofs of hen houses, roofs of barns, houses—(out of Rosemont one afternoon, under sky drowse, I felt peaceful, six bungalows got out their moorings and floated to midstream like duck brothers and sisters and proceeded to Lawrence and another Twi League)—

I stood there on the edge ledge.

It was a Monday night I'd first seen the floes, a terrible, bad sight—the lonely turrets of houses near the river—the doomed trees—at first it wasn't so bad. Pine families would be saved from the rock. None of the inhabitants of sorrow

162

in the orphanage across the way could drown in this deluge—

Nobody knows how mad I was— Tommy Dorsey's *I Got a Note* was out that year, 1936, just at the time the Flood mounted in Lowell—so I went around the shores of the roaring river in the joyous-no-school mornings that came with the flood's peak, and sang "I got a nose, you got a nose —(half octave higher:)—I got a nose, you got a nose," I thought that's what the song was: it also occurred to me how strange the songwriter's meaning must have been (if I thought of songwriters at all, it seemed to me people just got together and sang over the microphone)—It was a funny song, at the end it had that 1930's lilt so hysterical Scott Fitzgerald, with writhely women squirmelying their we-a-ares in silk & brocade shiny New Year's Eve nightclub dresses with thrown champagne and popples busting "Gluyr! the New Year Eve Parade!" (and there, huge and preponderant, sprung the earth's river devouring to its monstrous sea).

In gray afternoon my mother and I (it was the first no-school afternoon) took a walk to see why there was no school, the reason was not given but everyone knew it was going to be a bad flood. There were a lot of people on the shore, at Riverside Street where it meets the White Bridge near the Falls—I had every measurement of the river keen-etched in my mind along the rock of the canal wall—there were a few flood-measurements written, in numbers showing feet, and the marks of old moss and old floods— Derby-hatted Lowell had been there a hundred years, was grimed like Liverpool in its Massachusetts river fog; the huge

humus of mist that rose from the flooding river was enough
to convince anybody a flood, a great flood, was coming.
There was an improvised fence set up in the gloom near
the bridge, where the lawn went too close to sidewalk and
rail that once were summer dalliances, were now sprayed
by the mist from the great surging brown watermass roaring right there. So people stood behind that fence. My
mother held my hand. There was something very sad and
thirtyish about this scene, the air was gray, there was disaster (copies of *The Shadow Magazine* were dusting in the
gloom in the little hideaway junkstore across the street
from St. Jean Baptiste, in the paved Apachean alley, copies
of *The Shadow* in the dark gloom, the city's in flood)—

It was like a newsreel of 1930's to see us all huddled
there in gloomy lines with minstrel-mouths shining white
in the darkscreen, the incredible mud underfoot, the hopeless tangle of ropes, tackle, planks—(and seabags began
pouring in that night). *"Mon doux, Ti Jean, regarde la
grosse flood qui va arrivez"*—"tut-thut-thut-"with her cluck
tongue, (My goodness Ti Jean look at the big flood that's
going to happen)—*"c'est méchant s' gross rivière la quand
qu'y'a bien d'la neige qui fond dans l'Nord dans l'Printemps*
(It's bad those big rivers when there's a lot of snow that
melts in the North in the Spring)"—

"Cosse qui va arrivez? (what's gonna happen?)"

"Parsonne sai. (Nobody knows.)"

Officials in bleak windswept raincoats consulted ropes
and boxes of City equipment—"No school! no school!" The
little kids were singing as they danced over the White
Bridge— In a matter of 24 hours people were afraid to

even go on that bridge, it was concrete, white, it already had cracks in it ... the Moody Street Bridge was all of iron and racks and stone, gaunt and skeletal in the other part of the Flood—

In the bright morning of the gray afternoon after school was called off, me and Dicky Hampshire sallied forth at 8 A.M. to the scenes of wrath and destruction that already we could hear roaring over our Wheaties. People were walking on Riverside Street below Sarah with strange preoccupied airs. Those headed towards Rosemont understandably! Rosemont was low and flat at the river's basin, already half of Rosemont and its lovely Santa Barbara cottages were in six feet of brown water—Vinny Bergerac's home was a raft, they spent the first day him and Lou and Normie and Rita and Charlie and Lucky the old man on a lark in the flood and played rafts and boats around the front and back of the house, "Wheee! looka me Ma!" Vinny's yelling "The Goddam Navy's come to town, order up all the beetleskins, here comes purple Shadows McGatlin the Champ"—and the next morning at six they were ordered to leave the tenement crazy house in the Rosemont suburbs by a crew of booted policemen in rowboats wearing rain hats and gloomcoats, Rosemont was in a state of emergency, in another day there was hardly any of it left, spit and floodbubbles were at mylady's boudoir—

Dicky Hampshire's eyes gleamed with excitement. It was the greatest sight we'd ever seen when we crossed the back Textile field and came to its high-end plateau over the dump and the deep canyoned river quarter mile wide to Little Canada, and saw all the way there the huge mountain of ugly sinister waters lunging around Lowell like a beast dragon— We saw a gigantic barn roof floating in mid stream, jiggling with the vibration of the roar in the hump there— "Wow!" Hungry, tremendously hungry as we got on this excitement we never went home to eat all day.

—"The strategy is to snare one of them barnyard roofs and make a gigantic raft," said Dick, and was he ever right— We rushed towards the river across the dump. There, in brightest morning, where the great chimney loomed 200 feet high, orangebrick, overtopping the brick mass of Textile so nobly situated in height-vistas, there were our green lawn-slopes (the lawns of power houses neat and swardgreen) where we'd been playing King of the Hill for eternities, three years—there was the cinder path to Moody Street at the bridge (where cars were parked in this exciting morning, people were gathered, how many times I've dreamed of leaping over that fence at bridge end and in dream glooms rush down by the shadow of the iron underpinnings and the jutting rock of the shore, and bushes, and shadows, and Doctor Sax dreary ambiguities, something namelessly sad and dreamed and trampled over in the civil wars of the mind & memory— and further scene-dreams on the straw slopes cundrum-cluttered overlooking a little cliff drop to the waterside rocks)— We felt we'd grown up because these places and scenes were now more than child's play, they were now abluted in pure day by the white snow mist of tragedy.

Tragedy roared ahead of us—all Lowell with bated breath was watching from a thousand parapets natural and other-wise in the Lowell valley. Our mothers had said "Be careful" and by noon they too, huddled in housewife coats, locked the door and suspended the ironing of the wash to come and peek at the river even though it entailed a long walk down Moody across Textile to the bridge—

Billy and I surveyed this remarkable sunny morning. The river came boiling in brown anger from the rivulets of the valley north, on the Boulevard cars were parked to see the river waving trees in its claw,—down at the Rosemont end of the dump a crowd was lined to face the Netherlandic havoc there, our little shitty beach in the reeds was now the bottom of the sea—I remembered all the boys who had drowned—*"Tu connassa tu le petit bonhomme Roger qui etait parent avec les Voyers du store? Il s'a noyer hier —dans rivière—a Rosemont—ta beach que t'appele"*—(Did you know the little boy Roger who was related to the Voyers of the store? He drowned yesterday—in the river— at Rosemont—your beach you call it.)— The River was Drowning Itself— It came over the Falls at the White Bridge not in its usual blue sheen and fall (among white-caps snow) but sleered over in a brown and hungry slide sheen that only had to slip two feet and was in the foams of the bottom flood—the little children of the Orphanage on Pawtucket at the White Bridge were standing in watch-ful rows in the wire fences of the yard or down in the Grotto near the Cross, something huge and independent had come into their lives.

Dicky and I jumped down among the fenders and crap of the dumpslope, down to the water's edge, where the flood just lapped up and fendered away in a sunkjunk beach of 90 degrees— We stood on this edge of this watery

167

precipice watching with eagle eye of Indians in the plateau morning for a chickencoop roof to bump into our hands. It came pirouetting in bumps along the fendered shore—we hooked it at our mooring with a small piece of rope on one end (tied to a car bumper stuck in the ground for ten years) and the other end more or less held by a board bridge with rocks on it, temporarily—chicken feathers we found as we romped up and down the tin roof. It was a solid raft, wood on the bottom, tin on deck—it measured fifty feet by thirty, immense— It had slipped over the swollen Falls without damage. But we never bargained for any long trip on the Merrimac Sea—we thought we had it securely tied, enough anyway, and at some point the rope broke, Dicky saw it and jumped on the dump—but I was strolling along the outer, or flood, edge of the chickenroof and didn't hear (from eternity roar of river) what Dicky wanted to say—"Hey Jack—the rope broke—come on back." In fact I was dreamily standing surveying that tremendous and unforgettable monstrous rush of humpbacked central waters Flooding at 60 miles an hour out of the rock masses beneath the Moody Bridge where the white horses were now drowned in brown and seemed to gather at the mouth of the rocks in a surging vibration of water to form this Middle lunge that seemed to tear the flood towards Lawrence as you watched—to Lawrence and the sea—and the Roar of that hump, it had the scaly ululating back of a sea monster, of a Snake, it was an unforgettable flow of evil and of wrath and of Satan barging thru my home town and rounding the curve of the Rosemont Basin and Centralville Snake Hill by that blue puff figure castle on the meadow landlump in the rawmous clouds beyond— Also I was watching to see if the people in the Little Canada rock-cliff tenements that jutted over the river were evacuating their solidly founded homes at the hungry lip of the River's brown torrential roar— Back of Laurier park the dump and the dumpshacks of Little Canada Aiken Street and old pest heur with his poolhall shack and come-alleys of dirtybook hookey toss-a-coin days that came later to make men of me and Dicky and Vinny and G.J. and Scotty and Lousy and Billy Artaud and Iddiboy and Skunk— In fact I might have been dreaming of Skunk, as Dicky yelled to me, the time Skunk was supposed to fight Dicky in the park-trail and somebody intervened in the long red dusk of ancient heroic events and now Skunk was a baseball star on our team but also his house in Rosemont was probably floating away—*all of it was drowned* ... the dump, half the Laurier ballpark, tragic gangs of American Lowellians were gathered on the opposite shore watching—in the wild sun-excited day I watched it all from my foaming deck—higher than my head the deluge roared 200 feet away— The sun was one vast white mass of radiance suspended in the aurobus of heaven like an auriola, an arcade shaft penetrated it all, there were slants of heaven and bedazzling impossible brilliances illuminating all furyfied the tremendous spectacles of flood— High up there in the white of the blue I saw it, the silly dove, a *pippione*, an Italian love bird, returning from the Himalayas the other side of the world-roof with an herb wrap't round its leg, in a tiny leaf, the Monks of the Rooftop Monastery have sent Tibetan secrets to the King of Anti Evil, Doctor Sax,

Enemy of the Snake, Shade of Dark, Phantom Listener at
My Window, Watcher With Green Face of Little Jewish
Boys in Paterson Night Time when phobus claggett me
gonigle bedoigne breaks his arse shroud on a giant pitrock
black Passaic weyic manic madness in the smoony snow
night of dull balls— A young and silly dove is yakking in
the blue, circling the brown and slushy river with yaks of
pipsqueak joy, demoniac manic bird of little paradise, come
snowing from Ebon hills to bring our message herb—a pippione, weary with travel—now all eyes comes circling upon
the flood, then veers in blinding day to the woods of flooded
Lowell—a cape of ink furls upon the waters where Doctor
Sax rows—a car comes to the meadow mud edge of the
flood—Doctor Sax vanishes behind flooded bushes in a
gloor— Moisture from trees in the gray drops plipping in
the sullen moiling brown varnishy surface, full of skeel—
The Dove descends, aims fluttering heart straight for the
black arms of Sax upheld from his boat in gratitude and
prayer. "O Palalakonuh!" he cries upon the desolated flood,
"O Palalakonuh Beware!!"

"Jack! Jack!" Dicky is calling. "Get off the raft—the rope's
cut off—you're floating away!"

I turn around and survey the damage—I take a quick
run to the edge and look over at brown bottomless waters
of the 90 degree dump and its receding from the last shoe
hold fender at Dicky's feet, a four-foot jump in just a second... I knew I could barely make it and so I wasn't scared
but simply jumped and landed on my feet on the dump
and the raft went out behind me to join humps of the main

midstream, where it was seen pitching and diving like a gigantic lid—it could have been my Ship.

2

NEWS CAME TO US from subsidiary kids in the booming amazing morning like in a Tolstoy battle that the White Bridge was pronounced dangerous and nobody was crossing it, there were road blocks, and on the boulevard the River had found an ancient creek bed suitable to its new forward floodrush and used it to flow in a mad torrent across half of Pawtucketville and join its horror to Pine Brook deluges and a rush out back through already back-flooded Rosemont—further, news came of disasters in downtown Lowell, soon we couldn't even get there, the canals were overflowed into, the mills were swimming, water was creeping in the business streets, pools were forming of whole redbrick railroad switch alleys behind the mills—all of it was just mad great news to us— The afternoon of the gray tragic flood-warning with my mother, I later returned with the gang to see the sandbag operations at Riverside Street where it dipped down lowest. Right there lived one of our grammar school teachers, Mrs. Wakefield, in a little white cottage covered with rose vines. They were piling sandbags across the street from her white fence. We stood at the sandbags, at the ripple up flood swell, and poked our fingers at them—we wanted the Flood to pierce thru and drown the world, the horrible adult routine world. G.J. and I made jokes about it—scuffled with each other yakking in the tragic emergency flashlights and oilcup flares as the river rose—after supper we saw that the sandbag wall was higher. We wanted a real flood—we wished the workmen would go away. But next morning we came and saw the great snake hump roar of the river's strong left arm slamming through the sandbag place 20 feet high and pouring through the blind gawp windows of Mrs. Wakefield's brown vine weedy cottage with its last rooftop slipping over in the whirlpool—behind her a streetful of rushing water— G.J. and I looked at each other in astonishment and impossible glee: IT HAD BEEN DONE!

Doctor Sax stood high above the parapets of Lowell, laughing. "I am ready," he cried, "I am ready." He pulled his little rubber boat from his slouch hat and blew it up again and paddled away with his rubber oar and Dove in pocket through the dismal forest flood waters of the night —towards the Castle—his hollow laugh echoed across the desolation. A giant spider crawled from the flood water and rushed on sixteen legs rapidly to the Castle on Snake Hill—

also nameless little ones
did rush there.

3

PAUL BOLDIEU'S HOME that we used to climb rickety outdoor steps to—at the edge of the Cow Field near St. Rita's church,—his dismal house where his mother made beans for his breakfast in the morning—where poor dim religious St. Mary Calendars hung in brown door behind the stove

—Paul's bedroom, where he kept his records in red ink of all our baseball batting averages—crazy Kid Faro (because of his gold tooth and green tweed suit on Sunday afternoon at the Crown Theater with rats in the balcony and the time we threw boxes of ice cream at the miser in the movie foreclosing the widow's mortgage and a 90 year old cop came upstairs to try to find us)—Paul's house was flooded, six feet of water made it necessary to ride to his porch in a rowboat—

Tremendous excitement filled all the riverside streets of Lowell where people—in the clear air of holiday-like mornings—massed at the lapping beautiful flood-edge—"I got a nose, you got a nose"— I'm roaming both sides of the bank, singing—I go across the White Bridge which ordinarily I cross every day to go to Bartlett Junior High and there's the massive miraculous long-awaited monstrous flood-hump rolling thirty feet below at a speed of 60 miles an hour— massively more of the flood arcs down from New Hampshire, over highways sometimes—Paul's house was smack in the middle of the new waterbed across low-ground Pawtucketville— "I got a nose—you got a nose—" Poor Paul—I can't see him in all the crowd—there's a roadblock thrown across Riverside Street at the monument of World War I with Lauzon's uncle's name on it where the river is eating at the lawn-back of it, the monument's about to topple in the river—the river is not only roaring through Mrs. Wakefield's home but comes lapping almost beyond the monument to the very bridge head of Varnum Avenue—but Varnum Avenue is also flooded a few hundred feet beyond at Scotty's—out on the boulevard there's a new river— G.J.

173

and I congratulate each other that our houses are built
high on the rock of Pawtucketville—the Sandbank will
never get wet—Sarah Avenue and Phebe Avenue survey
immense vistas when you can see through the trees—the
flood might rise like Noah's flood and the mayor would
know the difference in lower Lowell—in Pawtucketville
Hump we could make a last ditch stand with a hastily
improvised ark—"Clear the way gentlemen!" G.J. is as-
severating at the sandbags as he tries to poke his fingers
through—"From time immemoriam's mortariums ye swabs
avast ye've swabbed them seabags to the fore myzen mast
god dam ye"—G.J.'s a regular Ahab at the Flood, a fiend
at the Levee— Hungrily we prowl up and down the flood
admiring the black madness, the demoniac river—it's eating
away everything that ever hated us—trees, houses, com-
munities are capitulating— Mad glee fires in our souls, we
hear now clearly the laugh of Doctor Sax penetrating the
roar of the middle river, we feel the hum and Vibration of
evil in the earth. When night comes we go striding with
wild arms swinging into the matted leaves and rocks of the
shore under Moody Street Bridge—we throw tiny feeble
rocks into the mass ... the rocks are hurled up—back—
Along the tragic granite wall of the canal we see no more
ancient watermarks of flood, or whitewashed numbers; the
flood has reached a record peak. A famous St. Francis Lock
in a Canal across town is saving the downtown District of
Lowell from complete inundation. As it is, six feet of water
fill my father's printing plant—he has taken several despair-
ing drives downtown looking at the water and even around
Pawtucketville—

"I'll never forget that time, Zagg, your father coughed" —G.J.'s talking to me as we prowl like rats—"in the alley wall, you know between the Club and Blezan's store on Gershom you get those two wood walls each side of the street, I was on one side, your father on the other, one early morning last week, cold as hell you remember, I'm sending up smoke screens from my mouth, suddenly a great explosion rocked me to my knees—your father had coughed and the echo had hit my wall and bounced right off me —my ears exploded, I fell down on *one knee* Zagg no shit— I said (to regain my senses, no one there to slap me you understand)"—(reaching out and goosing me—) "Zagg—so I says, innocently, 'Why Mr. Duluoz you do seem to have rather a bad cough there, don't you know?' 'N-o-o,' he says, 'no Gussie it ain't so bad—just a little rasp, Gussie, just a little rasp in my throat'- A-a-oo-ay—*Brash!*" he yelled, lifting a leg—an imitation of big burpers laying explosive farts at board of directors meetings.

The flood roared on, Craw River—it came Raining and Weeping from Six Thousand Holes in the moistéd Earth of all New England's spring. Newspapermen were out on the bridge with photographers taking pictures of the river— newsreels from Boston—visiting Red Cross journalists from the Hague Convention in Jersey City.

4

IT'S LENT AND PEOPLE GO ON WITH THEIR NOVENAS—I'm in there at gray dusk Tuesday evening (the afternoon after the raft fiasco with Dicky I spent hours simply on my back

175

in the riverside grass at the cliff precipice under Moody Bridge, surveying the flood with drowsy time's eye of summer and idly watching an airplane circling the river)—I'm at church, have to finish my Novena with which I can pray for anything I want later, besides they all told me to do my Novena, so I'm in church at dusk— More people than usual, they're afraid of the Flood. Dimly you can hear it roaring behind the candle silence walls.

5

BAGGYPANTS JOURNEYMEN INVENTORS OF THE WORLD couldn't have been able to solve the riddle of the flood even if they had a union— Make a study:—along the shore of the presdigitator water-measurer on the canal there was nothing but water, the gimmick was drowned, the alley between redbrick warehouses leading to the grimy door of my father's front floor hall-chamber with wagon wheels and wrinkly coaldust basement groundfloor for a red carpet to the Boss—it was all one vast and ghastly swimmingpool made of mud, straw, cotton, machine oil, ink, piss and rivers—

6

STAVROGIN HUNGRY MY FILIAL BROTHER was lost in the mud rats—I heard that Joe was off somewhere with a .22 rifle hunting rats, there was a bounty being paid, talk was up about a mass Typhoid inoculation—everybody had to take these shots, G.J. and I were terribly sick and arm-swollen from them that following week—

7

MY FATHER, Ma and Nin, and I, the car parked behind us, are standing on a high parapet street down by White Street surveying below us the brown water rising to the second floor level of houses just like our own on Sarah Avenue and the poor families like us that were out of a house,—well all they gotta do now is go bohemianing in the candlelight like all Mexico,—White Street was the name of Mrs. Wakefield's street, it was now Brown Street,—down towards the river you can see the arm of water inrushing and how it all happened, all coming from great seas of flood reported upriver—

"*Bon, ca sera pas terrible ca avoir l'eau dans ta chambre a couchez aussi haut que les portrats sur l' mur,*" said my father—(Well, wouldn't that be terrible to have water in your bedroom as high as the pictures on the wall!) I stood close to him for protection, love and loyalty. A fly buzzed.

8

MRS. MOGARRAGA THE IRISH WOMAN who lived in the little white bungalow in Rosemont was heard declaiming as she moved out of her piano parlor in a rowboat, "Bums and kit's kaboodles they are, the slimes of Arrah, to make trousers of themselves in the general pants bottoms Gomorrah

177

of their filthy hovel house—it's the Lord brought the Flood
to wash the wretches out like cockroach! Bottles in their
bedspreads, beans in their bedbugs, batty—I'd as soon
sweep them out with me broom"—(referring to her board-
ers) (clutching her cat to her bosom God bless her huge
delight)— A ripple of laughter rises from the floodside
crowd.

9

EUGENE PASTERNAK, mad with love of his stride-howl midnights, comes furiyating down the slime path in hod's man's
boots with a flume of essence in his air—"Geeyaw! The
groolemen make my flingle dole ring soul make out—con-
taint my comp! save my bomp!"—and disappearing in the
back shacks (in a shimmy dance like a comedian leaving
the stage).

10

IN SEARS ROEBUCK and hardware stores people stomped
around by the light of gray afternoon and bought boots,
rubbers, fiddled among rakes, cape, gloomrain gear—something like a dirty splotch of ink hung in the sky, the flood
was in the air, talk in the streets—views of water at distant
street-ends all over town, the great clock of City Hall
rounded golden silent in the dumb daylight and said the
time about the flood. Puddles splashed in traffic. Unbelievably now, I returned to see the flood still rising—after sup-

per—the mighty roar beneath the bridge was still there, casting mist up in an air sea—brown torrent mountains falling in—I began to be afraid now of watching under the bridge— Huge tormented logs came careening from the moil of upriver falls and consequence, lurched up and down like a piston in the stream, some huge power was pumping from below ... glistened in its torments. Beyond I saw the trees in the tragic air, the scene rushed on dizzily, I tried to follow filthy brown wave crests for a hundred feet and got dizzy and like to fall in the river. The clock drowned. I began to dislike the flood, began to see it as an evil monster bent on devouring everyone—for no special reason—

I wished the river would dry up and become the swimming hole of summer for the heroes of Pawtucketville again, right now it was only fit for the heroes of Punic War II— But it kept roaring and rising, the whole town was wet. Gigantic diving barn roofs suddenly submerging and rising again huge and dripping elicited "Ooohs & Aaahs" from watchers on the shore— March raged to her fury. The mad moon, a crescent hint, sliced thinly through the rayward crowds of cloud that boosted themselves in an east wind across the skies of disaster. I saw a lonely telephone pole standing eight feet deep, in thin rain.

On the porch of my house I knew in meditative revery that the roar I heard in the valley was a catastrophic roar —the big tree across the street added his multiform Voice of leafy to the general sigh sad of March—

The rain fell in the night. The Castle was dark. The knotty limbs and roots of a great tree growing out the side

of a pavement near the ironpickets of old downtown Lowell
churches made a faint glimmer in the streetlamps.— Looking at the clock you could envision the river behind its
illuminated disk of time, its fury rush over shores and people—time and the river were out of joint. Hastily, at night,
at the little green desk in my room, I wrote in my diary:
"Flood going full force, big brown mountain of water rushing by. Won $3.50 today Pimlico show bet." (I also kept
my bets going in the imaginary bankroll that lasted
years—) There was something wet and gloomy in the green
of my desk (as brown darkness flared in the window where
my mudblack apple tree branches reached in to touch my
sleep), something hopeless, gray, dreary, nineteen-thirty-
ish, lostish, broken not in the wind a cry but a big dull
blurt hanging dumbly in a gray brown mass of semi late-
afternoon cloudy darkness and pebble grit Void of sweaty
sticky clothes and dawg despair—something that can't possibly come back again in America and history, the gloom
of the unaccomplished mudheap civilization when it gets
caught with its pants down from a source it long lost contact with—City Hall golf politicians and clerks who also
played golf complained that the river had drowned all the
fairways and tees, these knickers types were disgruntled
by natural phenomena.

By Friday the crest had been passed through town and
the river starts going down.

"But the damage has been done."

BOOK SIX

The Castle

1

A STRANGE LULL took place—after the Flood and before the Mysteries—the Universe was suspending itself for a moment of quiet—like a drop of dew on the beak of a Bird—at Dawn.

By Saturday the river is gone way down and you see all the raw marks of the flood on wall and shore, the whole town is soaked, muddy and tired— By Saturday morning the sun is shining, the sky is piercingly heartbreakingly blue, and my sister and I are dancing over the Moody Street Bridge to get out Saturday morning Library books. All the night before I've been dreaming of books—I'm standing in the children's library in the basement, rows of glazed brown books are in front of me, I reach out and open one—my soul thrills to touch the soft used meaty pages covered with avidities of reading—at last, at last, I'm opening the magic brown book—I see the great curlicued print, the immense candelabra firstletters at the beginnings of chapters—and Ah!—picture of rosy fairies in blue mist gardens with gingerbread Holland skylark rooftops (with breadcrumbs on them), talking to wistful heroines about the mean old monster on the other bosky side of the dale —"In another part of the forest, mein princess, the lark's largesse is largely hidden"—and other sinister meanings— shortly after dreaming that I dive into dreams of upper hills with white houses slashed across by rays of a Maine sun sending sad redness over pines in a long highway that goes unbelievably and with ... remorse ... jump off the bus so I can stay in little Gardiner town, I bang at shutters, that sun's same red, no soap, the people of the north are silent, I take a freight train to Lowell and settle on that little hill where I rode my bicycle down, near Lupine Road, near the house where batty woman had the Catholic altar, where—where— (I remember the statue of the Virgin Mary in her livingroom candlelight)—

And I wake up in the morning and it's bright March sun —my sister and I, after hurried oatmeals, rush out in the fresh morning not unenlivened by the dew-residue of the river in its muddy slaw down by the tearful shore—Nature's come to pet and woo poor billywoo in the river valley— golden clouds of blue morning shine above the decay of the flood—little children dance along the washlined neigh- borhoods, throw sunny rocks in muddy rivers of the turtle day,— In a Susquehanna special river shore on Riverside Street-a-Dreams, legitimate, I saunter along with my sister to the library, throwing scaled rocks on the river, drown- ing their flight in mud floodwaters of greenly corpses bumping— Sailing along and jumping in the air we dally to the library, fourteen—

I come home from the library that morning, up Mer-

rimac Street with Nin. At one point we veer off to Moody
Street parallel. Ruddy morning sun on stone and ivy (our
books firm under our arms, joy)—the Royal Theater we
pass, remembering the gray past of 1927 when we went
to movies together, to the Royal, free because Pop's printing press that printed their programs was in back, early
days, the usher upstairs niggerheaven balcony where we
sat had raspy voice, we waited impatiently for 1:15 movie
time, sometimes arrived 12:30 and waited all that time
looking at cherubims in the ceiling, round Moorish Royal
Theater pink and gilt and crystal-crazy ceiling with a
Sistine Madonna around the dull knob where a chandelier
should be,—long waits in rickety nervous snapping bub-
blegum seat-scuff scattle tatter "*Shaddap!*" of usher, who
also had hand missing with a hook at the hump World War
I veteran my father knew him well fine fellow—waiting
for Tim McCoy to jump onscreen, or Hoot Gibson, or Mix,
Tom Mix, with snowy teeth and coalblack eyebrows under
enormous snow white bright blinding sombreros of the
Crazy Hollywood silent West- leaping thru dark and tragic
gangs of inept extra-fighters fumbling with beat torn vests
instead of bright spurs and feather-holsters of Heroes—
"*Gard, Ti Jean, le Royal, on y alla au Royal tou le temps
en?—on faisa ainque pensee allez au Royal—a's't'heur on
est grandis on lit des livres.*" (Look, Ti Jean, the Royal,
we used to go to the Royal all the time hey?—that's all we
thought about go to the Royal—now we are grown up we
read books.) And we trip along gaily, Nin and I, past the
Royal, the Daumier Club where my father played the
horses, Alexander's meat market on the canal now in the

185

Saturday morning all mad with a thousand mothers milling at the sawdust counters. Across the street the old drugstore in an ancient wood Colonial block house of Indian times showing jockstraps and bedpans in the window and pictures of the backs of venereal sufferers (made you wonder what awful place they'd been to get such marks of their pleasure).

"I never did forgive you for that time you hit me on the head with a marble Ti Jean," Nin is saying to me, "but I will never hold it against you—but you hit me on the head." I had, too, but if with Repulsion, champion of the Turf, she wouldn't be saying it without a lump on her head. Luckily I used a regular marble not the ballbearing—I flew into an awful rage because Ma had sent her up to clean my room, Saturday morning 11 o'clock when smells of boiling's on stove and I was settled for my game and cried when I saw the Meet (with 40,000 on hand) was going to be postponed, but she was adamant, so I confess before the judgment of the eternities I threw a marble (Synod, owned by S & S stables) right at the top of her head. She ran down crying—I was severely jostled by my irate mother and made to sit and sulk on the porch awhile—*"Va ten dehors mechant! frappez ta tite soeur sur la tête comme ca! Tu sera jamais heureux être un homme comme ca."* (Go on outside, bad! hitting your little sister on the head like that! You'll never be happy being a man like that!) Doubtful that I ever grew up, too. I'm worried.

"Eh bien Nin," I say, *"j'aura du pas faire ca."* (Well Nin, I shouldn't a done that.)

We come to the St. Jean Baptiste church and Nin wants

186

to go in for a second to see if the third-grade girls at St. Joseph for girls are having their Lenten exercises, wants to check on her girlfriend's little sister—ah the poor little girls of Lowell I knew that died, at 6, 7, 8, their rosy little lips, and little eye glasses of school, and little white collars and Navy blue blouses, all, all, underdusted in fading graves soon sinking fields—ah black trees of Lowell in your March glare—

We peek in at the church, at shuffling groups of little girls, at priests, people kneeling, doing the sign of the cross in aisleways, the prim flutter of front altar lights where a pursymouth youngpriest wheels sensationally to kneel and hangs knelt like a perfect motionless statue of Christ in the Agony of the Garden, budging for just an instant as he barely loses balance and all little kids in church who watched have seen, the sensational wheel failed, I notice all this just as I slip out the door—after Nin with a flick at the fount-waters and quick cap-on (my cap was an old felt hole-hat).

Bright morn blanked our eyelashes right there, inside the church perpetual afternoon, here: morning... But as we proceeded right on Aiken Street and left up on Moody the day stretched to noon with a faint whitish glare now come into the halyards of the blue and the trumpets have stopped sounding, half lost their dew—always hate morning going— The women of Moody Street were rushing and shopping literally in the shade of the Cathedral—at Aiken and Moody, center of traffic activities, it cast its huge bloat shadow on the scene—climbing a tenement or two in shadow-vertical-extenuation lengthening with afternoon. Nin

187

and I gaped at the drugstore window: inside, where neat black and white tiles made a golden sun floor for the drugstore, and where the strawberry ice cream sodas were foaming at the top in pink bubblous mist froth at the slavering mouth of some idle traveling salesman with his samples on the stool, soda in glass sitting in steel glass-grip with round clinky girderbottom, a solid soda, huge, oldfashioned, with a barbershop mustache on it, Nin and I sure wished we could get some of that. Joy of the morning was particularly keen and painful in the marble slab counter where a little soda was freshly spilled—I romped, we romped on up the Moody. We passed several regular journeyman Canadian grocery stores crowded with women (like our Parent's) buying hamburger and huge pork chops of the prime (to serve with hot mashed potatoes in a plate in which also hot porkchop fat is floating around beautiful with luminescent golds to mix with the mash of hot *patate*, add pepper). In fact Nin and I grow hungry remembering all our long hikes to the Royal, looking at sodas, walking, seeing the women buying sausage and butter and eggs in the grocery stores. *"Boy mué j'aimera ben vite, tu-suite,"* Nin says rubbing her dress over her belly (Boy me I'd like real soon, right away—) *"un bon ragout d'boullette, ben chaud* (a good porkball stew very hot) *dans mon assiette, j prend ma fourchette pis je'll mash ensemble* (in my plate, I take my fork and I mash it together), *les boules de viande molle, les patates, les carottes, le bon ju gras, après ca j'ma bien du beur sur mon pain pis un gros vert de la—"* (the balls of soft meat, the potatoes, the carrots, the good fat juice, after that I put a lot of butter on my bread and a big glass of milk—)

"*Pour dessert,*" I put in, "*on arra une grosse tates chaude de cerises avec d'la whipcream—*" (For desert we'd have a big hot pie of cherry with whipcream)—

"*Lendemain matin pour dejeuner on arra des belles grosses crêpes avec du syro de rave, et des sousices bien cui assi dans l'assiette chaude avec un beau gros vert de la—*" (The next morning for breakfast we'd have some nice big crêpes with maple syrup, and sausages well cooked sitting in the plate hot with a big beautiful glass of milk—)

"*Du la chocolat!*" (Chocolate milk!)

"*Non non non non, s pas bon ca—du la blanc— Boy sa waite bon.*" (No no no no, that's no good—white milk— Boy it's gonna be good.)

"*Le suppers de ce jour la, cosse qu'on vas avoir?*" (The supper of that day, what we gonna have?)

"*Sh e pa—*" (Dunno)—she's already turned her attention to other things, to watching the women hang up the area-ways of wash in the great shining alleys of famous Moody Street—

"*Moi j'veu un gros plat de corton—*" (Me I want a big bowl of corton) (meatspread)—"*des bines chaudes, comme assoir, Samedi soir—un pot de bines, du bon pain fra de Belgium, ben du beur sur mon pain, du lards dans mes bines, brun, ainque un peu chaud—et avec toutes ca du bon jambon chaud qui tombe en morceau quand tu ma ta four-chette dedans—pour dessert je veu un beau gros cakes chaud a Maman avec des peach et du ju de la can et d le whipcream —ca, ou bien le favorite a Papa, whip cream avec date pie.*"

(—And hot beans, like tonight, Saturday night—a pot of beans, good fresh Belgium bread, lots of butter on my bread, lard in my beans, brown, just a little hot—and with all that some good hot ham that falls apart when you put your fork in it—for dessert I want a beautiful big cake, hot, made by Mama, with peaches and the juice from the can and some whipcream—that, or else Pa's favorite, whipcream with date pie.)

Thus we rushed along, and came to the bridge . . . we'd almost forgotten the Flood—

2

HUGE WASHED OUT NOON's shining on the river day. Great marks show how high the river was. Forests in the pebbly shore are all mudbrown. A cold high wind blows, the sign of the store at the end of the bridge, on Pawtucket, creaks and cringes. Whipping bright skies wash over the sight of the earth. Over in Rosemont you see great pools of despair still reflecting clouds . . . six blocks long some of them. All Lowell sings beneath our sight as we dance across the bridge. The flood is over.

I look to see towards the Castle on Snake Hill and I see the gnomic old figure gnarled in its vlump on the keen desirable hill far away. Blazing heavens shine on its knobs.

3

THE CASTLE IS REALLY DESERTED—no one lives there—an old sign sags in the overgrown grass by the front gate—not

since Emilia and her pals in the 20's did we see any signs
of a car or a visitor or prospective buyer— It was a heap.
Old Boaz endured in the woodsmoke cobweb hall—the only
inhabitant of the Castle who could be seen with mortal
eye. The kids who played hookey, and the occasional people who walked around in the moldy cellarly ruins inside
did not realize that the Castle was Totally occupied— In
the Reality of the dark dust the Vampires slept, the gnomes
worked, the black priests prayed their Litanies of the per-
fidious Damp, the attendants and Visitors of the Nark said
nothing but just waited and workmen of the underground
mud local were ever loading trucks with bare shoulders
below— When I walked on the Castle grounds I always
felt the vibration, that secret below— This was because
the location was not far from my birthplace hill Lupine
Road... I knew the ground whereof I thought & tread.
That sunny afternoon I visited the Castle, kicked at a
broken glass in the side cellar window, and then retired
to a bed of grass beneath a crabapple tree by the lower
picketfence—from where I lay I could see I could see the
regal slope of the Castle lawns with their hints of last
October's ruddy-spot leaves (O great trees of the Versailles
castle of our souls! O clouds that sail our Immortalities!—
that tear us to the Voom, beyond the ledge and massive
widow, O fresh paint and marbles in a Dream!)—the gentle,
graceful grass, the weaving waving in the drowsy afternoon, the kingly slump and slope of the earth of Snake
Hill, and then sensationally out of the corner of the eye
a whole wing and corner and facade of the Castle—wild,
noble, baronial home of the soul. This was an afternoon of

191

such bliss that the earth moved—actually moved, I knew why soon enough—Satan was beneath the rock and loam hungry to devour me, hungry to sleek me up through his portal teeth to Hell—I lay back and innocently in my boyhood barefoot sang "I got a nose, you got a nose—" Nobody passing in the road beyond the wall asked what I was doing there little boy—no paint trucks, no women with children —I was relaxed in my day in the yard of the homely old Castle of my play.

Late that afternoon, almost dusk, very cold, I made my way down Snake Hill via the little cart road through the jackpines in the sand not far from the sooty old coal shute of the Centralville Bee Coal Co.

4

AFTER SUPPER I WANDERED up to the sandbank and stood on top till dark,—looked at the coal shack below, the sand, Riverside Street where the sand road crossed, the rickety Voyer grocery store, the old cemetery on the hill (homerun centerfield in old games against Rosemont Tigers on their own grounds), the backyard viney and autumn-like of the Greek brothers Arastropoulos (faintly related to G.J. thru relatives working a lunchcart on Eighth Avenue New York)— The vast fields towards Dracut Tigers, distant pines, stonewalls— The trees of Rosemont, the great river beyond—far off, across Rosemont and over the river, Centralville and its darkening Snake Hill. I stood on sandbank top like a meditative king.

The lights turned on.

Suddenly I turned. Doctor Sax was standing there.

"What do you want Doctor Sax?" I said immediately—didn't want the shade to overcome me and I pass out.

He stood, tall and high and dark in the bushes of the night. The feeble Lowell night lights, and the early stars of 8 o'clock evening, sent up and down a gray luminescent aura to illuminate the long green face beneath the shroud slouch down hat— "Staring with mute sun eyes were you at the drop of day in your billygoat town—think old men ain't traveled and seen other shepherds and other gray goat pies in the meadow by the wall— You didn't read a book today, did you, about the power of drawing a circle in the earth at night—you just stood here at nightfall with your mouth hanging open and fisting your entrail piece—"

"Not all the time!"

"Ah," said Doctor Sax rubbing his cane against his jowl, his shroudy cane popped up from black pedestal bases in his stomach dark—he leered—"now you're pro-*test*ing—" (turning away to do a sudden smirking grin with himself in the palm of his black glove)—"Look, I know you also saw the little children of that Farmier family running up and down the log at the river's flooded edge and complimented yourself for the keenness of your eyes and thought of mowing them down with a distance scythe didn't you!"

"Yes sir!" I snapped.

"That's better—" And he pulled out a mask of W.C. Fields with David Copperfield Mr. Swiggins hat and put it over the black part where his face was under the slouch hat. I gaped,— When I'd first heard the rustle of the bushes I thought it was The Shadow.

5

AT THAT MOMENT I KNEW that Doctor Sax was my friend.

"When I first saw you on the Sandbank I was scared— the night Gene Plouffe was playing the Moon Man—"

"Gene Plouffe," said Doctor Sax, "was a great man—we must pay him a visit. I've been watching Gene for years, he was always one of my favorites. As a phantom of the night I get to know and see a lot of people. I once wrote a story about one of my madder adventures which I've since lost."

Neither one of us at that time knew Amadeus Baroque or that he had found that ghostly manuscript.

"The Flood," said Doctor Sax, "has brought the thing to a Head."

When I heard him say that, even though occasionally through my being struggled the wonder of his holding the W.C. Fields mask to his face and it makes not my mind whirl but settle in obvious understanding— I knew what he meant about the flood, but by the same laws I couldn't piece it. "The understanding of the mysteries," he said, "will bring forth your understanding in the maples"—pointing at the air.

He started out of the bushes with a mighty shudder but suddenly stopped and stood silent beside me, so high, thin and tall that I couldn't see his face unless I looked all up— From way up there came his famous sepulchral laugh, I tingled in my toes.

DOCTOR SAX: "Stately Queens of evil rock caves come slomming in the slush of the underground, dripping ... all

194

the swimmers of hell are poking and sticking skinny arms thru the iron grates of the River Jaw, the underground river beneath Snake Hill—"

ME: "Snake Hill? You don't mean where I was this afternoon—"

DOCTOR SAX: "The hill of the blue balloons, same."

And with these words he started off and pointed, turning. "Say goodbye to your view of the sand hills of where you call your home—we're going through these bushes and down to Phebe Avenue."

And tragically he led me through the bushes. On the other end, where Joe and I and Snorro had spent a whole afternoon running and sailing thru the air till we got dizzy and faint landing in the hot sand like parachutists—here Doctor Sax looked up and a great dark eagle of the night swooped low to salute us with Uncle Sam fiercy eyes leadening at us in the silver darkness. "That was Tantalus Bird —flew in from the higher-than-Andean heights of the Tierra del Fuegan Princess—she sent a packet of herbs in his horny claw leg, I unwrap't it—it has brought a blueish tinge to the state of my current powder—"

ME: "Where are all these tinges and powders sir?"

DOCTOR SAX: "In my ammenyuosis shack, madame" (he chewed viciously on a cud of tobacco and sunk the chawcake in his inner blackpockets till later).

I realized that we were both crazy and had lost all contact with irresponsibility.

The eagle flamed in heaven, I saw that his claws were made of water, his eyes were burning sand-storms of gold, his sides were solid shiny silver bars luminescent in flame, blue shadows at his rear, guards—seeing the Eagle was like suddenly realizing that the world was upside down and the bottom of the world was gold. I knew that Doctor Sax was on the right track. I followed him as we pitched down through the soft sand of the bank and came stomping softly in the thinner sand at the edge of the halo-lamp light foot of Phebe—"Hup," said Doctor Sax handing out his arms from which a great drape fell shrouding me to my feet, as we stood there melted in a black statue of ecstasy. "No Nadeaus in the Road?—forgot about them didn't ye—no Ninips, poor little boy—no little frantic Drouins pigglywiggling in the dust before bedtime there where the brown supperlights stretch on sidewalk—"

"No sir."

"Nevertheless one of the Code laws of the dark, is, never let yourself be seen by shroud or self, sands have messengers in that starlight ink."

And off he glided, shroud and soft, I right beside him, bent, head down, zooming to the next shadow, I'm a great veteran at it as Sax well knows already—we hit the darkness of the last-house yard.

"We're paying a call on Gene Plouffe," he said in a low sepulchral whisper. We leapt over the first fence, over violet bushes, and came to the Nadeau backyard crawling low— Not a sound, just the Saturday night Hit Parade on the radio, you hear the clash of cymbals, and the announcer, and the fanfare of the orchestra, and the crash of thunderous triumphant music, *No, No, They Can't Take that Way from Me* song hit of the week, and it makes me sad remembering my little dead Bouncer that got lost and then recovered and then died when they put flea-powder on it and I buried it in right field in my backyard near the cellardoor—buried her six inches deep, she was just a little kitty, little dead kitties are poor.

The music is coming out of the Nadeau radio raspy and distant— Doctor Sax and I glide thru the backyard shadows silently— At the next jumping, he puts a shroudal hand on my shoulder and says "No need to worry—mix your mud with elephant flowers, adamantine boy—the hook and curl in the crook of eternity is a living thing." All his statements knock me on the head *Come In* even though I don't understand them. I know that Doctor Sax is speaking to the bottom of my boy problems and they could all be solved if I could fathom his speech.

"Grawfaced travelers have been this way, came waiting grayly and meekly at doors to the committee room and consulting booth at the Castle—they were all turned away."

"When are you gonna go there?"

"Now—tonight," said Doctor Sax—"you might as well be with me tonight as with anyone anywhere—for your own safety—" A fiery eye suddenly contemplated us in the dark, on the rail of the fence. Doctor Sax brushed it aside with his shady whip-cane-shroud. I couldn't see when the Eye had vanished—for a moment I thought I saw it flying thru the sky, and the next thing I knew I saw a flashing speck in my eye and it closed-up again.

Far ahead of me, low along the fence, Doctor Sax glided and led the way.

We come to the Hampshire's backyard, I can see the light in Dicky's room where he's drawing cartoons that he'll be showing me Sunday at the house when my mother makes caramel pudding— I know Dicky will never see Sax or me with his weak eyes. "Punk," I say, cursing up at his house—we'd had a fight after the raft episode—we'd make up in three days meeting gloomy and unwilling eyes on the irrevocable path in the park, and exchange *Shadows*.

The Hampshire barn was dark and huge—Sax was interested in it, glided to the door edge, we looked in at the groomus ceiling and suddenly a bat started from its revery and flapped away, dropping little red fire balls that Sax blew away with his breath, laughing like a young girl.

"Our good friend Condu," he said in a burbling aristocratic voice, as though pleased with the recollection of his chi-chi castle friends and enemies.

In back of the Delorge house, where the old man had died and the night G.J. and I were wrestling along in the rain suddenly six men in black carrying a shrouded black box came out and deposited it, with Mr. Delorge in it who'd screamed at us one sunset of puddles over some ball, into the hearse, and with black feet stood in the rain—as Doctor Sax and I hurried under the vines, lattices and darkeries of the yards a car passed on Phebe casting brown thirties headlights towards my house and Sarah Avenue, crunching over the sand road with tufts of sandbank pines leaning within the up-lights dismal and strange in the Saturday Night— Sax coughs, spits, glides on; I see that he's right in the world, things happen around him, he responds only to his own life in the world—just like an auto mechanic. I'm gliding behind him slanted and leering, at one point, tripping over a rock garden, slanted and leering like vaudeville comedians shooting drunk into the wings from a matinee performance for forty-seven bums half sleeping in seats— "Moo-hoo-hoo-ha-ha-ha" came the long, hollow, sepulchral sound of triumphant Doctor Sax's profound and hidden laughter. I made my own cackle-laugh, with hands cupped, in the excruciatingly exciting dark shadows of Saturday Night—women were ironing the snow ghost wash in shroudy kitchens. The children scream-ed a race on the cobblestones of Gershom. A raucous woman who just heard a dirty joke lofts a shrieking big laugh in the humming neighborhood night, a door slams in a shed. Tall weepy Bert Desjardins' brother is coming up Phebe from work, his footsteps are crunching in the peb-bles, he spits, the starlight shines in his spit—they think he's been to work but he's been to skew his girl in a dirty barn in the Dracut Woods, they stood against the raw drippy wood of the wall, near some piles of kidshit, and kicked some rocks aside, and he lifted her dress over the goose pimples of her thighs, and they leered together in the dark pant barn—he's coming from her, where he kissed her goodbye on a windy hill, and came homewards, stop-ping over only at church where his shoes crunched on grit of basement churchfloor and he did a couple *Notre pères* and looked at backs of sudden devout kneelers pree-ing in their dark shave, among sad fluttering naves, silence except for echo pew-coughs and distant frabbles of wood benches dragging on stone, frrrrowp, and God broods in the upper hum-air—

Gliding together in the dark shadows of the night Doctor Sax and I knew this and everything about Lowell.

6

WE CROSS THE BACKYARD IN THE DARK SHADE of Mrs. Duffy's cherry tree—in two months, when they run the Kentucky Derby, the cherry blossoms will be in bloom— She wanted to have it cut down, she said, because she didn't want nobody to hide behind it in the dark. Lounging, hand in pocket, in the day time, as everybody laughed at her, I nodded and agreed she was silly to want that tree cut down. The Doctor flattened into its Shadow like a passing thing; I brought up the rear, shh.

We crossed on tiptoe to the fence and leapt cleanly into the yard of my old Phebe Avenue house— Another family lives there, man and eight kids, I look swiftly as I pass under green porch at haunteds in the brown gloom of rakes, old balls, old papers. Up, I look at my ancient bedroom window where once, within, in light, I had begun my gray and hoary Turf (1934) (Westrope the first Jockey) —the rattling doom glooms of other deaths we've died. Triumphant laughter snickered from the immense nasalities of Doctor Sax as he led striding low thru the grass and weeds of the yard—and we vaulted Marquand's, tiptoed in gardens, came to the gloomy brown side of the Plouffe house and looked in at Gene Plouffe's window. I saw the Shadow of Sax far ahead, I hurried to follow—he was looking for the wrong room, it turned out, he hurried swiftly to rectify mistakes.

"Ah!" I heard him say (as I fumbled and turned around in circles and he bumped into me coming around the other way and the force of his bump carried us in one shroud to the window). There we were, chins on the windowsill, looking in under a foot of no-shade at Gene Plouffe reading *Shadow Magazine* in bed.

Poor Gene Plouffe—looking at the dark window to make a speech to an enemy cowboy but realizes void, nobody there—Sax and I were well concealed by his Shroudy Cape. It hung in great black velvet folds in the cubular shadows of the high wall yard. Mr. Plouffe's house had brown shingle-planks and strange tar alleys he made himself you'd think. He was asleep in his own part of the house that night— It was probably the one or two nights out of the week Gene slept there— A lot of Lowell families had several houses, several bedrooms, and wandered sullenly from one to another under great swishing trees of Eternity's summer. Gene had the quilt up to his chin, only his wrists stuck out to hold the *Star Western* in his hand—on the cover you can see reddish brown riders shooting bluegray Colt .45's in a milky snow background sky, with the words Street & Smith that always took your mind away from red-brown buttes of stark West and made you realize a redbrick building, somehow sooty, with big sign STREET & SMITH on it, in white, dirty white, near Street & Smith Street in the downtown section of Pittsburgh New York. Sax chuckled, poked me in the ribs. Gene was engrossedly eyeing a beautiful sentence about "Pete Vaquero Kid riding up a dry arroyo in the mesquite desolations of a flat table near Needle, the road to Needle angling off like a wriggly snake thru the brush humps of the desert below, suddenly 'Crack-Ow' a

201

bullet pinged in the rock and Pete leveled with the dust in a flap of brushbeaten chaps and spurjingles, lay still as a lizard in the sun."

"How eagerly the youth doth pursue his legends, with a hungry eye," whispered Doctor Sax much amused. "Would now the Ko-*ranns* of the grown up gulpitude make keen misery of that hitch. A hitch will disgust your mind in time. A hitch is called time in jail. You'll come to rages you never dreamed."

"Me? Why?"

"You'll come to when you lean your face over the nose will fall with it—that is known as death. You'll come to angular rages and lonely romages among Beast of Day in hot glary circumstances made grit by the hour of the clock —that is known as Civilization. You'll roll your feet together in the tense befuddles of ten thousand evenings in company in the parlor, in the pad—that is known as, ah, socializing. You'll grow numb all over from inner paralytic thoughts, and bad chairs,—that is known as Solitude. You'll inch along the ground on the day of your death and be pursued by the Editorial Cartoon Russian Bear with a knife, and in his bear hug he will poignard you in the reddy blood back to gleam in the pale Siberian sun—that is known as night-mares. You'll look at a wall of blank flesh and fritter to explain yourself—that is known as Love. The flesh of your head will recede from the bone, leaving the bulldog Deter-mination pointing thru the pique-jaw tremulo jaw bone point—in other words, you'll slobber over your morning egg cup—that is known as old age, for which they have benefits. Bye and bye you'll rise to the sun and propel your

mean bones hard and sure to huge labors, and great steaming dinners, and spit your pits out, aching cocklove nights
in cobweb moons, the mist of tired dust at evening, the
corn, the silk, the moon, the rail—that is known as Maturity
—but you'll never be as happy as you are now in your quilt-
ish innocent book-devouring boyhood immortal night."

Gene went on reading—we looked fondly awhile at the
way his prognathic jaw stuck up, his hawk nose came down,
almost suffocating his ecstatic mouth with its thin round
of breath whistling thru it—Gene sure got high on a good
magazine story. "Ain't nothin I like better, podner, than to
wrap mah entrails round a good mess of heapin vittlin Star
Western or Pete Coyote westerns or The Shadow when
dark he come peramgulatin his long soral laff in the Vault
of the Bank shade, yes—"(at times Gene, to imitate prose
of pulp magazines, began to sound like W.C. Fields). This
is what he had said to me the day he led me down to the
brown gloom of his father's drear house cellar and we
found *Shadows* and *Thrilling Detectives* and *Argosies* lying
around in cobweb bins. "Edify ye mind, me bye," says
Gene, remembering lines from some *Argosy* sea-story.

On go the Shadow Sax and I, to blacker things in the
night beyond— We skirt the Paquin house, glide swiftly
without transparency but vaguely and without sound along
the fence across the street, at the Boongo house, go on
under immense roars of the huge tree above (still buzzing
with its insect selves over the flood excitement), and pause,
only for a moment, to look at and give homage to my house
... the lights of which, on Saturday night, were now tragically dark, I knew there was something wrong. There is

nothing worse than the great weeping face of houses, a family house, in the mid night.

7

"FEAR NOT THE GREEN LOSS—every twig in your cerebular tree is aching to return to you *now*. No particular loss is there in the use of the loss—by same token no gain by use of gain, habit gain, habit loss—all and every moment is yearning to stay grown to you even as the pee-rade passes it—you'll take up your place in the hierarchal racks of vege-tabalized heaven with a garland of carrots in your hair and still you won't know you ever suffered such sweet wishes —in your death you'll know the *death* part of your life. And re-gain all that green, and browns."

Thus did Doctor Sax me give counsel as we furled on into the darkness past my house—Ah! there's my mother now, she's been out shopping at Parent's, late, has bought extra subsidiary pork chops to go with the roast beef, the baked beans (with molasses), the boiled ham, the French bread—the holiday weekend walnut bowl—the Saturday morning sausage and eggs and *crêpes* with Vermont maple syrup—the big boiled stew of Saturday noon lunch—the beans and ham of Saturday night—but now, at this junc-ture, she realizes Shammy and Pop are going to have a get together in the house and Blanche is coming, also others, old Joe Fortier, so she rushed hastily to Parent's to buy latenight snack meats (it's now 9 P.M.)—she hurries, with big festive packages, on solid peasant feet, no wavering, like the mothers of Mexico hurrying barefoot in the rain with little babies bundled in little balls in their shawls. Sax and I hide back in the Coongo fence shadows to watch her pass—I feel like running and throwing my arms around her— But in the shroud of Sax I am frozen into objective humility and just stand there looking at my mother, just barely a small, shadowish, but more gleeful cackle escapes me— In the street walking beside her I see her Guardian Angel. It is a huge angel, very solemn, slightly hurt, with lowered mouth, but with great shining wings, that drop rich showers of cool flame rolling and merling in the Gershom cobbles— My mother walks right along, any old guardian angel'll do and she will bless them when her time comes Holy Mother, Blest on High—

"'Tis an odd old saying, my boy—in my travels from one jungle to another in the fetid marshes of the South, and my treks in the Plateaus of the Gold North, I've had enough occasion to recognize this truth: women own the earth, women own heaven too—it is a tyranny without words— and without swords—"

And there's Nin, hurrying down Gershom hill from the brights of Satnite Moody and's calling my mother *"Hey Ma-a-a, attend mué"*—(Hey Ma-a-a, wait for me)—and her cry rings with the cries of a hundred other daughters in the air, the wild scuffledowns of old eve-sun-down go-mammy-by-the-river-blues, the tired trumpet that must blow in the blues of little boys when they hang their head from a curbstone and hear their Maw's a callin them—the Bloop Moon shining by a jackpine in Pawtucketville.

And my sister joins Ma, and they hurry home, talking

about Sister Teresa at the convent and Blanche and the price of the new stockings in the window and—in fact—

MA: *J'achetez des beau poids*—(I bought some beautiful peas)—(fishing)—*gard*, (look)—

NIN: *Oooh je veux le plus belle tite robe aujourdhui Ma!*— (Oh I saw the most beautiful little dress today Ma!)—*a l'ava des belles boules d'or sur une epaule*—(it had beautiful golden balls on one shoulder)—

MA: *Way—way—des boule d'or—pi?* (Yay, yay, golden balls, and?)

MRS. BISSONNETTE (shaking out her mop from her porch): *Ayooo Madame Duluoz—Angy?—ta achetez ton manger tard!* (Ayooo Mrs. Duluoz, you bought your groceries late!)— Heeyah heeyah! (laughing)

MA: *Oui Madame Bissonnette—j'm'ai faite jouer un tour* (Yes, Mrs. Bissonnette I got played a turn)—(We later lived in Mrs. Bissonnette's flat, six rooms) (corner Gershom and Hilltop Fairytown Garnier St.)—Doctor Sax and I crept on thru the buzzing arletarian tenement night, hearing a thousand voices, a thousand greetings and comments in the March night air—the roll of bowling balls from the alley, there's my father in the door, talking to Zagg the Pawtucketville own drunk who looked exactly like Hugh Herbert and staggered around saying "Woo Woo!" because he knew it, but was really drunk— There's Zagg with a mashed cigar in his face protesting with my father about how he won the high score, he bowled 143 and won the high score prize, where was the prize, and my father's smiling and saying "I know Zagg, goddamit, I know you bowled 143—I seen it in

every strike you threw down the gutter—I seen it on that
Japanese scoresheet you wrote—ha ha ha ha! (cough,
cough)—Zagg, it's aw-right, won't hold against you" and
above, in the screen window of the top floor of the Club,
old Joe Fortier, Joe's pop, who's been playing pool with
Senator Jack the Bullshitter, looks down at Emil and Zagg
in the yard and yells "Fer crissakes what are you two
fuckin bums doin down there! Emil, *poigne le par l'fond
d'culotte pis leuve le ici, on va y'arrachez la bouteille* ...
(Emil, grab him by the asspants and lift him here, we'll
take his bottle) ... *Zagg vieux chian culotte va't'couchez!!*"
(Zagg, you old shittypants, go to bed!)—In Blezan's store
twelve guys are massed at the pinball machine, tilting it—
some are scanning thru the *Shadows* and *Operator Fives*
and *Masked Detectives* and *Weird Tales*—(*Weird Tales*
were such a wig, there were moss invasions of the earth, lava
rivers of moss were coming to engulf us). The Shadow Sax
and I are hard against the alley wall between LeNoire's and
Blezan's, watching, listening, a thousand ululating dis-
tractions in the living human night. In Parent's across
Moody interior glimpses of big Mr. Parent himself wield-
ing his butcher knife at the hock counter, the log chop-
pery, fwap, Mr. Parent with his great benign and rosy
face, saying, and smiling, "*Oui, Madame Chevalier, c'est
un bon morceau d'boeuf*"—(Yes, Mrs. Chevalier, it's a
good piece of beef). The hanging sausages and joy of the
golden inside on Saturday night—I remembered cold,
whipping October nights with lamp lights waving and
leaves flying, the corner of Moody and Gershom, Parent's
casting its material gold glow across the sidewalk with its

few forlorn packing cases in front—and suddenly you see a little kid is sitting on one of them, eating an Oh Henry and a Powerhouse.

"All your America," says Sax, "is like a dense Balzacian hive in a jewel point."

And suddenly, right there, for no forewarned reason, he reared up and seemed to explode, or up-burp like a bull about to throw five gallons of blood, "Bleu-heu-heu-ha-ha-ha" he erupts, hugely, "Mwee-hee-hee-ha-ha" he comes again from around the other side, sweeping me off my feet with fear—I jump two feet dodging the scythe of his laugh— Then I see his gigantic leer lowering as he laughs again— and utters his sepulchral sibilance—"Fnuf-fnuf-fnuf-fnaa," he says, "this is the night of the destruction of the Snake. —The Wizard of Evil with his Nittlingen pain-gnomes, the faulty Decadent Dovists in their pillows and books of the dead, the bloodsucking unagrarian flap-wavers and aristocrats of the black sand, and all devoted monsters, spiders, insects, scorpions, gartersnakes, blacksnakes, blindbats, cockroaches and blue worms of the Snail—tonight the erupting head will sweep you with it—roses know herbs better than you—you'll fan out in love-letters blown from an aeroplane forge in the center of my earth."

I shivered to hear him, not knowing what he meant, nor capable of understanding. Indian file we stalked across a falling shadow in the street and jumped through yards, the park, yards, came and mingled in the ironpicket shrouds of Textile on Riverside—

"Behold them," says Sax, "your fields, your dark, your

208

night. Tonight we make the worms unite in one pot of destruction."

I take my last look—there, in the corner door steps, the old wrinkly-dinkly tar corner where I'd oft been too, but was no more . . . stood G.J. surveying the street, twirling a stick, thin little boy in the early evenings of his doomed lifetime, his massive curly Greek hair flying up, his big searching almond white eyes looking out like the eyes of a Negro but with Greek fierce and mad ambitioned intensity—calling on the night for love and faith, getting no answer from the wall— And Scotty was sitting on a step, picking slowly at his Mr. Goodbar peanut by peanut—with a wry, faint smile; he's weathered the crisis of the Flood, he'll weather others, he'll rise at bleak dawn in a thousand lifetimes and duck his head to walk to work, chastised by labor into huge humilities beneath the sun, big-fisted godly-silent Scotcho was never going to eat his own hands nor chaw his own soul to bits—letting pass a March Saturday night by the wry regard of his attention, storing up, just sitting there, letting the eagle of eternity fly his own nose. Vinny's walking home, up Moody, across the street—carrying groceries—flooded out, they're staying at Charlie's sister's on Gershom—twenty feet behind smiling laughing shrieking skinny Vinny comes Lou, with bags, solemn; then Normie, striding, smiling, carrying a box; then Charlie and Lucky, for once walking down the street together, smiling, in the soft breeze of the evening's events they went downtown to buy some groceries, traveled it and did it on foot like a country family, an Indian family,

209

a crazy family in a happy street—G.J. and Scotty wave at the Bergeracs. Cars pass; Shammy walks home, spitting and patting his belly where he just lodged a few brews, passing the boys with a polite nod. Tomorrow morning he'll be in church; tonight, at Emil Duluoz's, he'll be loaded on Tom Collins and singing at the piano okay.

"Well," says G.J. turning to Scotty, as Lousy ghostly comes up-flailing in the leafwild shade of Riverside with his funny sounds and little pebbles he is throwing, approaching us out of eternity, a riddlic being, headed the other side—elf—G.J. is saying "I wonder where Jacky is tonight."

SCOTTY: Dunno, Gus. He may be over to Dicky Hampshire's. Or down in the alley spottin.

GUS: Here comes Old Lousy—whenever I see Old Lousy coming, I know I'll go to heaven, he's an angel Goddam Lousy—

Doctor Sax and I suddenly fly into the upper air like we were dodging some tremendous black force that would have knocked us far—instead we veer up, and *over* a great deal, so I don't know where we are, and can't see how far down, or up, or over, and what precipice and shelf it is. But it's familiar: it's not a baptismal font, but it's in the shrouds and holy hands V-clasped,— Doctor Sax, elongated like a long scorpion, is flying across the moon like a demented cloud. Fiendish, teeth shining, I fly after him in a minor flare of ink— We come to the red-works of his shack, we're standing in the middle of his house looking down at an open trap door.

"Into that innocent land go as you are now, naked,

when you go into the destruction of world snakes. Leery-head may moan, go ahead and do your groan, Leda and the Swan may moan, go a lone groan, listen to your *own* self—it ain't got nothin to do with what's around you, it's what you do inside at the controls of that locomotive crashing through life—"

"Doctor Sax!" I cried "I don't understand what you're saying! You're mad! You're mad and I'm mad!"

"Hee hee hee ha ya," he gaggled gispled, "this is the Moan victory."

"How mad can you get?" I thought. "This old hero of the shroud is a crazy old fool. What'd I let myself in for?"

We're standing there staring at the red glow in the trap door; there's a wooden ladder.

"Go down!" he says impatiently. I jump down that ladder fast, the rungs are hot; I land on a hard dirt floor like clay upon which there are several great straw rugs and scrapes all stretched and torn but keeping your feet from the cold clay—all bright with designs skimmed in and wove, but dancing in the red fire light. Doctor Sax had a forge, it was well nigh impossible to hear the clang of your own heart for the hearty meaty clang of that harp-fire, it was a sodden bum-down red bed of coals, and a blower, a batwing blower, fue, powders were made to undergo hardening and boiling down tests in these works. Doctor Sax was making the herb powder that was going to destroy the Snake.

"Anoint thee, son—" he hallooed in the mud cellar—"we're going into Homeric battles of the morn—over the dew tops of every one of your favorite pines of Dracut

211

Tigers slants the far red sun that's just now rising from a
bed of night-blue to a day of bluebells in the crime—and
the shores of oceans will crash, in Southern Latitude
climes, and the bark will plow thou hoary antique sea
with a vast funebreal consonant splowsh of bow-foams
—you're in on no mean squabble the butcher's devil."

8

SUDDENLY I REALIZED his great black cat was there. It stood
four feet tall from ground to spine, with big green eyes
and vast slow swishing tail like eternity on a fly—the
strangest cat. "Got him in the Andes," was all the Sax
ever told me, "got him in the Andes, on a chestnut tree."
Parakeets he also had, they said exceedingly strange
things, "Zangfed, dezeede leeing, fling, flang"—and one that
cried in proud Spanish learnt from old bushy brow pirate
who farted in his rum, "Hoik kally-ang-*goo*—Quarent-ay-
cinco, señor, quarent-ay-cinco, quarent-ay-cinco." A vast
perwigillar balloon exploded over my head, it was a blue
balloon that had risen out of the blue powders in the
Forge, and so suddenly everything was blue.

"The Blue Era!" cried Doctor Sax, dashing to his kiln—
His shroud flew after him, he stood like a Goethe witch
before his furn-forge, tall, emasculated, Nietzschean,
gaunt—(in those days I knew Goethe and Nietzsche only
from titles in faded gold paint imprinted on the backs
of soft brown or soft pale green old velvety Classic books

in the Lowell Library)— The Cat swished his great tail. There was no time to lose. The jig was up. I could sense flurrying excitements in the air, as though a flight of ten thousand angels in small-soul form had just flown through the room and through our heads in their heavy tearful destination ever farward round the earth in search of souls that haven't yet arrived— Poor Doctor Sax stood drooped and sad at his forge works. The fire was blue, the blue cave roof was blue, everything, shadow was blue, my shoes were blue—"Oooh—Ah-man!" I heard a whisper from the cat. It was a Talking Cat? Doctor Sax said "Yes, it was a talking cat once I suppose. Help me with these jars."

I uprolled me sleeves to help Doctor Sax with the jars of eternity. They were labeled one after another with bright blue and obviously other colors and had Hebraic writing on them—his secrets were Jewish, mixed with some Arabic.

"Introversions! torturous introversions of my mind!" screamed Doctor Sax jumping up and down as hard as he could and screaming at the top of his lungs, his great shroud flapping. I hid in the corner, covered my mouth and nose with fear, my hands ice cold.

"Yaaah!" screeched Doctor Sax turning and protruding his great leering green face with red eyes at me, showing blue teeth in the general blue world of his own fool powders. "Screeeech!" he hollered—he began pulling his jaw cheeks apart to make worse faces and scare me, I was scared enough—he bounced back, head down, like a hip tap dancer pulling his bops away, on swinging heels—

213

"Doctor Sax," I cried, "*Monsieur Sax, m'fa peur!*" (You scare me!)

"Okay," he instantly said and reared back to normal, flattening against a cellar stanchion pole in a black bereaved shadow. He stood silently for a long while, the Cat swished his mighty tail. The blue light vibrated.

"Here," he said, "you see the chief powders of the preparation. I have been working on this amazing concoction for twenty years counting ordinary time—I've been all over the world son, from one part of it to the other—I sat in hot sun parks down in Peru, in the city of Lima, letting the hot sun solace me— In the nights I was every blessed time inveigled with some Indian or other type witch doctorin bastards to go into some mud alley in back of suspicious looking sewer holes dug in the ground, and come to some old Chinese wisdom usually with his arms hanging low from a big pipeful of World Hasheesh and has lazy eyes and says 'You gen'men want some-theeng?' 'Tis a pimp, son, hides at the secret heart of mystery—has big thick lace curtains in his loot room—and herbs, me boy, herbs. There's a blueish weird smoke emanates from a certain soft wood to be found far South of here, to be smoked—that when mixed with wild Germunselee witch brews from Orang-Utang Hills in crazy Galapoli—where the vine tree is a hundred foot high, and the orchid bunches knock your head off, and the Snake does slither in the Pan American slime—somewhere in South America, boy, the secret cave of Napoli."

Whirl bones rattled from the arrangement he had with the forge pull—every time he yanked, and blew on the

214

coals, the string-chain also pulled the tripod on the ceiling that made the rattling bones whirl. There were a thousand interesting things to notice—

Reverently Doctor Sax bent on his knees. Before him was a little glass vacuum ball. Inside of it were the powders he'd taken 20 years of alchemy and world travel to perfect, not to mention everything he had to do with round-the-world doves, the trusteeship of giant secret society black cats, certain areas of the world to patrol, North and South America, for sight of Snake's suspicious presence—manifold duties on every side.

"When I break this bubble ball and these powders come into contact with the air at the Parapet of the Pit, all my manifold duties will have melted into one white glow."

"Will everything stay blue till we get to that Snake White?" I asked swiftly.

"No—even from inside the vacuum glass my potent powder will change the atmosphere several times this night as we jostle to our work."

"Is the cat coming with us sir?"

"Yes—Pondu Pokie they called him in the Chilean mines —you'd never guess what his Indian name meant— It my boy meant 'Great Cat Full of Waiting'— A beast like that is born to be great."

He took the glass ball with its terrible innocent looking morphine-powder-like spoonful, and thrust it in his holy heart's pocket.

He raised his face to the dark ceiling.

"——" His mouth was wide open for a great cry and he only awped with his neck muscles upstrained to the ceiling—in blueish glows of fire.

He ducked slightly, the cat stiffened, the room shook, a great cranging noise rang across the sky towards the Castle—

"That's the Eagle's Lord and Master coming to the fray."

"What? Who?"—terrified, an air raid of horror everywhere.

"They say there's a mighty force no one of us knows about and so the eagles and birds make a great to-do and noise and especially tonight when the Invisible Power of the Universe is supposed to be nigh—we don't know any more than the Sun what the Snake will do—and can't know what the Golden Being of Immortality can do, or will do, or what, or where— Huge batallions of loud snake-decorated birds it was you just heard above, rattling their sabers above the Lowell night, heading for the duel with the Crooges of the Castle—"

"Crooges?"

"No time to wait son!—figs and Caesar don't mix—run to the fore with me—come and see the moo mouth maw of death—come get your ass through the western gate of Wrath, come ride the rocky road to orgone mystery. The eyes of those who have died are watching in the night—"

We're flying in a sad slant whirl right over Centerfield Dracut Tigers, came up-chawing from the cannon of his mad activity and balled across the air talking.

"What eyes?" I cried, leaning my head on a pillow of air; it was dew, & cool.

"The eyes of eternity, son— Look!"

I looked and suddenly in the night it was all filled with floating eyes none of them as bright as stars but like gray plicks in the texture cloak of fields and nightskies—unmistakable, they drooped and dreared to see Doctor Sax and I pass in the wake of the clanging nightbirds ahead. The eyes without seeming to move followed us like flying saucer armies as we fanned out all in great raw wild flight over the fields, sandbank and still-brown foamed river to the Castle.

9

AND THEN IT BEGAN TO RAIN, Doctor Sax deposited himself sadly on a rock right down by the river at the part where Snake Hill lawns stretched down bushy and wild to the rocky eternal Merrimac shore. "No, son," said Sax, as the first drops pittered and I look all around at the suddenly dark night with its rainshrouds and listen for spooks from the Castle, "no, me boy, the rain comes to peter me out. Years of my life have piled a great woe-weariness in a one-time worry-house soul that stood on vibrating but solid pillars; no, now it's doubt returns to flagle me in my old age, where once I'd conquered in youth—sun-lizard days— No this woe and rain makes me want to sit down on a rock and cry. O waves of the river, cry." He sits down, be-shrouded— I see a little corner of his rubberboat sticking out of his cardinal black hat above its frightening cargo blackbody in drape. The river laps and ululates on rocks. Night creeps across its misty surface to a meet with dumpshores and factory pipes. All Lowell is bathed in blue light.

The usually blue windows of Boott Mills in the night are now piercing, heartbreaking with a blue that's never been seen before—terrible how that blue shines like a lost star in the blue city lights of Lowell—yet even as I look, slowly the night turns red, at first a horrible red suede red with evil shitty river and then a regular deèp profound night red that bathed everything in dim soft restful glow but very death-like,—Doctor Sax's vacuumed powders had created an Ikon for the Void.

And he sat glooming. "No, 'tis and will be true, the Snake can't be real, husk of doves or husk of wood, it will swirl from the earth an illusion, or dust, thin dust that makes the eyelids close—I've seen dust gather on a page, 'tis the result of fire. Fire won't help the heat of embarrassment and folly. Foo-wee—what shall I do?" He mungled with his ponder fists. "I'll go through the motions ... because this sad rain that now gathers to its intensity ...patting the solaced but not chastised river with its manifold spit-hands you might say—no, the Snake's not real, tsa husk of doves, tsa tzimis, tsa rained out. I talk—how? howp?" He looked up distracted. "But I'll go through the motions. I've waited 20 years for this night and now I don't want it—'tis the paralysis of the hand and mind, 'tis the secret of no-fear... Somehow it seems the evil thing should take a care itself, or be rectified in organic tree of things. But these deliberations ah-vail not my old Sprowf Tomboy Bollnock Sax—listen to me, Jacky, kid, boy that comes with me—though doubts and tears are roused up by the rain, wherein I know the rose is flowing, and it's more natural I lay me down and make peace with bleak embattled eternity, in my rawer bed of dolors, with eyes of the night and soul shrouds, to keep my balanced fingers in—among the shades of arcade shafts, friends and fellow Evangelians of the Promised North—ever promised, ever-never-yielding North shroud ghost of upper snow, ralc of snowy singers wailing in the Arctic-speared, solitude night—I go and make my mention, I go and seek my tremble."

10

WE WENT ON TO THE CASTLE.

Everything began to happen to prevent us from reaching our goal, which Doctor Sax said was the *pit*— "The pit, the pit, wha do you mean the pit?" I keep asking him as I race after him with more and more fear. I feel like I did on the raft, I can jump or I can stay. But I don't know how to construe the simple action of the raft with these powders and mysteries, so foolishly I grope along in black life and folly my Shadow. I yearn for the great sun after all this doom and night and gloom, this rain, these floods, this Doctor Sax of the North American Antiquity.

We start up a narrow alley between two sudden stone walls in the yards—rain is dripping from the rocks.

"The sun worshippers go through dank caves for their

snake-heart," cries Doctor Sax, leading far ahead with his
hood. Suddenly at the end of the stone alley I see a huge
apparition standing.

"It's Blook the Monster!" cries Doctor Sax coming back
my way in the narrow alley and I have to flatten to re-
ceive him. Blook is a huge bald fat giant somewhat ineffectual who cannot advance through the alley but reaches
over his 20-foot arms along the wall tops like great glue
spreading, with no expression on his floury pastry face—an
awful ugh—a beast of the first water, more gelatinous than
terrifying. Sax joined me in his Shroud and we flipped
over the wall in the wink of a bat-wing. "He's mad as
hell because we caught him burying an onion in the
garden!" Blook emitted a faint, thin whistling noise of
disgust that he missed us. We ran like hell through a
drippy bush wet garden, over rills, mud hamps, rocks and
suddenly I see a huge spider like four men tied to each
other at the back and running in the same direction, a
gigantic beast, running like mad across the glow of the
rain.

"There's one of the Mayan spiders that came with the
Flood. You ain't seen nothing till you've seen the Chimu
centipedes in the dongeons of green bile, where they
threw a couple of Dovists last week."

"Yock! Yock!" cried a strange thing that suddenly dove
at our heads from the rainy air. Sax waved aside with a
claw of his great red-green fingers in the general reddish
dark of everything— It was like Hell. We were at the
portals of some awful hellhole full of impossible exits.
Straight ahead, was our Pit,—in the way, a hundred an-

noying barriers. We even came to a giant scorpion that lay scat on a wall big and black red, full six feet long, so that we had to go around—"Came with the Flood," explained Sax, throwing his head over to me with a smile like a young secretary explaining to the visiting boss on the Set.

Suddenly I see Doctor Sax's red eyes shining like wild buttons in the general river night, and loops of red shrouds around his hidden face. I look at my own hands ... I can see the red veins threading through my flesh; my bones are black sticks with knobs. All the night, drowned blood red, is relieved by the angular black framesticks of the living skeletal world. Great beautiful livid orgones are dancing like spermatazoa in every section of the air. I look and the red moon's come out from the rainclouds for an instant.

"Onward!" cries Sax. I follow him as he barges head first straight through a green pile of moss or green grass of some kind, I bowl through after him and come out on the other side covered with bits of grass. Down a long hall, I realize with horror, stand a long file of gnomes pointing spears alternately at us and then at themselves in a solemn little ceremony— Doctor Sax emits a wild "Ha ha!" like the jolly Principal of a Parochial Boarding-school and dashes capes-a-flying along the wall beside them as they melt to one side in sudden fear with their spears—I dash after. I pushed the wall and it caved in like paper, like the papier-mâché night of cities. I rubbed my eyes. Suddenly we were exploded into a golden room and ran screaming up a flight of stairs. Doctor Sax struggled with a moss-covered trapdoor in the dripping gray stone above our heads.

"Look!" says Sax pointing at a wall—it's like a cellar window, we see the ground outside the Castle illuminated by some kind of oil lamp or flare near there—just the ditch along the cellar stone—thousands of slithery little garter snakes are tumbling in a shining mass in the half grass half sand of the cellar ditch. Horrible!

"Now you know why it was known as Snake Hill!" announces Doctor Sax. "The snakes have come to see the King of Snakes."

He heaves up the terrible trapdoor, dropping mud and dust, and we climb up into an intense black. We stand for one whole minute not seeing or saying anything. Life is actual: darkness is when there is no light. Then slowly a glow emerges. We're standing in sand like the beach but damp, thin, full of wet sticks, smells, shit—I smell masonry, we're underground of something. Doctor Sax knocks against a wall of stone as we pass. "There's your Count Condu, across these rocks, his bloody sleeping box—by now it's night, he must be off shenanigansing with his little beastly wing." We pass a great under alleyway. "There's your dungeons, down there, and entrances to the mine. They succeeded and dug the Snake out a hundred years before its time." How milky-soft the blackshrouds of Sax! —I'm hanging on to them, filled with sadness and premonition.

The ground shuddered.

"There's your heaving Satan now!" he cried, raspy and

whirling. "A procession of mourners in black, son, move aside—" And he pointed far off down a dim shaft alley where it seemed I saw a parade of black shrouds with candles but couldn't see because of the unnatural red glow of the night. Through another cellar window I caught a glimpse of Redblood Merrimac flowing around in brown-red bed-shores. But even as I looked everything trembled to turn white. The milky moon was first to send the radiant message—then the river looked like a bed of milk and lilies, the rain beads like drops of honey. Darkness shivered white. Ahead of me in snow white raiment Doctor Sax suddenly looked like an angel saint. Then suddenly he was a hooded angel in a white tree, and looked at me. I saw waterfalls of milk and honey, I saw gold. I heard Them singing. I trembled to see the halo pure. A giant door opened and a group of men were standing at a rail in front of us in a gigantic hall with cave like walls and impossible-to-see ceiling.

"Welcome!" was the cry, and an old man with a beak-nose and long white hair lounged effeminately against the rail as the others parted to reveal him.

"The Wizard!" I heard these words sibilantly cracking from the empurpled lips of Doctor Sax, who was otherwise all white. In the whiteness the Wizard shone all over like an evil glowworm out of the dark. His white eyes now shone like mad dots of fury . . . they were blank and had snowstorms in them. His neck was twisted and strung and streaked with horror, black, brown, stains, pieces of tortured dead flesh, ropy, awful—

223

"Those marks on his neck, boy, are when Satan tried to expose him first—a wretched ningling underling from nittlinging."

"Flaxy Sax with his Big Nax—" said the Wizard in a strangely quiet voice from the parapet rail. "So they finally are going to dispose of your old carcass anyway? Got you trapped this time?"

"There are more ways out of this maze than you realize," spat back Sax, his jaws pulling down his mawkish old face. I saw the bulbous pop of dumb doubt in his eyes for the first time; he seemed to swallow. He was facing his Arch Enemy.

"Everything's milk under the bridge *this* night," said the Wizard, "—bring your boy to see the Plaything."

A kind of truce had been made between them—because it was "the last night," I heard it whispered. I turned and found handsome courtiers of all kinds standing around in lounging attitudes but deeply, wryly attentive— Among them stood Amadeus Baroque, the mystery boy of the Castle; and young Boaz with a group of others. Opposite the parapet rails, in another part of the Castle I saw with amazement *Old Boaz* the castle caretaker sitting at an old stove with an old bum's overcoat, heating his hands over the coals, impassive-faced, snowy— Not long after, he disappeared and came back in a minute peering up at us unpleasantly with old red eyes from a cellar grate or gutter-bar-window in the hall— Ripples of comment rose from the spectators; some were frightening black-garbed Cardinals almost seven feet tall and completely imperturbable and long faced. Sax stood proudly, whitely, before all of them;

his grandeur was in the weariness and immovability of his position, coupled with the wracked fires that emanated from his plunging frame and he stalked up and down for a moment in temporary deep thought.

"Well?" said the Wizard. "Why do you withhold from your self the great joy of finally seeing the Snake of the World your lifelong enemy."

"The thing's ... just struck me ... *silly—*" said Sax, emphatically pronouncing every syllable, through thin unmoving lips, the words just expressing out through a grimace and a curse-curled tense tongue—

"The Thing's bigger than you loom, Orabus Flabus. Come & look."

Doctor Sax took me by the hand and led me to the Parapet of the Pit.

I looked down.

"Do ye see those two lakes?" cried Doctor Sax in a loud madvoice that made me wish there weren't so many people to hear him.

"Yes sir." I could see two distant sort of lakes or ponds sitting way below in the dark of the pit as if we were looking down through a telescope at a planet with lakes —and I saw a thin river below the lakes, flicking softly, in a far glow—the whole thing mounted on a land hump like a rock mountain, strangely, familiarly shaped,—

"And do ye see the river below?" cried Doctor Sax even louder but his voice cracking with emotion and everybody even the Wizard listening.

"Yes sir."

"The lakes, the lakes!" screamed Sax leaping to the parapet and pointing down and cruelly grabbing me by the neck and shoving my head down to see and all the spectators primming their lips in approval—*"those be his eyes!"*

"Hah?"

"The river, the river!"—pushing me further till my feet began to leave the ground—*"that be his mouth!"*

"Howk?"

"The face of Satan stares you back, a huge and mookish thing, fool!—"

"The mountain! The mountain!" I began to cry.

"That—*his head.*"

"It's the Great World Snake," said the lizard Wizard, turning a wry face to us with its impossible snowy brilliance and eye shroud—a waxy faced dead man turned flower in his moment of Power.

"Oh sir, Oh sir, no!" I heard myself crying in a loud littleboy voice above the rippling amused laughter of all the courtiers and visiting princes and kings of World Evil from every corner of the crawling globe—some of them heaving thin handkerchiefs to their mouths, politely—I looked up and saw that thousands of Gnomes were ranged in the galleries above in the stone hollow of the Cave— The mining snake beneath was coming up, inch an hour. "In another few minutes," said the Wizard, "possibly thirty, possibly one, the Snake will reach the redoubt our miners have built for it in their now-ended labors in my service —well done, well cherished!" he cried in a hollow voice that cracked like a public address system with its own echoes— "Hail to the Gnomes, Singers of the Devil Spade!"

There was a great clatter of spades above—some wood,

some iron. I could only see vague masses beyond the crowded antennaed gnomes. Among them wildly flew the Gray Gnome Moths that made the air multiform and crazy as their pinched tragic visages looked out from their night up on the flowing fretworks of the fire, in all heaven's dark cave soundless, wild, and listening. The Angels of the Judgment Day were making great tremendous clang across the way. I could hear some of the rattling birds that we'd seen at Dracut Tigers. Hubbubs were rising by the minute outside the Castle. The ground again shuddered, this time shook the leaning Wizard off a foot.

"Old Nakebus wants to maw up his earth too fast."

"And you'll ride his back?" grinned Doctor Sax with one hand elongated dramatically on the faded wood edge of the rail—

"I'll lead him through all the land, a hundred feet ahead, bearing my burden torch, till we reach the alkalis of Hebron and you'll never make a move to stitch my path. It was a fore-ordained path, and one, that you, particularly among the unselected unchosen kind, but willing to put on the wrong regalia and think you are, don't know your own madness—*why you breathe when the sun comes up*—Why oo breathe in the morning Ootsypoor—I'd rather lead my candle Satan soul with my Promised Snake dragon-ing the earth in a path of slime fires and destruction behind me— meek, small, white, old, the image of a soul, leading my candlelight brigades, my wild and massive Cardinals that you see here ravened like hawks along a line-wall hungry to eat the stones of Victory—with bare sand to wedge and wash it down— Pilgrimages of the Snake— We will darken

227

the very sun in our march. Hamlets will be gobbled up entire, my boy. Cities of skyscrapers will feel the weight of *this* scale—won't sit to weigh, or not for long,—and scales and Justice have nothing to do with a dragon's sides— whether she holds alms, or balms, in her milky embowered palm— Or your Seminal Dovists, half of whom arrested now rot below—I see them floating in the lake of milky slime— Fires shall eat your Lowells—the Snake'll make the subways his feeding-place—with one coy flick he'll snop up whole Directories and lists of the census, liberals and re-actionaries will be washed down by the rivers of his drink, the Left and the Right will form a single silent tapeworm in his indestructible tube— No avail your ordinary fire de-partments and dull departments—the earth's returned to fire, the western wrath is done."

And Doctor Sax, weakly smiling, held a long pale hand over his heart, where the vacuum ball was pocketed—and waited.

Now a mighty sigh rose from the Pit, it grew in size, rumbled, shook the earth—a great stench rose, all the noble-men covered their noses and some turned away and some ran out the door. The horrid stench of the ancient Snake that has been growing in the world-ball like a worm in the apple since Adam and Eve broke down and cried.

"No need to save your little flijabets—Nature's got no time to dally-hassel with its insects—" sneers the Wizard. The stench of the Snake reminds me of certain alleys I've been in—mixed with a horrible hot scent that no bird has ever known, comes up from the bottom of the world, the middle of the earth's core—a smell of pure fire and burning vegetables and coals of other Epochs and Ages—the brimstone of the actual brimstone underground shelf—burning now but in the nibble of the Great Snake of the World it has acquired a strange reptilian change—the blue worms of the underworld devoured and sending up their flaw— I didn't blame some of the Noblemen becoming disgusted even with a spectacle for which they'd waited years. Great clouds of dusty mud fell from the invisible living ceiling of eyes and souls—in a plipping rain—when the ground shuddered again, the Snake had inched his hour. Now I knew why there had been earth tremors at Snake Hill. I wondered if this had anything to do with the crack I had seen in the park—and with the dream of the Cannibals rushing over the brow of the hill—the strange afternoon in which I saw all that, and the afternoon just passed when I lay looking at the golden clouds of yesterday-today fanning in solemn mass across the afternoon balloon—

Suddenly there was a new commotion among the Noblemen not Sax, I or the Wizard could fail to notice— Boaz Jr. had instructed nearby guards to capture Amadeus Baroque in a sensational *coup* that was the climax of weeks of plotting and chawing over logistical problems of nonsensical action. I recognized Boaz Jr. from his long black shoes. One day that past summer, not long after the treeing of Gene the Moon Man, on the night I'd first seen Doctor Sax in the shroud of the sandbank, we'd made a trap, a hole in the sand, six feet deep, with twigs across, a newspaper, and sand— Doctor Sax came very close to falling in, he later confessed. But Boaz Jr. who (as I now learned) was stalking around the neighborhood looking for talent for his puppet show, fell in—half in—lost a shoe (long, long black shoe, when I saw that thing I shuddered) and ran off red with embarrassment into the night . . . went back to the Castle, was curt to his father and went immediately to bed with the bats in the attic. He was a young man who wanted to be a vampire, and wasn't, but was trying to learn—he took instructions from several ineffectual Black Cardinals, the Spider Committee would have nothing to do with him, so he adjusted himself to deep mystical studies, long conversations with the brilliant Condu—and at first was a close friend of Amadeus Baroque who was the only occupant and emissary of the Castle from the city of Lowell. But Boaz Jr. who was ambitious, began to suspect Baroque of Dovist tendencies— Dovism was the idealistic left of the Satanic movement, it claimed that Satan was enamored of doves, and therefore his Snake would not destroy the world but merely be a great skin of doves on coming-out day, falling apart, millions of come-colored doves spurting from it as it shoots from the ground a hundred miles long—most Dovists in fact were impractical and somewhat effeminate people—that is, their idea was absurd, the Snake was real enough— They finally had to go underground when the Wizard issued his Black Decree the year the Gnome Miners revolted but were subdued by Blook the Monster and his trained corps of Giant Insect Men—trainers, with sticks and antennae, they lived in huts along the underground Jaw River, next to the insect Caves—giant Spiders, Scorpions, Centipedes and Rats too. The Black Decree forbade Dovism and poor hapless Dovists (including La Contessa it turned out) were rounded up and sent to live on rafts

in the Jaw River moored to the huts and insect caves.
There the helpless innocent Dovists wept in an eternal gray
darkness and mist. Boaz Jr., in his disappointment at not
being able to be a vampire, since he wanted none of his
evil *literal*, turned to a black art—he kidnapped boys and
paralyzed them from a freezing drug that turned them into
puppet dolls—an old secret learned from one of the Egyp-
tian Doctors in the Castle. With these puppets (he shrunk
them in a shrinking furnace to proper doll size) he pre-
sented his own gala Puppet Show to anybody who wanted
to watch—built his own stage, sets and drapes—but it was
a horrible and obscene performance, people walked away
in disgust. Never the success he wanted to be, Boaz Jr.
turned to anti-Dovism and was now having Baroque arrested at the crucial moment to prove to the Wizard that
he was a great Solomon statesman and should at least be
made his secretary—especially now with the Snake thundering to rise. He had also a tremendous vengeance to pay
Baroque—Baroque, early an idealist in his first efforts to
get into the Castle among the Wizard's Forces after that
initial discovery of an innocent Doctor Sax manuscript in
the winter night that led him, by speculation and investiga-
tion, to further discoveries—Baroque became disillusioned
and a Dovist, when he saw how really evil some of the Evil-
ists were— Finally when he learned how Boaz Jr. got his
puppets he revolted and had the news brought to the Wizard. The Wizard wearily ordered a stop to the puppet shows
—Boaz Jr. had by this time finally wormed his way into an
amateur show at the Victory Theater on Middlesex Street
near the depot and was being booed off the stage by the par-

ents in the Saturday afternoon audience as he snickered in
his long black shoes at the footlights, tall & strange—Dicky
Hampshire was the usher— Things were thrown at him,
he had to run: the little kids who'd been in other acts of
the amateur show with him were now running into the
audience to join their parents. And that was when the news
came that the Wizard was giving orders: no more puppet
shows—so Boaz Jr. plotted the end of Baroque— His next
plan was to make blood illegal so the Vampires could be
jailed to make it ten years' mandatory sentence for posses-
sion. The commotion we were now witnessing was the
culmination of Boaz Jr.'s first great triumph— But soon it
was apparent that none of this would matter, up heaved
the parapet of the pit as an earthquake seemed to strike
the Castle and Snake Hill.

Howling roars from the snake pipes rose.

11

GREAT MOLE CAME FARTING FROM THE GROUND. Everybody
ran. Milky white horror flowed in the air. Only Sax wasn't
afraid. He ran back to the parapet, which was now uptilted,
and stood gripping one crazy rail and reached for his magic
herb powders. All the whiteness vanished when Sax jolted
that vacuum ball—normal gray of the world returned. It
was like walking out of a technicolor movie and suddenly
on the gray suit grit of the sidewalk you see small shining
bits of glass in the neon lights of disappointed Saturday
night. Screech went a wild honk, it rose like a siren from

the hot pit, there was an answering deeper rumbling sub-
terranean honk, more like a burp of heavy sounding hell
in his Huge Goop— Some courtiers flung anguished hands
across their eyes to hear the Snake make voice. It was a
tremendous experience full of shuddering and general horror in my bones and in the stones of the Castle. The earth
swayed. I wondered what all Lowell was doing—I saw that
it was daylight. Sunday morning, the bells of Ste. Jeanne
d'Arc calling Gene Plouffe, Joe Plouffe and all the others—
There were no explosions in Pawtucketville Peaceful Sunday Morning—impossibility in the choked out grass outside
the church where the men stand and smoke after Mass—Leo
Martin comes up to St. Louis the Shadow who's been saying
his Rosary with his hawk lips, says "*A tu un cigarette?*"
(Got a cigarette?)

But Doctor Sax stood at the Parapet, leering down with
an insane laugh—his cloaks were black again, his figure was
half hidden in the gloom. "Ah priests of the hidden Geth-
semane" he was shouting. "Oh molten world of jaw-fires
drooling lead—Pittsburgh Steelworks of Paradise—heaven
on earth, earth till you die— Law's amighty as they said
in Montana—but these old Doctor Sax eyes do see a horrid
mess of snapdragon shit and pistolwagon blood floating in
that wild element where the Snake's made his being and
drink for all nigh on ta— Saviour in the Heaven! Come and
lift me up—"

He sounded delirious and incoherent even to me.

All the guards and Noblemen who a moment before had
been wrangling around the arrest of Amadeus Baroque
were now lost in swirls of crowds of them, it amazed me to

233

see the extent and numbers of the Wizard's Evilist Colony.

Then I heard the screams of thousands of gnomes in the unbelievably immense cellar beneath the Castle, a cellar so enormous, so full of coffins, and levels, and shaftways that you try to crawl out of and they get increasingly narrower —there were gnomes dying down there.

The Parapet heaved up farther, it was about to gulp itself up, rocks and dust and sand flew, Doctor Sax took his suction cups and climbed the sheer wall of the Parapet and came to the edge howling.

I saw the mad frustrated puppeteer with the long black feet running under falling boulders. "There must have been a lot to what Doctor Sax said if *he* used to stand in the door of the Castle bowing from the waist," I said to myself in a daze. Boaz Jr. went up, climbed several balconies: he was safe, sitting on another parapet with old shriveled Wizard with his white hair. An updraft from the Pit made all their hair stand wild and flamelike.

Doctor Sax was bellowing in the fury "And now you will know that the Great Snake of the World lies coiled beneath this Castle and beneath Snake Hill, site of my birth, a hundred miles long in enormous convolution reaching down into the very bowels and grave of the earth, and for all the ages of man has been inching, inching, inch an hour, up, up, to the sun, from the unspeakable central dark depths to which originally he had been hurled—now returning and now only five or four minutes from breaking the crust of earth once more and emerging in the breaking boil of evil, full flaming fury of the dragon into the golden sunshines of Sunday morn as bells of men ring around the countryside, to crawl across the land in a path of fire, destruction and slime, to make horizons blacken with his huge and horizontal crawl. Yah, mad shriveled wizard that falmigates around the Cee—famous fuckface of history— come back from detestable grave to gather vampires, gnomes and spiders and committees of the black mass ecclesiasts and werewolves of the soul aspiring to destroy mankind again with evil, final evil,— Yaah fiend of dirty fires—"

The gnomes below began to crawl out of the Pit in groups like cockroaches running out of a hot stove—years of labor, awful drudgery in secret barges and tiny dirt-carts in the undergrounds of Old Swift Waters Merrimac —the whole thing exploding now in their faces.

Now more than ever I saw there were an infinite number of levels in the Castle, millions of candles which I now saw were held individually each one by gnomes, no end to those, and various levels above the parapet that had rows of black-garbed figures of the Wizard's mad and evil church, heretics in black smoke, on other levels there were women with wild scraggly hair, on other levels spiders with funny eyes looking down almost human—the whole mad gallery swaying in the demented gloom. There were things going on I couldn't fathom, a big slide of some sort, a rack of neckties hanging—the enormous complexity. Just one level above the parapet where we were I saw a boat floating by, and people on it sitting in easy chairs under reading lamps talking. And they had no idea what was below. It was like old women rocking on the porch in New England, who don't realize that the goddam thing is underneath the earth, placidly reading the *New England News*. And I saw everything, I saw a colored porter cleaning out ashtrays, cutting along and taking a nip out of a bottle in his backpocket and disappearing thru the swinging doors. He didn't know where he was. Farther up I saw distant parapets that were so far away and so far up I doubt that the people up there could see as far down as to see the Snake, or see anything but a blur or maybe they were able from that great height to see that it was a Snake's head better than I could— I wondered that the people of Lowell had thought this an abandoned Castle—I looked far down the hall, and couldn't see across, except for vague movements like parades in India bringing up the incense for the Wizard— I called to Doctor Sax "Is this the Castle of the World?"

"It is fitting for the snake of the world, yes," he said, —"My son, this is judgment day."

"But I only started to stand on the sandbank—I didn't want no JUDGMENT DAY!" Everything else was vibrating as I said these words—I wanted to grab Doctor Sax's cape, hide myself, but he was up on the parapet furying and waving his arms in the fires of hell.

I saw distant moilings of activity of other kinds, and the light increased. The Wizard's face was paling as he prayed in the big moment, arms aloft showing incredibly skinny wrists and little waxy stick hands trembling with ague.

I heard the word dawn, and there was a clamor, and a great crack appeared in the side of the bulging parapet. And a Roar overtook the scene, mountainous rocks began to fall from the roof of the Castle down in the Pit to hit the Snake. Doctor Sax braced himself with a suffering cry: "The rocks will enrage it! O Wizard, Idiot, Fool, King!" he was screaming.

"O Doctor Sax," the Wizard was hallooing faintly from the other side of the Pit. "Poor innocent Sad, go crawling around don't you with your little ideas of this and that and destiny, believe in dreams come true— Agonies of the mad!"

"O Wizard," replied Sax—a greater, now agonized roar rose. "Wizard Wizard maybe so—but mindful I am ... of the sleep of little infants ... in their fleecy beds ... and of their lamby thoughts—something so far from snakes —something so sweet, so downy—" And the Great Snake sent up screams. And steam hissed and billowed from the pit. "—Something so angelic—something something something!" Sax was screaming in the steam—I could see his mad red eyes, the glint of the vial in his hand.

Suddenly he spread his legs wide and opened his arms and yelled "God offers man in the palm of his hand dove-like seminal love, embowered." There were confusions, the Dovist dungeons had been upheaved, Dovists were swarming around the parapet praying for Doves— In Sax they saw their mad liberator, their crazy hero—they heard his words. Joy! Sneers descended from the Wizard and his men. Everybody was hanging on to something now as the earth pulsed.

"What are the poor people of Lowell doing now!" I moaned—"They must be sounding the fire alarm from Lawrence clear to Nashua, they must be scared shitless," I thought. "Oh God I never knew that a thing like that could happen to the world." I leaned on a stone, the Pit yawned below, I looked down to face my horror, my tormentor, my mad-face demon mirror of myself.

And so the Castle of the World was Snaked.

Because then I began to look, I said to myself "This *is* a Snake" and when the consciousness of the fact that it was a snake came over me and I began to look at its two great lakes of eyes I found myself looking into the horror, into the void, I found myself looking into the Dark, I found myself looking into IT, I found myself compelled to fall. *The Snake was coming for me!!* And I began realizing that slowly like a distant landslide of an enormous mountain what I saw was the torpid malicious monstrous flick of its green tongue and Venom. Screeches rose on all sides. The Castle Rattled.

"Ah the Great Power of the Holy Sun," called Sax, "destroy thy Palalakonuh with thy secret works"— And he offered up his vial to the Snake. I see the contraction of his fingers as he begins to squeeze. Suddenly he staggered—as if faint he swooned and drooped in his poor shroud ... then the powders which immediately burst into a beautiful explosion of blue mist, huge!, flupped up a big blue conical flame and showered in particle-clouds into the luminous red pit. Soon the whole pit was boiling with a green rage. His powders were most potent, his *pippiones* had brought strong leaves on feeble stick bones. The Snake seemed to shudder and groan in his confining-pit, the world tumbled over— Sax disappeared from my sight in a big heave. My eyes flew to the stars in the ceiling of the Castle which was having its own night in broad daylight. I heartbroken saw the perfectly pure heaven softclouds sitting in their regular Sunday morning blue stands—early morning clouds, in Rosemont young Freddy Dube wasn't up yet to go spend his day selling fruit and vegetables in the country, his sisters haven't yet cleaned the crumbs from early-communion breakfast, the chicken was standing on the Funnies on the porch, the milk was in the bottle—Birds luted in the Rosemont trees, no idea of the horror I was dark and deep in across the warm rooftops. I was propelled in a great arc through my space. I got up and ran like hell and only fell down when I got tired, not when the earth shocked. A great screaming cleek of howk-horns made me turn—it was the Snake rising Nigh.

And there went the Castle collapsing. And there, out came the great mountainous snake head slowly seeping from the earth like a gigantic worm coming out of an apple, but with great licking green tongue spilling fires that were as big as the fires of the biggest refineries you've ever seen on man's earth... Slowly, hugely piling out with the Castle spilling off its scales like scale itself— On all sides I could see tiny people flying in the air and bats and circling eagles and noise and confusion, showers of noise, things falling, and dust. Count Condu was in his box, was being skewered to Eternity in the coals of the Pit where he and ten thousand gnomes fell headfirst moaning—with Baroque, Espiritu, Boaz Jr., Flapsnaw, La Contessa, Blook the Monster, nameless countless others— Old Boaz ran down to the river, lassoed a piece of float-

ing something that was taking up the rear of the flood
but very slowly and profoundly dragged him into the
river—he had the misfortune of having tied the rope
around his waist—nobody knows why, what it was— Dust
of the uproars, dark world—

And suddenly I saw Doctor Sax standing behind me.
He had taken off his slouch hat, he had taken off his cape.
They were on the ground, limp black vestments. He was
standing with his hands in his pockets, they were just
poor old beatup trousers and he had a white shirt underneath, and regular brown shoes, and regular socks. And
hawk nose—it was morning again, his face was back to
normal color, it turned green only at night— And his hair
fell over his eyes, he looked a little bit like Bull Hubbard
(tall, thin, plain, strange), or like Gary Cooper. And he's
standing there saying "Goddam, it didn't work." His normal voice is rueful. "Funny thing is, I never knew that I
would meet Judgment Day in my regular clothes without
having to go around in the middle of the night with that
silly cape, with that silly goddam shroudy hat, with that
black face the Lord prescribed for me."

He said "Ah you know, I always thought there'd be
something dramatic in dying. Well," he says, "I see that I
have to die in broad daylight where I go around in ordinary clothes." He had wrinkles of humor around his eyes.
His eyes were blue and like big sunflowers in Kansas.
There we are, on this poorass field, watching the tremendous spectacle. "The herb didn't work," he said, "nothing
works in the end, you just—there's just absolutely nothing
—nobody cares what happens to you, the universe doesn't

care what happens to mankind... Well, we'll let it go at that, there's nothing we can do about it."

I felt sick. "Why can't we have another—why can't we have some more—why do we have to go through all this—"

"Well I know," said Doctor Sax, "but—"

We both watched. Showers of black dust made a shroud of wings and droop-drape bierlike background in the clear sky like a thundercloud without sense, in the center of its darkness darkly and more high rose the Mysterious Head twirling and squirming with a dragon's felicity, the hook and curl was sure alive. I could hear girls of eternity as if screaming on rollercoasters; over the water came the hysterical symphony honks of some sad excited commotion in the bustling bosom earth. Into the beautiful glary pale of giant massclouds that had come to cover the sun, leaving a snow White hole, rose the mighty venom headed Serpent of Eternity—clouds formed at his slowly emerging base. I sat on the ground completely stunned, legs spread. Unbelievably slow heaps of castle were flowing down the Mountain Head's sides... Shuddering huge roars.

12

BUT SUDDENLY GRAY CLOUDINESS came over—a swift darkness flew in from the South. Doctor Sax and I looked up into the sky. At first it was a massy thunderhead and then it was a strange flagellous maw cloud like a huge grooked hooded bird with a solemn beak, but unbelievable, not moving—

Then we realized that it was not a cloud, there in the blinding white sky of churchbells and wild disaster hung this huge black bird that must have been two or three miles long, two or three miles wide, and with a wing spread of ten or fifteen miles across the air—

We saw that it ponderously moved... It was such a big bird that when it flapped and flew with a mighty slowmotion in the tragic shrunken sky it was like watching waves of great black water going C-r-a-s-h with a heavy slowness against gigantic icebergs ten miles away, but up in the air and upside down and awful. And banners were streaming from its Feathers. And it was surrounded by a great horde of white Doves, some of them belonging to Doctor Sax—*Pippiones, pippiones,* the young and silly doves! And the great shadow fell over everything. Our eyes were amazed by the luminescent waving banners still wrangling in the wrong haze yet retaining flashes of the sun in them on the shade side of the Bird —how tremendously these gorgeous feathers of Heaven gleamed and drew Aaaahs and Awwws of hope in the people below who were privileged to be there. It was the Bird of Paradise coming to save mankind as the Snake upward protruded insinuating itself from the earth. Oh its huge grave beak!—its mewing wave leak, the architectural pisses falling, enormous structures of wing and joint, and gone All-Hosannah Golden fowl-flesh curly-ongs in his vast assembled flight— Nobody, not Sax, me, the Devil's assistant or the Devil himself could keep from seeing the horror and the power roaring in upon this phrale of Lowell. Tortured earth, tortured snake, tortured evil, but this Implacable Bird, with the same huge creaky movement, a million myriad feathers slowly waving in its own breeze, turned down, hood-eyed. Masters of the Hood were there, frowning. As I looked up at that descending World of Bird I felt more fear than I've ever felt in all my life, infinitely worse than the fear when I saw the Snake, I instantly remembered the Big Bird I played with my hands chasing the Little Man when I was five years old—the Little Man was about to be caught and his name was Satan— This could not be Judgment Day! There was still hope!

The Snake, as if torn to turn in its own agony and fire to see what haps beyond in that burgoyne air just penetrated and become—and though having no eyes but blindness—the Giant Serpent did accomplish a green tongue licking at the sky with a huge slowmotion futility, I heard and felt a sigh cross the field—

Down came the Bird, slowly, wings at ease, descending with majesty and unbelievable with slow immense ringlets of gilded broadsides, black as Jonah, thunderousfaced, mute beaked.

And just as the Snake had wound itself out to coil once around the rim of the Parapet and was trying to ease his ass out a hundred miles of hugeness and slime—the mighty green coil turned in the sun slithering with underworld masses and vapors, whole slivers of evil cakes toppled from the Snake's side and fell in the turmoil of its unfoldment— Things fled in terror from that vicinity, it shot out its own cannon clouds of detonation and disaster—and all the whole river was blackened—

243

Just as this happened—the Great Black Bird came down and picked it up with one mighty jaw movement of the Beak, and lifted it with a *Crack* that sounded like distant thunder, as all the Snake was snapped and drawn, feebly struggling, splashing sweat—

Lifted it in one gigantic movement that was slow as Eternity—

Heaved skyward with its ugly burthen— Rollypolly mass of snake, curlicue, thrashing in every way upon the imprint heavens of poor life—how could anything take it in its beak—

And raised up into the bedazzling blue hole of heaven in the clouds as all birds, eagles, feather brains, sparrows and doves Squakked & Yakked in the golden bell ringing morning of the Curlicue, the wild May Time rope was being thrown across the Belfry, the bell was clanging with a ding dong, the Lord rose on Easter morning, daisies rejoiced in fields beyond the churches, almighty peaces settled in the clover—up rose the huge monstrosities that have left our Spring! Our Spring is free to fallow and grow wild in its own green juices.

Off—up——up the bird rises farther, diminishes into the original Giant Bird Cloud, up into the sky I look and I look and can't believe the feathers, can't believe it, can't believe the Snake— The sailing objects in that distant Up are peaceful and very far—they are leaving the earth—and going into the ethereal blue—aerial heavens wait for them —they specken and grow dotty—calm as iron, they seem to have an air of funniness the smaller they get— The sky is too bright, the sun is too mad, the eye can't follow the

244

grand ecstatic flight of Bird and Serpent into the Unknown—

And I tell you I looked as long as I could and it was gone—absolutely gone.

And Doctor Sax, standing there with his hands in his pockets, his mouth dropped open, uptilted his searching profile into the enigmatic sky—made a fool of—

"I'll be damned," he said with amazement. "The Universe disposes of its own evil!"

That bloody worm was ousted from his hole, the neck of the world was free—

The Wizard was dissatisfied, but the neck of the world was free—

I have seen Doctor Sax several times since, at dusk, in autumn, when the kids jump up and down and scream —he only deals in glee now.

I went along home by the ding dong bells and daisies, I put a rose in my hair. I passed the Grotto again and saw the cross on top of that hump of rocks, saw some old French Canadian ladies praying step by step on their knees. I found another rose, and put another rose in my hair, and went home.

By God.

Written in Mexico City,
Tenochtitlan, 1952
Ancient Capital
of Azteca